FUJINO OMORI

ILLUSTRATION BY SUZUHITO YASUDA

123

VOLUME 19

FUJINO OMORI

ILLUSTRATION BY SUZUHITO YASUDA

NEW YORK

IS IT WRONG TO TRY TO PICK UP GIRLS IN A DUNGEON?, Volume 19
FUJINO OMORI

Translation by Dale DeLucia
Cover art by Suzuhito Yasuda

This book is a work of fiction. Names, characters, places, and incidents are the product of the author's imagination or are used fictitiously. Any resemblance to actual events, locales, or persons, living or dead, is coincidental.

Original Japanese edition published in 2023 by SB Creative Corp.
This English edition is published by arrangement with SB Creative Corp., Tokyo in care of Tuttle-Mori Agency, Inc., Tokyo.

Yen On
150 West 30th Street, 19th Floor
New York, NY 10001

Visit us at yenpress.com · facebook.com/yenpress · twitter.com/yenpress · yenpress.tumblr.com · instagram.com/yenpress

First Yen On Edition: August 2024
Edited by Yen On Editorial: Ivan Liang
Designed by Yen Press Design: Andy Swist

Library of Congress Cataloging-in-Publication Data
Names: Ōmori, Fujino, author. | Yasuda, Suzuhito, illustrator.
Title: Is it wrong to try to pick up girls in a dungeon? / Fujino Omori ; illustrated by Suzuhito Yasuda.
Other titles: Danjon ni deai o motomeru nowa machigatte iru darōka. English.
Description: New York : Yen ON, 2015– | Series: Is it wrong to try to pick up girls in a dungeon? ; 17
Identifiers: LCCN 2015029144 | ISBN 9780316339155 (v. 1 : pbk.) |
ISBN 9780316340144 (v. 2 : pbk.) | ISBN 9780316340151 (v. 3 : pbk.) |
ISBN 9780316340168 (v. 4 : pbk.) | ISBN 9780316314794 (v. 5 : pbk.) |
ISBN 9780316394161 (v. 6 : pbk.) | ISBN 9780316394178 (v. 7 : pbk.) |
ISBN 9780316394185 (v. 8 : pbk.) | ISBN 9780316562645 (v. 9 : pbk.) |
ISBN 9780316442459 (v. 10 : pbk.) | ISBN 9780316442473 (v. 11 : pbk.) |
ISBN 9781975354787 (v. 12 : pbk.) | ISBN 9781975328191 (v. 13 : pbk.) |
ISBN 9781975385019 (v. 14 : pbk.) | ISBN 9781975316105 (v. 15 : pbk.) |
ISBN 9781975333515 (v. 16 : pbk.) | ISBN 9781975345655 (v. 17 : pbk.) |
ISBN 9781975373917 (v. 18 : pbk.) | ISBN 9781975393403 (v. 19 : pbk.)
Subjects: | CYAC: Fantasy. | BISAC: FICTION / Fantasy / General. | FICTION / Science Fiction / Adventure.
Classification: LCC PZ7.1.O54 Du 2015 | DDC [Fic]—dc23
LC record available at http://lccn.loc.gov/2015029144

ISBNs: 978-1-9753-9340-3 (paperback)
978-1-9753-9341-0 (ebook)

10 9 8 7 6 5 4 3 2 1

LSC-C

Printed in the United States of America

VOLUME 19

FUJINO OMORI
ILLUSTRATION BY SUZUHITO YASUDA

BELL CRANELL

The hero of the story, who came to Orario (dreaming of meeting a beautiful heroine in the Dungeon) on the advice of his grandfather. He belongs to *Hestia Familia* and is still getting used to his job as an adventurer.

HESTIA

A being from the heavens, she is far beyond all the inhabitants of the mortal plane. The head of Bell's *Hestia Familia*, she is absolutely head over heels in love with him!

EINA TULLE

An adviser and a receptionist for the Guild, the organization in charge of overseeing the Dungeon. She has bought armor for Bell in the past, and she looks after him both officially and personally.

NINA TULLE

A half-elf student of the School District. A member of *Balder Class*.

LILLILUKA ERDE

A girl belonging to a race of pygmy humans known as prums, she plays the role of supporter in Bell's battle party. A member of *Hestia Familia*, she's much more powerful than she looks.

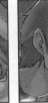

WELF CROZZO

A smith who fights alongside Bell as a member of his party, he forged Bell's light armor (Pyonkichi series). Belongs to *Hestia Familia*.

MIKOTO YAMATO

A girl from the Far East. She feels indebted to Bell after receiving his forgiveness. Belongs to *Hestia Familia*.

HARUHIME SANJOUNO

A fox-person (renart) from the Far East who met Bell in Orario's Pleasure Quarter. Belongs to *Hestia Familia*.

CHARACTER & STORY

The Labyrinth City Orario——A large metropolis that sits over an expansive network of underground tunnels and caverns known as the "Dungeon." Bell Cranell came here to pursue his dream of becoming an adventurer. After meeting the goddess Hestia, he joined her familia and began to spend his days in the Dungeon, hoping to win the respect of his idol, the Sword Princess Aiz Wallenstein. Not long after, the supporter Lilly, the smith Welf, the Far Easterner Mikoto, and the renart Haruhime have joined *Hestia Familia* alongside him.

Overcoming the Goddess Freya's charm, *Hestia Familia* and the familia coalition challenged *Freya Familia* to a war game.

Though tossed about by the einherjar strategy and strength, Bell, Lyu, Mia, and Hedin managed to take down Ottar, and Bell reached Freya. When he plucked the flower from her breast, the war game was brought to an end—

LYU LEON

Formerly a powerful elven adventurer, she now works as a waitress at The Benevolent Mistress.

SYR FLOVER

A waitress at The Benevolent Mistress.
She established a friendly relationship with Bell after an unexpected meeting.

CHLOE LOLO

A catgirl waitress at The Benevolent Mistress who talks and acts like a goddess. Chases after Bell.

AHNYA FROMEL

One of Lyu and Syr's coworkers at The Benevolent Mistress, she's something of a foolish catgirl.

MIA GRAND

The owner of a tavern called The Benevolent Mistress. Relatively tall, despite being a dwarf. Strong enough to send adventurers running away in tears.

RUNOA FAUST

A human waitress at The Benevolent Mistress. Although she seems to be a commonsense type, she has a troubled side.

AIZ WALLENSTEIN

Known as the Sword Princess, her combination of feminine beauty and incredible strength makes her Orario's greatest female adventurer. Bell idolizes her. Currently Level 6, she belongs to *Loki Familia*.

HERMES

The patron god of *Hermes Familia*. A charming god who is quick on his feet and is careful to maintain neutrality among the various factions. Is he keeping tabs on Bell for someone…?

ALLEN FROMEL

A cat person who belongs to *Freya Familia*. A Level 6 first-tier adventurer known as the fastest in Orario.

OTTAR

The captain of *Freya Familia*. The strongest adventurer in Orario. A boaz.

HEDIN SELLAND

An intelligent magic swordsman who has put his faith in Freya. His alias is Hildsleif.

HEGNI RAGNAR

A dark elf and Hedin's old foe. His alias is Dáinsleif. The truth is he actually has trouble speaking to others…

HÖRN

The goddess's attendant who has sworn loyalty to Freya. Known as Nameless, she has no alias.

ALFRIK GULLIVER

An adventurer who managed to reach Level 5 despite being a prum. Has three younger brothers named Dvalinn, Berling, and Grer.

BALDER

The patron god of *Balder Class*. Founder and headmaster of the School District.

LEON VERDENBERG

An instructor at the School District.
A member of *Balder Class*.

PROLOGUE
A STORY FROM THE SEA

"That was so amazing!!!" Misha shouted.

Eina had heard her say that more times than she could count.

"*Hestia Familia* and *Freya Familia*'s war game was sooooooo crazy!!!"

"M-Misha, not quite so loud..."

They were in the Guild Headquarters and it was about noon. Most adventurers were already in the Dungeon by this hour, and there weren't many visitors.

Inside the office next to the reception counter, Eina stopped her paperwork and looked up from her desk to ask Misha Frot to calm down a bit, but it was futile.

"Everyone's thinking the same thing, so it's fine! See? That's just how impressive it was!"

The other Guild workers and receptionists were nodding earnestly. They'd spent every free moment talking about exactly one thing: the war game that had taken place five days ago. It had been the fight of the century, pitting a motley coalition up against the mighty *Freya Familia*.

"It was incredible no matter how you look at it! The first-tier adventurers were completely dumbfounded, too! And in all that insanity, that kid and his pals managed to defeat Warlord—*the* Warlord!"

Misha's peach-pink hair bobbed up and down as she bounced around and gestured excitedly like a child. She had been like that ever since watching the fight.

How is she still this worked up about it?

"When Gale Wind joined the fight, it was like *BABABABAM*!!!"

"I couldn't believe it when Hildsleif switched sides, but I was almost numb by that point."

"Warlord is just way too strong!"

"But seriously, your Bell was the star of the show!"

And on and on it went. Misha kept recalling the explosive events with eager commentary.

Not that I don't understand.

Nearly a whole week had passed, and the city was still roiling. It was probably the same wherever the news had reached beyond the city walls.

Defeating the legendary *Freya Familia* was worthy of that sort of uproar. Eina understood that on a logical level. At the same time…

"Aren't you proud after seeing how well he did, Eina?"

"Proud? Of myself? It's not like I personally did anything."

"Oh come on, don't be modest! I'm sure you're finally going to get that raise, you being his adviser and all! Jealous!"

Misha praised Eina without a hint of irony. The other receptionists had also been teasing her recently, calling her the new rising star. All she could do in response was awkwardly smile.

"I wasn't really thinking about any of that."

"Eina…?"

"Even when I woke up today, I wondered if it was all just a dream and felt terrified. Or maybe worried? I'm not really sure myself."

That was how she really felt.

An adventurer under her supervision had been directly involved in an incredible string of incidents that had led him straight into that massive familia war. Too much had happened too quickly. It felt like she was still walking on eggshells. Her heart hadn't stopped racing since the war game had begun and she wasn't getting any sleep.

Bell had faced impossible odds in the war game, and it had seemed like he was destined to lose. Eina had watched from start to finish, pale as a ghost, and there hadn't been a single moment where some part of her body wasn't trembling. She'd cried several times that day. And the moment Bell's side had won, she remembered slumping to the ground on the spot.

Even now, after everything was over, she could not help wondering if her memories had been tampered with again…

In any case, she was far too tired to celebrate. The stress had been exhausting.

"Hmm, interesting. I guess you do love him a ton!"

"L-love…? M-Misha!"

It wasn't clear how well Misha understood her friend's true feelings, but she laughed at Eina's red face and loudly said, "Looks to me like you should give Rabbit Foot a proper congratulations! Especially since you've been cheering him on all this time!"

Whatever angry retort Eina had been about to say disappeared like smoke the moment she heard that suggestion. Part of her still wanted to be mad, but she was already falling deep in thought, and her face was more pensive than pouty.

Misha's not wrong. I was completely out of it and in no state that day, but…The next time I see Bell, maybe it wouldn't hurt to tell him what a good job he did.

After the fighting had ended, Bell and Eina had both been too busy dealing with the aftermath to meet. She would have to think about what to say to him the next time they saw each other.

Should I go with the default good job? *Or* I was worried? You were amazing *is also an option.*

Or maybe…

You worked so hard.

My heart was racing.

You were so handsome.

I love you—

"Wait, what?!?!?!" Eina clutched her head and buried her face in her desk.

"Eina?!" Misha's eyes were wide open. The other Guild workers looked just as surprised by Eina's weird reaction.

The last of those thoughts was definitely too much, and she wasn't totally sure where it had come from, but Eina knew that there was a very distinct possibility something crazy might slip out if she found herself near Bell with nothing more than a table separating the two of them. She might even throw herself at him.

After considering how it would be impossible to express any of those feelings if Freya's plan to have Bell all to herself had succeeded, Eina decided to live without any regrets going forward. So hugging him or even making a pseudo-confession was in the cards, and maybe it wouldn't be so bad to invite him out to dinner, just the two of them.

A-anyway, I need to plan this carefully so I don't do anything weird.

Her long ears and her cheeks were just a little bit flushed as she adjusted her glasses and finally raised her head.

"Don't take too long, Eina. The School District's going to arrive soon."

As Eina's thoughts were filled with the boy, Misha's comment stopped her in her tracks.

"Once it's back, we're going to be so busy again!"

"........."

In a sudden shift from her excitement, Misha let out a strange groan.

Eina looked silently out the window.

"Right...It's already that time of year?"

It was almost the first day of winter.

Even Orario, on the westernmost edge of the continent, was starting to cool down, and it was beginning to feel like winter.

As the final traces of the autumn sun fell from the blue sky, Eina looked out into the distance, her emerald eyes narrowing.

"She's coming to Orario..."

A tower rose in the distance. It was a white, marble spire that pierced the blue sky and reached toward the heavens.

This was Babel, the tallest building in the world, visible even out at sea.

And at its base sat the city of heroes. The one and only Labyrinth City, considered by many to be the center of the world.

That was her destination. It was a place she did not want to visit, even as she hoped going there would change something.

"Orario..."

Below her feet, a gargantuan ship intrepidly cut through the waves. She stood on its deck with a wistful look in her emerald eyes.

"Sister..."

CHAPTER 1 V-V-V FOR VICTORY PARTY

As the sun sinks behind the mountains in the west, magic-stone lamps spring to life, filling the night with glittering lights as numerous as the stars in the sky. This is why everyone knows Orario as the city that never sleeps.

Recently, it's been even more lively than usual because of a certain huge battle. A nonstop stream of shouts and cheers can be heard on any of the eight main streets of the city. Grinning adventurers and giddy deities eat and drink as much as they like while all the many bars and taverns keep serving up their best, fueling the city's party atmosphere.

And The Benevolent Mistress is no exception.

"Here's to our victory in the war game! Cheeeeers!!!"

"WOOOOOOOOOOOOOOOOOOOOOOOOOOOOOOOOOOOOOO!!!"

On Lady Hestia's cue, countless cups rise together for a toast.

The tavern's filled with people, people, and more people. There's loads of gods and goddesses, too.

Tonight, the whole place has been reserved for *Hestia Familia* and our friends. It's dead obvious, but this is a celebration for winning the war game.

"You drinkin', Little Rookie?!"

"No, we just started, and…! Oh, also, my alias is Rabbit Foot now, Mr. Mord…"

"Don't be stupid! When are you gonna drink if not now?!"

I feel a thick arm around my neck and hear a gravelly voice as the smell of alcohol hits my nose. Mr. Mord is very red-faced as he raises his cup high while hanging onto me with his other arm.

"We woooon!!! Against *Freya Familiaaaaa*!!!"

"""""*Yeaaaaaaaaaah!!!*"""""

Mr. Gyle, Mr. Scott, Mr. Bors, the people of Rivira, plus Mr. Dormul and the dwarves of *Magni Familia* all roar in response.

Lots of the adventurers who lent us their strength in the war game have been partying hard from the get-go.

I understand why they want to celebrate. Our accomplishment is truly incredible. We defeated *Freya Familia*, which is considered as powerful as *Loki Familia*. Everyone who fought has earned the right to get drunk on the glory of victory.

...Even if they're maybe a little too unreserved.

"Tonight's on me!!! I got a mountain of cash from *Freya Familia*!!! Eat all you want! Bottoms up on those drinks!!!"

"Wooooooo!"

"Yeah, Bors!"

Overjoyed by their reward—a share of *Freya Familia*'s massive fortune—Mr. Bors and Mr. Mord and the others have loosened their purse strings and are dropping coins all over. I watch them throw back their drinks with a wry smile.

"They'll burn through their prize in no time at this rate. I can see it now."

"Ah, Mr. Luvis."

"Don't mind them. Let's celebrate in our own way, noble friend of the elves."

Mr. Luvis holds out a glass filled with ice and pure Alv Spring Water. I feel a little embarrassed as I gently clink it with my own cup.

I'm not old enough to drink just yet, but...I can still celebrate with the people who fought by my side.

"More food, meow!"

"Ale first! There's not enough ale, meow!"

With Mr. Luvis's help, I escape the crowd around Mr. Mord as catgirl waitresses rush around.

The Benevolent Mistress is arranged differently from usual. Tonight, it's set up buffet-style. All the chairs have been put away, making the interior feel more open. Really, if it wasn't set up like this, it would be almost impossible to fit everyone inside.

While all the people here are friends of *Hestia Familia*'s, a lot of them can get pretty rowdy, like the people of Rivira. Other mortals and deities who fought with us in the war game have also stopped by. It's rare to see so many different groups mingling like this outside Denatus.

Speaking of, I go over to give my thanks to *Takemikazuchi Familia*.

"Mr. Ouka, Ms. Chigusa, and Ms. Asuka and everyone else, too. Thank you so much for helping us in the war game!"

"Not at all! If anything, I'm sorry we weren't able to help you when you were in such a critical spot before!" Ms. Chigusa quickly says as she waves her hands.

"That's right. We were simply following Laurus Fuga's order to let the enemy cut us down, after all," Mr. Ouka bemoans.

Ms. Daphne almost does a spit take with her beer before she manages to chime in.

"Hey now! Don't make it sound like I got you killed! I spent more than my fair share of time getting carved up by Dáinsleif too!!!"

"C-calm down, Daph!"

I struggle to hold back a laugh as I watch Ms. Cassandra desperately soothing Daphne. Then I turn my attention to the pair next to them.

"Umm, Ms. Nahza...What are you and Lord Miach going to do about your broken prosthetic...?"

"It's fine...We got our share of the reward too, so we should be able to make a new airgetlám..."

"It's not enough to also pay off the loans for the last one, though, so we're basically net even. Well, we did get to help you in the process, so let's call it net positive."

Ms. Nahza and Lord Miach wear warm smiles. I notice Ms. Nahza's right sleeve is tied up. I heard her airgetlám broke during the war game, so I'm relieved to hear they seem to be handling it okay. I did consider going into the Dungeon to pay her back for it.

"It rubs me wrong having to pay Amid...but Lord Miach's right, the return was well worth the price. I even reached Level Three..."

"Huh?! Really?!"

"Mhmm. So we're celebrating...Not that it's much use when I can't fight monsters, though."

Any excelia you earn under the effects of a Level Boost are supposed to be halved! And according to Ms. Nahza, Ms. Samira, Ms. Lena, and several other Berbera also leveled up. Seems like there were plenty of gains aside from the usual fortune and glory.

That stunning report reminds me how the opponents we fought were truly absurd.

"Bell Cranell? You know you don't need to go around greeting everyone, right?" Lady Hephaistos assures me.

"Yes. You fought harder than anyone else—and got more wounded as well," Lord Takemikazuchi says in agreement.

Ms. Tsubaki bellows, "Quit stumblin' around and stand up straight, man!"

"Umm..." I take a moment to put my feelings into words. "I just wanted to let everyone know how grateful I am...The battle was *a lot*."

I'm not doing this because I feel obligated. It's simply what I want to do.

Lady Hephaistos's heartwarming gaze suddenly disappears as her eyes blaze and she snaps, "Then have Hestia do it! She's your patron deity!"

I freeze up and weakly respond with, "Y-yes, ma'am."

The others chuckle as I excuse myself and continue making the rounds.

I don't see Miss Eina anywhere in the crowd. Mostly just adventurers. Apparently, it's not ideal for people from the Guild to join big gatherings of adventurers—or in this case, whole familias. The other notable absence is Lord Hermes and his familia. They turned down the invitation since they didn't directly participate in the war game. In exchange, we got an expensive bottle of wine and a message that read, *Enjoy the victor's feast!*

They aren't the only ones being missed. Fels, Mr. Finn, Ms. Tiona, Ms. Tione...a lot of people who helped us aren't attending today.

"Aiz cheered for you until her voice was hoarse! It got so bad she's too embarrassed to see you right away! Don't worry—she'll come find you once it's healed, Argonaut!" is what Ms. Tiona told me.

The reason we can enjoy this happy moment is because we had the help of so many people. I can't pretend that we won this by ourselves.

"I still can't believe we beat *Freya Familia*...It doesn't seem possible, even now! It feels as if I might wake to discover it was just a dream...!"

"Please don't say something so ill-omened, Ms. Mikoto! Lilly had to perform an extended tightrope walk down into hell and back four whole times! Never again! Lilly is never doing anything like that ever again! Never, ever, everrrrr!!!"

"C-calm down, Lady Lilly!"

After I finish seeing everyone, I return to the table at the center of the tavern where my familia is chatting. Ms. Mikoto clearly hasn't fully processed everything that's happened. Meanwhile, Lilly is ranting almost hysterically, and Ms. Haruhime is doing everything she can to calm her down.

We may have won, but Lilly is still having constant nightmares, and just this once, she desperately wishes she could drink herself senseless. She swore off alcohol after the incident with Divine Wine, but apparently "who could stay sane after all that *without* drinking?!" are her thoughts on the matter.

"Mgh, mgh...mhaa! That's just how crazy things got! We had to win no matter what it took. It was a true life-or-death battle!"

Our goddess simply nods as she reaches out for more food like it's a competition. As I watch her, I can feel my awkward smile growing.

Of course, I understand where Lilly is coming from. I'd rather not remember the war game too vividly. Being battered, beaten, pummeled, pounded, smashed, and crushed by Mr. Ottar for so long has probably left some scars. Just thinking about it makes the smile on my face twitch a little, even now...

"That's all well and good, but..." Welf starts, only for Lilly to roar back with, "It is neither well nor good!!!"

After taking a swig of his drink, Welf glances to the side and continues.

"...Why is the losing side here?"

While Lilly has been decidedly not looking in that direction, the rest of us follow Welf's gaze. Standing there are the four prum brothers carrying giant plates and a massive number of bottles of ale.

"It's just a bit of service."

"It's just humiliation."

"I'll never forget this disgrace."

""""I'll never forgive you, Bell.""""

"Why me?!"

Hearing their four overlapping voices use the same exact tone, I reflexively respond just like I did when I was *Freya Familia*'s Bell Cranell.

The Gulliver brothers are wearing their usual imposing sand-colored armor and helmets. But they also have white aprons on, covering the armor as they work diligently as waiters.

And it's not just them—it's all of *Freya Familia*.

"Thus was our sin, thus is our fate. The reparations of the defeated...to die banquet slaves. Heh, the humiliation beneath so many gazes is unbearable. My material form must retreat to the holy kitchen...! ...P-please...?"

"No can do. The kitchen is already covered. This place is crazy, though. Hard labor comparable to Folkvangr..."

Mr. Hegni is shy enough that he's reaching his limits, but Ms. Heith casually cuts off his line of retreat, scooting by carrying platters of food in both arms. It looks like she's already gotten the hang of waiting tables, and I could swear I've seen her like this before in Folkvangr...How do I put it...? Her exhausted eyes look like they belong to someone much, much older.

"Whew, this is definitely easier compared to normal! Only a little bit, though!"

"That's right! Thanks to the slaves we got our hands on, it's a liiiiiittle bit better, meow! Move it along, losers, work hard to make up for our share too, meow!"

Ms. Runoa and Ms. Chloe are smirking as they watch the Gulliver brothers, Mr. Hegni, and the others working all around the tavern... Well, that's how it goes.

Freya Familia is being forced to work at the banquet celebrating the coalition's victory. Now that their familia has been effectively disbanded, Ms. Mia has been dragging all the former members, particularly the Andhrímnir, to work in her restaurant. Or maybe it would be more accurate to say she forced them to join? From what I heard, she said something like, "That stupid goddess went on an absolute rampage, and her idiot children made a damn mess of my stupid girls. They better settle up with me, or else!"

I guess it's sort of natural given her personality, but casually putting einherjar and first-tier adventurers to work…Ms. Mia really is unbelievable. They're not visible from out here, but all the Andhrímnir working in the kitchen probably make for an incredible sight.

As it happens, there weren't any staff uniforms for men, so Mr. Hegni and the other male members of *Freya Familia* are just wearing their normal battle clothes, while the women are wearing the iconic The Benevolent Mistress outfit.

The reactions to seeing *Freya Familia* working in the restaurant have been varied, to say the least.

Some like Welf find it almost disturbing. Some are even terrified. At the same time, people like Mr. Mord and his buddies are enjoying the view with big smirks on their faces.

Undoubtedly, the goddess of beauty's familia members are renowned for their looks, and seeing many of them in waitress outfits is a treat, but it's plain to see that if anyone tries anything untoward, they'll be swatted to the ground in an instant, so even as drunk as Mr. Bors and the others are, all of them are very careful not to do anything foolish. It's a delicate balance of excitement and cold sweat.

Just then, a terrifyingly icy voice skewers my brain.

"—What are you staring at, filth? You're hideous. Put out your eyes and fall into hell. Animal."

"I'm not staring! I'm not! So please stop glaring at me like you're going to kill me with your eyes alone, Ms. Hörn!" I don't need to look to know who just said that. Her long ashen hair is covering the right half of her beautiful face, which is currently frozen in an expression as cold as ice.

Calling her the Witch's Disciple is a perfect description. Like Ms. Heith and the other women, she's currently wearing the restaurant's uniform. And now she's standing right behind me.

She usually wears a long black dress, so seeing her in the cute, green uniform is really refreshing…is what I would be thinking if I wasn't so terrified. My neck is coated in sweat and my jaw is insanely tense. Under her withering gaze, I just barely manage to offer a pathetic, polite smile.

"I-it…looks good on you, Ms. Hörn…that outfit…"

Her eyes widen, and her face turns so red I can almost hear her steaming.

"Beast! Beast! Beast!!!"

"Why?!"

Ignoring my cry, Ms. Hörn desperately pulls at the skirt that already reaches past her knees and isn't exactly short, trying to cover her slender legs, which are also covered by black tights.

"How dare you leer at me with your vulgar gaze when I'm already enduring so much! Have some shame! Ugh, why do I have to wear this…? It suits Lady Syr, but it doesn't fit me at all…!"

"We effectively lost because of your betrayal, so it makes perfect sense that you are first in line for punishment. Please keep up the swift work, Hörn." Ms. Heith mercilessly cuts her down.

"Heith…! Gaaaaaaah!!!!"

Ms. Hörn glares as hard as she can at Heith, but her stare isn't very effective when she's still bright red and can't even get a proper word out.

The rest of their familia initially branded her as a traitor until their goddess insisted she be formally pardoned. But even if she has technically been forgiven, the rest of the familia believes she still needs to atone, which is why she was the very first one to go to work at The Benevolent Mistress.

Because Ms. Hörn was the goddess's attendant who hardly ever appeared in public, she has become the center of curious attention for quite a while now. The male gods are all singing the praises of the picture-perfect pretty-girl psycho.

"It really is all your fault! All because you are alive! Have some shame!" she shouts at me, making her long, tied-up hair swing wildly. I think I can see a tear in the corner of her eye.

"Hiiiii?!" I cry when I realize she's holding a fork in her hand like she has some sort of murder-suicide planned.

Thankfully, Ms. Heith comes over and says, "All right, that's enough," before dragging her away. Even then, Ms. Hörn keeps looking right at me, like she might be able to kill me if she glares hard enough.

"This staffing choice is definitely messed up...How am I supposed to enjoy my drink like this?"

I'm still deathly pale as Welf sighs and mercifully props me up with one arm.

"It's fine, I guess," Ms. Samira says with a laugh. "They're making themselves useful in other ways, too."

"Yeah! After the war game, Haruhime's been targeted constantly! If *Freya Familia* hadn't been around for protection, who knows what would have happened?!" Ms. Rena agrees with animated gestures.

These Berbera Amazons are, of course, talking about the current situation surrounding Ms. Haruhime and her Level Boost ability.

"With her Level Boost out in the open thanks to the war game, all sorts of people have their eyes on her. That's why I told you to keep that under wraps, you useless fox," Ms. Aisha says as she musses up Ms. Haruhime's hair.

"Auuugh. My humblest apologies...!" she says while doubling over.

Ms. Haruhime used Uchide no Kozuchi over and over during the war game and all of Orario was watching, so her ability is essentially public knowledge now. Even if it's only temporary, magic that can break all the rules and raise your level is something that a lot of people won't overlook...Ms. Haruhime has had to endure kidnapping attempts, shady offers, and all other sorts of dangerous activity recently.

Ms. Mikoto and I, plus Ms. Aisha and the other Berbera, have all been on guard...but *Freya Familia* has also been very helpful.

"All is as the heavens have decreed...What a pitiful fox, destined to be sacrificed on an altar. Severing that doomed fate is our duty, as our sin was the root of such misfortune..."

"What are you even talking about?"

Welf turns a sour eye on Mr. Hegni's rambling as he walks by.

If I had to guess, he's probably saying, "Ms. Haruhime is getting targeted because of our fight, so we're taking responsibility by protecting her." I think. Probably...

"Umm, Mr. Hegni? Out of curiosity, how many times has Ms. Haruhime been targeted...?"

"That's hard to say...Until today, Hedin and I took turns watching over her. Just during my shifts, I crushed seventy-one different attempts."

"Ugh."

It hasn't even been a week since the end of the war game, and even if they didn't get off the ground, that is a crazy number of attempts.

Ms. Haruhime's Level Boost is undoubtedly incredible, but this is also a reminder that Orario is a truly dangerous place. I'm sure there's people and places outside the city that aren't much better, but...

"...I have to say this to Ms. Samira and the other Berbera as well, but thank you for protecting Ms. Haruhime, Mr. Hegni."

"Mmm...You're going to make me blush, so you don't have to be so formal with me." His cheeks redden just a bit, and he briefly looks away. I've noticed that Mr. Hegni isn't quite so awkward when he talks with me recently. "Also...if you're feeling grateful, then be grateful to her, not us. It's all because of what she asked of us."

I don't have to see where he's looking to know who he means.

The girl with blue-gray hair has been the hardest worker in the entire restaurant.

"Syr, dear! Can I get another plate of this tomato pie?"

"Of course, Lady Demeter!"

"Some more beer, Syr!"

"Of course, Lord Njǫrðr!"

""""Syrrr! Pour us some beer!""""

"Uuuuugh! Right away!"

Ms. Syr is running all around, answering the constant orders from the gods and goddesses, looking like she's on the verge of giving up and staring at the ceiling in exhaustion. Lady Hephaistos smirks sadistically, thoroughly enjoying this, while Lord Takemikazuchi and Lord Miach share a wry smile.

The great goddess of beauty who once brought Orario to its knees is no longer here. She left the city days ago. That's the official story.

Possibly because of the far-reaching and devastatingly powerful charm, hardly any mortal residents of the city have retained their memories from when Orario was her sandbox.

In other words, very few mortals know Lady Freya is actually Ms. Syr.

However, her true identity is now known to basically all the deities. With the city no longer threatened by her charm, many of them are nonchalantly stopping in to tease and bully Ms. Syr. Speaking for the whole coalition, Lady Hestia has allowed Ms. Syr to remain here, but this level of shaming is considered appropriate.

And Ms. Syr has obediently accepted. She's already apologized to lots and lots of people, listened to all their complaints—and even been slapped more than a couple times. Even now, she is still taking her punishment.

There are apparently many people who think this is far too lenient, especially among the goddesses, but...she doesn't have any status, honor, or wealth left to her name. As such, she is serving her penance not as a goddess, but as a normal girl.

I think the reason *Freya Familia*'s members are working here is not just because of Ms. Mia, but also because they want to lessen Ms. Syr's burden. To share in her punishment. They are still her faithful followers.

"Syrrrrr! Where's my brother, meow?! Today's the day we're supposed to have a proper talk, meow! We're going to be family again, meow!"

"Umm, is he not on the roof? I think he's looking out to make sure no bad people get close."

"Got it, meow! Then I'm going to cut work to go see him, meow! Take care of my share, Syr!"

"Eh?! Wait, Ahnya! I'm at my limit here! Seriously, please wait! Ahnya?!"

Ms. Ahnya sprints into the back of the restaurant, and not long after, everyone can hear a thudding set of footsteps that don't sound anything like a cat's running across the roof. Then two voices that don't sound much like cats meowing ring out.

"Stay away from me!" and "Quit hugging me!" and "Brother!" That sort of thing.

The voices quickly fade into the distance, meaning those two cats probably started a game of tag across the rooftops.

Thanks to Ms. Syr, Ms. Ahnya has really cheered up.

I'm not so naive that I believe everything will simply go back to the way it was, just like that...but I think it's safe to say The Benevolent Mistress has reclaimed a little normalcy.

"...Ms. Syr, should I help out too?"

I've been trying to just watch over her with the best smile I can muster, but seeing how busy she is, I can't help but offer to help.

"No, Mr. Bell. You promised to keep an eye on me, right?" She politely declines and goes on, saying, "Since I can't be a good girl, if you disappear, I might turn into an evil witch again. So just keep your eyes on me all the time as I do my best. That was our promise, my Odr."

She smiles merrily. Not like a goddess, but like a happy, normal girl.

...A smile I have to protect.

It's just like the promise I made with Wiene and the Xenos. A selfish promise that I can't break.

As the tavern swells with the excitement of a banquet, I realize Ms. Syr and I have been smiling together like the first day we met.

"—That's right, Bell!!! This scheming, troublesome Syr-what's-your-face is far more dangerous than Wallen-what's-her-face, and she doesn't need you going easy on her!"

"Gwah?!"

All of a sudden, I get tackled at high speed by my goddess and reflexively catch her in my arms.

"Listen up, Syr-what's-your-face!!! Bell isn't your Odr or whatever, he's *miiiiiiine*!!! *My prrrecious Bell!!!* If you eeever try to seduce my sweet, gullible boy again, I'll hit you with the purifying flames agaiiin!!!"

Sidling up to me like a child clinging to a mother, my goddess is really not holding back with Lady Freya, not even using her name. She just keeps calling her *Syr-what's-your-face* and slurring her words.

And I'm pretty sure that even Ms. Syr is finding Lady Hestia's triumphant grin annoying.

"Ack! Ahem…uh, G-Goddess, I'm sure Ms. Syr is sorry about what she did. You really shouldn't…"

"You're too sweet, Bell! Sweeter than a red-bean cream Jyaga Maru Kun! This Syr-what's-your-face is like the ultimate hidden boss! Leave a single opening, and she'll sic that Warlord on you with a snap of her fingers! You'll be abducted again!" my goddess says with a glare.

"Ah-ha-ha, that's not true," I say with a laugh.

"Ha-ha, of course not— Oops, my finger slipped."

Ms. Syr has a big smile on her face as she suddenly snaps her fingers.

"—Here are the extra dishes. Sorry to keep you waiting."

Before I can even blink, a giant boar appears like he teleported.

"Uwaaaaaaaa! You can *actually do that*?!?!?! And what kind of joke is this? Warlord, serving dishes with a body like that?!"

"——*Glub glub glub glub…*"

"Wait, Beeeeeeeell?!"

The instant his massive, boulder-like body appears in front of me holding a tray, my consciousness slips into darkness. Mainly because of nightmarish flashbacks of being battered, beaten, and blasted.

"What are you doing, Lady Hestia?!"

"Sir Bell's eyes have rolled back and his mouth is foaming!"

"Damn, that's some serious trauma!!!"

"M-Master Bell?!"

I think I can hear Lilly, Ms. Mikoto, Welf, and Ms. Haruhime shouting all at once, but I have no way to tell for sure because I've fallen down.

"Oh my, Mr. Bell! Oh no! He isn't breathing! I'll perform rescue breathing!"

"Like I'd let you!!! You aren't sorry at all!!!"

"Lady Frey—Lady Syr! You mustn't bring your lips near such filth! S-such a terrible, awful burden should be borne by a sinner such as myself…!"

"It's fine, Hörn. If it's a healer you need, then there's one standing here. Pucker up, Bell."

"What are you all doing so casually?! Mr. Welf, burn this coven of witches to ash, please!!!!"

"As if I could…"

I have no idea what happens next because I promptly pass out. Who knows what sort of uproar this is going to turn into or if a fight is brewing. I have no way of knowing.

"How long are you planning to sleep? Fool."

"Ghfu?!"

I wake up to something mercilessly slamming into my cheek. I sit up immediately and quickly gather that it's the tip of a shoe.

Swinging around, I notice a certain pair of eyes peering down at me.

"Ah, Master…"

"Get up. Do not cause me any more trouble, stupid rabbit."

Intensely relieved by the fact that Master is acting just like usual, I nervously look around.

The celebration is still going strong, and Mr. Bors is raising yet another toast. Who knows how many rounds they've already gone through?

How long have I been unconscious?

I'm currently lying up against the wall, and Master is the only one nearby…

"Umm…Why are you…a-apparently taking care of me…?"

"It was decided I would be the most neutral toward you. Quit making more work for me, you dolt."

Neutral…? In what sense? Did they mean cruel—

"What are you thinking?"

After briefly suffering from a fresh kick, I finally realize something. Master, whose face is as pretty as any lady's, is covered in bruises and cuts.

"U-um...where did you get those wounds...?"

"It's my punishment for disgracing my goddess. From Allen and the other first-tier adventurers. And Heith. And everyone else in the familia."

"Eh?!"

"After the second punch, I fought back."

"Oh..."

"I accepted the first blow, but there was no reason to quietly take any more."

Uhh...right. I can imagine him doing that. That's basically a whole new Folkvangr...Yeah, that's exactly what would happen.

It's hard to tell with their armor on, but the Gulliver brothers also seem to be nursing some fresh injuries. I guess I know why now...

But...If it weren't for him...

Master...Mr. Hedin. We were only able to win the war game because he sacrificed himself, knowing full well his familia would hold it against him and that this punishment was waiting for him.

Of course, that wasn't the only reason we achieved victory, but without him, we would have definitely lost, and I wouldn't have been able to save anyone.

"Master...Thank you very much. For lending us your strength."

"Don't misunderstand, you nitwit. I simply used you. I didn't help you."

"Even so, thank you."

Master is still standing and I'm still on the floor. Leaning against the wall, I look out at Lady Hestia and everyone else partying in the middle of the tavern, where Ms. Syr is being assailed from all sides. Her smile never falters even as she goes along with all their unreasonable requests.

"If it weren't for you, Master...I don't think Ms. Syr would be able to laugh like that."

Instead of looking at each other, we keep our eyes on her as a brief silence passes between us.

After a moment, he snorts.

"Stupid rabbit."

It's faint. So faint it's almost imperceptible. But I could swear he just smiled, though I don't know for sure because I'm still looking forward.

Master finally steps away from the wall with an annoyed look on his face.

"Your stupidity is contagious. I'm leaving."

"Yes, Master."

"Do not break the promise you made her."

"...Yes, Master."

With that, Master's long, blond hair sways as he turns toward the kitchen. As I watch him go, I finally get the sense that the long, difficult battle has ended at last.

"Is the booze here?! Then let me tell the tale of my heroic deeds!"

"*Yeaaaaaaaaaaaaah!*"

The banquet goes on. Mr. Mord and everyone else is enjoying themselves to the fullest with drinks and stories.

This is definitely going to last until morning.

With one last glance at the mortals and deities letting loose, I slowly stand up.

"Bell."

It's a cool voice.

When I turn around, there's an elf standing there. Instead of the waitress uniform, she's wearing travel clothes. My eyes widen a bit when I realize who it is.

"Ms. Lyu..."

She must have just gotten back.

"Could I have a moment of your time?"

We've stepped outside and gone a few steps into the back alley.

The laughter spilling from the tavern and the bustle of the main street has faded a bit. After struggling with my words a moment, I ask my question.

"Ms. Lyu, did you do what you wanted? With your goddess, I mean..."

"Yes. I finished saying my good-byes to Lady Astrea."

Ms. Lyu stops and turns around.

Her patron goddess, Lady Astrea, rushed to Orario to make it in time for the great familia war. To see off the goddess who no longer lived in the Labyrinth City—and to make sure Lady Astrea made it safely back to her current home—Ms. Lyu had left Orario for a short while.

Together with the second-generation *Astrea Familia*.

"I was able to escort her to Zolingam safely. I was allowed to perform that final act of familial piety."

With the help of Lord Hermes and his familia, she left the city. She called it her final selfishness, a final responsibility. Following her strict sense of honor, Ms. Lyu guarded her patron goddess and her new familia on their final journey.

Part of me thought she might never come back. So even though I am relieved that she came back, I also can't help but ask.

"Is this really for the best? To not return to Lady Astrea..."

Lady Astrea's blessing is still engraved in her back. No matter how painful the past, Ms. Lyu is still a follower of justice. She should have been able to follow her goddess.

If I were in her position, I'm sure I would waver.

Just thinking about having to say good-bye to Lady Hestia...

If it were me, if I could be forgiven, then I think I would choose to be together with her again.

"Yes, this is fine. I abandoned justice once before. To ask her to welcome me in again after I pushed her away is too selfish."

"B-but! That's—!"

"Besides, Lady Astrea has built a new home. A new familia follows her now."

I start to lean forward, but like an older sister explaining things, Ms. Lyu smiles. She is at peace.

"And I have found a different home, too. With Syr and the others. And with you. I chose this, Bell. I want to be here."

"Ms. Lyu..."

"Here, with all the people who saved me."

In no uncertain terms, Ms. Lyu declares that she is choosing the future instead of standing still and looking toward the past.

She used to dye her hair. The natural blond hair she's growing out in the open now seems to echo her answer.

"Besides, this isn't farewell for good. I can go see her whenever I feel like it. And I promised to send her letters once I got back. My bond with Lady Astrea and Alize and everyone else will never disappear."

Ms. Lyu's eyes wander toward her back, where her goddess's ichor is emblazoned. She's wearing an expression I've never seen before. No darkness clouds it. No doubt. Ms. Lyu and Lady Astrea have decided this is for the best.

It isn't my place to keep asking, so I stop leaning forward and smile at her. There's only one thing left for me to say.

"Welcome back, Ms. Lyu."

"...I'm back, Bell."

Lit by the gentle, magic-stone light, we share a quiet smile. What should be a gloomy, dark alley almost feels bright and warm.

"Bell, shifting to the main topic..."

"Ah, right. You said there was something you wanted to talk about. What is it?"

After spending that moment together, Ms. Lyu quickly changes the topic, and I remember why we're here.

Outside the tavern, it's just the two of us. She must want to talk about something important. Something she doesn't want anyone else to hear—the moment that thought crosses my mind, a shudder runs through me. My shoulder trembles.

"Bell, there is something I have to tell you first."

"Yes?"

"I love you."

"Yes... Wait, what?"

With everything going on, I somehow managed to forget that Ms. Lyu confessed her feelings for me!

"I love you…as a man."

She made sure there was no room for misunderstanding about whether she meant as a friend or a pet or anything else!

The temperature of my face shoots up. The instant I remember I'm here alone with a beautiful older woman, my heart starts racing.

And at the same time, the color drains from my face.

Bell Cranell is an absolute fool who can't turn his back on his idol.

If she wants an answer to that confession, there's only one response I can give!

I'm starting to get scared by the idea of affection from women, and I know I can't just go around saying this, and I don't have the right to, either, but after the incident with Ms. Syr, the idea of rejecting someone is just a bit traumatic.

If Gramps were here, he'd probably say, *Quit gettin' ahead of yourself. If you don't want it, trade with me, you disgrace!* but I can't help it! It's hard!

Ms. Lyu's sky-blue eyes are staring right at me!

I can't escape! Well, I mean, I *could*, but that would be *wrong*!

"…Ordinarily, I should probably discuss this with Lady Hestia instead of you, but…"

She wants official permission from the head of the family?!

While my foolish thoughts are running wild, Ms. Lyu stares at me with a dead serious look in her eyes.

The two of us, alone in a stone-paved back alley.

The perfect place for a secret chat. Her thin lips part.

"Bell—"

"W-wait, I'm not ready!"

My pathetic cry echoes in vain as Ms. Lyu finally reveals what she wants.

"I would like to join your familia."

"……………………………………….Huh?"

Needless to say, all I can do is stand there agog, looking like an idiot.

"Lady Lyu is joining us?!"

The next morning, Ms. Mikoto's surprised shout echoes across the clear, blue sky.

"Yes. I have received permission from Lady Astrea to convert."

Not just Ms. Mikoto, either. Ms. Lyu's straightforward statement has stunned Lilly, Welf, Ms. Haruhime, and our goddess.

We're all currently in the courtyard of *Hestia Familia*'s home, Hearthstone Manor.

As captain, I'm acting as the mediator, creating a space for negotiation.

"You're crazy powerful, and I know you're a solid, sensible elf, so from my perspective, I'd gladly welcome you, but..."

"That means quitting the restaurant, right? I'm amazed that dwarf allowed it..."

"Syr...no, Mama Mia told me, 'If you've got a place you wanna be, then get on and go.'"

Lady Hestia and Welf were both thinking of the scary dwarf, but Ms. Lyu just answers with the declaration she was given before—from back around the incident with Wiene and them.

"You've got that troublesome sense of justice, so you won't be able to stand still in one place for too long."

Apparently Ms. Mia has grumbled before, saying something along those lines with a tired sigh after Ms. Lyu left the tavern one too many times to come help us. As the primary reason for those frequent excursions, I definitely feel a bit bad...but Ms. Lyu told Ms. Mia her intentions after the war game finished.

"If you've found a place for yourself, then hurry up and go there. Stupid girl."

That's what she said, not even looking up as she kept preparing food. Ms. Lyu gave her one last thanks before she left.

"Thanks to the Andhrímnir, the restaurant has enough staff now… Also, it seems they are more efficient and adept than I ever was."

I laugh a little as Ms. Lyu supplements her explanation, looking down in embarrassment, maybe even seeming a little dejected. That only lasts for a moment, however, and she quickly collects herself.

"Lady Astrea has already performed the purification ceremony. I am an elf who has made a great deal of mistakes, but if you would be willing to have me…I would like to join this familia."

The Falna on her back is no longer connected to Lady Astrea. Not sealed. Just in a sort of tentative state, waiting for conversion. And even after a conversion, Lady Astrea's ichor would remain in her back. Her bond with Ms. Alize and everyone else will never be lost.

Ms. Lyu gently grabs her left shoulder with her right hand and looks at us with clear eyes.

Ms. Mikoto answers first.

"Of course! It would be an honor to be in the same family as you, to embark on the same adventures together!"

Ms. Mikoto has looked up to the elf who can Concurrent Cast ever since the battle with the Black Goliath on the eighteenth floor, and now her cheeks are flushed with a childlike excitement.

"There isn't any familia who would turn down a first-tier adventurer who comes knocking, right?"

"Yes! And we have received Lady Lyu's aid many times already. There is no reason to refuse her!"

"If a Level Six joins, and Mr. Bell is already Level Five…Our familia rank…The Guild tax…Ugh…my head…!"

Welf and Ms. Haruhime smiled as they agreed. Our familia's top mind is groaning and cradling her head, but…I'm sure it'll be fine.

And everyone already knows what I think.

It's unanimous.

"All right, then it's settled! We'll take care of the conversion ritual in a bit, but first—welcome to our familia, elf girl!"

Our goddess welcomes Ms. Lyu with open arms as Ms. Mikoto and the rest of us celebrate.

Ms. Lyu smiles and says, "Lilliluka."

"Hmm? …Ah, yes!"

Lilly seems a little caught off guard by Ms. Lyu using her first name instead of the "Ms. Erde" that she always used before. That surprised all of us.

"Welf, Mikoto, Haruhime…and Bell. And Lady Hestia. Please take care of me."

It seems like an important distinction for Ms. Lyu. This is how she plans to talk to us now that we live under the same roof as a family. As equals.

I smile, feeling just a tad embarrassed that Ms. Lyu is already talking to us the way she used to with *Astrea Familia*.

This strong, beautiful paragon of justice is our comrade now.

Hestia Familia has just grown a little bit larger.

"You're a good kid, elf girl! As expected of one of Astrea's followers! Unlike a certain cat burglar, I can trust you to look after Bell!"

"Why are you looking at me while you say that, Lady Hestia?!"

"Because you try to get the jump on me every chance you get! And Haruhime is even worse because she does it naturally without even meaning to!"

"Eeep?!"

"In that regard, this upstanding elf is wonderful. If anything happens, don't hesitate to tell me! I'm expecting great things!"

Goddess is singing Ms. Lyu's praises from the rooftops, prompting Lilly to complain, "This is discrimination!" And for some reason, Ms. Haruhime got caught in the cross fire. Welf looks tired by all this, and I'm a bit concerned how Ms. Lyu will handle this sort of mood when she's normally so serious.

"…I am sorry to bring something up so soon, but there is one thing I should mention."

As everyone else freezes, Ms. Lyu starts to elaborate.

"There is one issue with me joining a familia…or rather, a demand from the Guild. I have been asked to change my name."

"Hmm? What do you mean?"

"Officially, Gale Wind is dead."

Our goddess cocks her head, but I get the gist. In the aftermath of the

Juggernaut incident, Gale Wind was officially recorded as dead. However, since the war game was broadcast throughout the city, Ms. Lyu basically announced that she's still alive in a way that can't be ignored...

"The situation is complicated, but...as it was a formal Guild decision, for the sake of appearances, they have asked me to not register as an adventurer under the name Lyu Leon."

The gods seem to find this peculiar situation hysterical, and the people of Rivira are helpfully playing along, saying, "What are you talking about? Gale Wind is already dead, so of course that wasn't Gale Wind!" Of course, plenty of people know the truth. Even though her offenses were technically expunged when she was declared dead, it wouldn't be very convenient for the Guild to have someone who was on the blacklist openly walking around.

Out of consideration for her efforts to protect the peace during the Dark Ages and the practical considerations of not letting a valuable Level 6 go to waste, the Guild has requested that she at least change her name.

"So basically, the Guild wants to have a fake name in the adventurer registry, huh? Make it seem like you're a new adventurer with an unknown past rather than a transfer from *Astrea Familia*." Lilly mulls over the situation.

"Level Six *rookie* is an insane string of words..." Mikoto says as a bead of sweat trickles down her brow.

"Well, I guess that's fine. It's just for paperwork, so it's not like you have to actually change your name," Goddess summarizes.

It's not like we have any real reason to say no, so Ms. Lyu says her thanks and we start thinking of a name she can use.

"Umm, the whole name doesn't have to be different, right?"

"Yeah, just the family name should be fine. If I could, I would love to ditch Crozzo..."

"So, Lady Lyu Leon, changing just the family name..."

"Borrowing from Lady Mia, what about Lyu Grande...?"

"Hmmm, that's a little foreboding..."

"Elf girl, is there anything you'd like?"

Sitting in a circle on the courtyard grass, me, Welf, Ms. Haruhime,

Ms. Mikoto, and Lilly start playing with the idea while Goddess casually asks Ms. Lyu directly.

Sitting formally with her legs under her, Ms. Lyu pauses for a few moments before she glances at me and starts fidgeting.

After a couple more furtive glances, her cheeks go red, and she says, "Lyu...Lyu...Lyu Cranell..."

SMACK!!!

Goddess moved behind Ms. Lyu at lightning speed, a sandal in her hand, and a loud crack rang out as she hit Ms. Lyu in the back of the head.

"You were supposed to be *different*!!!"

"I-It's not like that. If I'm joining a familia, borrowing the name of a deity would be too irreverent, so I thought I should borrow the name of the captain...!!!"

"I can see right through your lies, you hapless elf!!!"

"Calm down, Lady Hestia!"

Ms. Lyu desperately tries to explain herself while rubbing the back of her head.

There is a certain logic to it...But it doesn't really feel quite right, either...

Ms. Mikoto is desperately trying to hold back Lady Hestia, who looks like she might kick out the newest member of our familia. Lilly quickly agrees with our goddess while Ms. Haruhime sways nervously back and forth as a noisy clamor fills the courtyard.

It's interesting seeing Ms. Lyu frantically try to explain herself. She always seemed so cool and pretty and gallant...but suddenly there's this clumsy side to her.

"...I think she'll fit in better than I thought."

"Yeah..."

I nod at Welf and do my best to stay out of it for as long as I can.

"*Lyu Astrea*...I know it's not really my place, but you aren't trying very hard to hide it, are you?"

That's Miss Eina's wry response as she takes the paperwork for a *new* adventurer from me as we enter one of the Guild Headquarters's consultation boxes. The cleanup following the war game is almost finished, so I made several reports and came to talk with Miss Eina today.

"Yes, we ended up deciding it would be nice to just name her after Lady Astrea..."

Once we're inside the mostly soundproof room that we've used so many times before, we sit down at the table, and after sharing a polite laugh, I sit up straight.

"Miss Eina, with this...our familia is now..."

"...Yes. Here is the official notice from the Guild."

I feel like a defendant standing before a judge, waiting for a verdict, as Miss Eina passes the single slip of parchment in her hands over to me. It bears the official Guild seal, and written on it is...

"*Hestia Familia* has been promoted to B rank. Congratulations."

...B...

...All the way to B from D, huh...?

"Even with Ms. Lyu, our familia still only has six people, though..."

"Mhmm. We know that, but...the Guild cannot classify a familia with two first-tier adventurers as anything lower. Especially not when one is a Level Six..."

I had to mention that, even though I knew what she would say. But after giving me the formal response, Miss Eina has a troubled look on her face.

"More than a few were arguing it should be A and not B, you know."

When she puts it that way, there isn't much I can say.

Loki Familia is S, and *Ishtar Familia* was A before it was disbanded, so the significance of being put into B rank instead is obvious. Lady Loki's faction and Lady Ishtar's Berbera are incredibly powerful groups that boast quantity and quality.

A small, elite faction. That's apparently the niche *Hestia Familia* finds itself in now. To think that just a little while ago, we were completely insignificant...

And despite our new rank, we're still holding a significant debt (that the goddess adamantly insists is her personal loan…)

A-anyway, the new tax we'll have to pay the Guild is going to be a painful jump. I can already imagine Lilly wailing in despair. As captain, lately I've also been looking over the familia's finances, but… all I can do when I look at the numbers is laugh nervously. We gave most of the prize from the war game to *Miach Familia* and the other familias, too.

"The level distribution of your members is part of it, but the biggest factor is, well…Goddess Freya has become Goddess Hestia's subordinate…"

Even though she knows we're in a soundproof room where no one will overhear us, Miss Eina still leans in close and lowers her voice to a whisper.

She's right, of course.

Officially, *Freya Familia* was dismantled, but it would be more accurate to say Lady Freya—or rather, Ms. Syr—has been placed under Lady Hestia's care.

The last thing Orario wants to do is give up an asset as powerful as the einherjar. At the same time, they're terrified of a goddess who could charm the entire city. Their answer to those two big issues was to make her subordinate to Lady Hestia.

As Lady Hestia managed to burn through her playhouse before, she's considered a deterrent if the goddess of beauty ever tries anything in the future. Plus, as long as our goddess is officially in charge of Ms. Syr, then Mr. Ottar and her other followers won't leave the city and will continue being useful in clearing the Dungeon.

For appearances' sake, they are nothing more than scary employees at a tavern and followers technically available for a conversion (though they'll never accept any offers).

…Anyway, that's apparently what the top brass of the Guild decided. The reasons are mainly political, so I probably only half understand at best.

The point is, in a certain sense, *Hestia Familia* has absorbed the enormous power of *Freya Familia*. Of course, we can't give them orders, let alone get them to fight alongside us…or rather, we're too scared to even try.

So if we're being precise, *Hestia Familia*'s rank is B (S). Officially, it's B, but in the upper levels of the Guild, we're treated as S.

I don't really understand the full implications myself, but that's the rough idea.

"Apparently, this is a fairly common system in Rakia and other country-level familias, but it's not done much here in Orario…At least, I don't think I've ever heard of it. That's just how much *Freya Familia* stretches the rules, I suppose."

"Oh right, you mentioned the Guild had trouble dealing with the aftermath surrounding Lady Ishtar, too."

"That's right. So…how has it been? Your relationship with *Freya Familia*?"

Miss Eina sounds a little concerned, so I smile to reassure her.

"I don't think we're going to be happily exploring the Dungeon together anytime soon…but outside of that, they've been really, really helpful."

What immediately comes to mind is the security they provided during the banquet the day before yesterday. Ms. Syr asked Mr. Hegni, Master, and the Gulliver brothers to keep watch around the clock, paying special attention to Ms. Haruhime.

Another thing is that lots of people who hold a grudge against Ms. Lyu have been popping up recently ever since word got out that Gale Wind is alive and well. One word from Ms. Syr was enough to eradicate them all. Master and the others did it before we even realized, clean and fast.

Hestia Familia is effectively under the protection of some of the strongest first-tier adventurers and the einherjar. After the Guild confiscated Folkvangr, Mr. Van and the others officially made their base of operations in the Dungeon, exploring every day and taking turns staying at Hearthstone Manor—or rather, standing watch from the shadows.

In a way, Hearthstone Manor is probably the safest place in the world right now because it's being guarded by the strongest, most terrifying bodyguards you could possibly have.

"This isn't atonement or anything of the like. It is just taking responsibility."

That's what Ms. Syr said as she refused to accept any thanks, but… it's thanks to her Ms. Haruhime and Ms. Lyu can live freely out in the open. If it weren't for them, it would have been quite difficult for Ms. Lyu to even join our familia.

"There's no need to worry. Thanks to Ms. Syr, there won't be any problems."

"Really? That's good to hear…"

Miss Eina has a bit of a troubled look on her face when she hears me use *that* name.

She probably has some lingering doubts due to what she experienced in the walled garden. I understand that it might not be easy for her to get over that. It isn't like either of us is a saint.

All I can do is smile apologetically.

"…Sorry. If you've decided to accept it, then it's not my place to say anything. So, shall we discuss what to do going forward?" Miss Eina asks.

"Yes! Please!" I say with a firm nod.

Once she's collected herself, Miss Eina spreads a Dungeon reference book out on the table.

Time to discuss our future plans in the Dungeon.

"What is your familia thinking?"

"We've been out of the Dungeon ever since the Goddess Festival, so we discussed easing back in by going to the middle floors first. We were thinking that setting up base on the eighteenth floor and staying in the Dungeon for a while could be an option."

Lilly, Ms. Haruhime, and I all leveled up, and the Level 6 Ms. Lyu has joined us. The *Hestia Familia* from before the Goddess Festival and Elegia is a completely different party from what *Hestia Familia* is today. Our current plan is to test ourselves in a relatively safe area to get a measure of our new strength and confirm what we can and can't do.

"When you add a new member to your party, you need to adjust your tactics and teamwork."

That's the advice Ms. Lyu gave us as a seasoned adventurer. Our commander Lilly completely agreed.

"Yes, that would be best," Miss Eina nodded. "What is Ms. Leo—Ms. Astrea's position in the party? Magic swordsman?"

"Umm…she said she can basically do anything, so she would cover whatever position we're missing. Vanguard, back line…she said not to expect too much, but she could even be a healer apparently…" I say, stumbling a bit on my words.

"Umm……………She really is an incredible adventurer, isn't she?"

Miss Eina's glasses almost slip off her face, but she manages to keep them on as she jots down a note with her quill.

Ms. Lyu has always been able to use healing magic, but thanks to her new Astrea Record skill, she can access the magic of all her fallen allies from *Astrea Familia*, including a dedicated healer's area-healing spell.

Without dancing around it too much, Ms. Lyu can essentially do everything herself.

Despite also being a first-tier adventurer, she's clearly a cut above someone like me who only knows how to charge in from the front.

With her addition to *Hestia Familia*, we have a lot more options in how we deploy. Lilly said it would be ideal for Ms. Lyu to fight as a pure mage or healer so she can move around freely, but…that might be asking a bit too much.

Either way, thanks to Ms. Lyu, we have long-range offense and healing covered. Between Welf's magic swords and Ms. Nahza's items, we don't have any gaps to speak of. That's why Lilly and I have concluded that *Hestia Familia* can move to the next stage.

"What do you think, Bell?"

Miss Eina almost seems like she's reading my mind, so I answer plainly.

"I want to move on to a new floor…beyond the twenty-seventh."

There was the incident with Juggernaut, so while we haven't completely explored the Water Metropolis, we should be able to go further.

With Ms. Haruhime's Level Boost, the entire party could be Level 3 or higher. More than enough to safely advance all the way to the thirty-sixth floor without too much issue, even going by the Guild's suggested level requirements.

Ms. Lyu made it to the forty-first floor with *Astrea Familia*, so with her experience and knowledge, there shouldn't be anything to fear even on floors the rest of us haven't seen—and unlike me, Lilly and the others have a better feel for the lower floors because they made it to the thirty-seventh floor with Lido and the Xenos by their own strength.

Of course, we have no intention of pushing ourselves too hard. I don't want to expose the familia to danger just because I'm in a rush.

Only after proper preparation and learning how our party works in the Dungeon…only then will we be ready to brave new territory. Safely, surely, steadily.

"…Right. Your party is more than powerful enough. In fact, it's almost excessive. That's what it means to have two first-tier adventurers in a party. I don't think passing the twenty-eighth floor safe point and pushing into the twenty-ninth floor would be a mistake."

The region beginning at the twenty-ninth floor is known as the Jungle Glens.

It is a heavily forested area where bloodsauruses and other dinosaur-type monsters begin to appear. Level 3 is a requirement for survival there.

After recalling what I learned about that part of the Dungeon in lectures, I nod in affirmation, only to notice Miss Eina suddenly smiling with a quiet look on her face.

"It's hard to believe it was only half a year ago you were being chased around by a minotaur on the fifth floor."

…Does she mean that it feels like that only happened yesterday?

Or that feels like forever ago?

I can't bring myself to ask, but she continues slowly.

"A lot has happened, and many things have happened to you that I don't know about…You're an adventurer, Bell. A full-fledged adventurer."

Her gaze seems tranquil, but also slightly lonely. Rather than an older sister happy to see how much her brother's grown...it's almost like a mother watching a child getting ready to leave the nest.

Before I realize it, I feel her emerald eyes pulling me in.

"Is it rude to say something like that to a first-tier adventurer?"

"Oh, uh, no, not at all...! Honestly, I still don't really feel like a first-tier adventurer myself..."

"Ha-ha...The truth is, I don't feel that way about you either," she says with a small chuckle, like she's finally coming to grips with her true feelings on the matter. Then she continues, saying, "I don't think you need my advice anymore."

"!!!"

"More like, I don't think I can help you anymore. I can teach you what's written in books and records, but...you're a first-tier adventurer now. You can think for yourself and find the answers on your own."

—So anything I can think of to tell you, you should already be thinking, too.

Without saying it explicitly, Miss Eina explains that all she can do is give harmless, noncommittal advice now.

"That's not—!"

"No, it is true. Because I'm not an adventurer."

"!!!"

"What you see as a first-tier adventurer is different from what I see."

She's still smiling as she says this, and I can't force myself to deny it.

The way Miss Eina sees the world and the way we adventurers—especially upper-class adventurers—see the world is fundamentally different.

"An adventurer must not risk adventure."

Miss Eina's standard advice, the golden rule for lower-class adventurers, applies less and less as an adventurer grows more capable and experienced. There comes a day for all of us when we have to risk something. A day when we delve ever deeper into the Dungeon and brave new dangers.

What I see and what Miss Eina sees are no longer the same.

"That isn't the only reason, but..."

Miss Eina grasped that fact far more firmly and quickly than I did, so as a final bit of advice, she suggests, "Why don't you rest for a while, Bell?"

"Huh...?"

"So much has happened. Too much. And you risked more than anyone...That's why I want you to take it easy for a little bit."

My eyes widen.

"I know you have a goal...That you look up to Ms. Wallenstein, that you want to chase after her. You talked about it with me before anyone else. I remember."

"........."

"So rest. Even if it's only for a short while. You've been pushing yourself so hard and for so long. If you aren't careful, you might wear yourself down completely before you even realize. Especially when you've been making progress toward your goal and feel like everything is going smoothly."

After the Xenos incident, and after returning from the deep floors, I took proper breaks before going back to the Dungeon—but that's not what Miss Eina means.

She's saying...

"You should reward yourself...and also, maybe try something new."

"Something new..."

"Mhmm. Based on my own experience, when things don't seem to be going right, and especially when you've been working really hard, it's good to try something different. It can change your perspective, and you might even notice that it connects back to your goal in surprising ways."

So why not try looking at something outside the Dungeon?

That's what she's saying.

"*Hestia Familia* is rank B now, so you will be given expedition missions. You will be facing the Dungeon sooner or later. So until then, take this chance to give yourself room to breathe, broaden your horizons, and take things slower...That's my suggestion."

With our new familia rank and the problem of higher taxes, it would be difficult to remove ourselves from the Dungeon entirely. And there's definitely a part of me that's tempted to sprint forward now that I've become Level 5—now that the woman I've been chasing has finally come into view.

But that might be all the more reason why I should take a deep breath and take stock of things.

With the great familia war over and the title of first-tier adventurer hanging over me, I realize that I've subconsciously been getting a bit hasty.

"Sorry for raining on your parade right when you were feeling so eager to rush ahead."

"...No, not at all."

Miss Eina looks apologetic, but I shake my head.

She might be feeling a bit down after declaring that she doesn't have anything more to teach me now that I'm a first-tier adventurer. But that simply isn't true. No matter my level, it doesn't change the fact that I only have half a year of experience as an adventurer.

Compared to Ms. Aiz and the other first-tier adventurers, I'm incredibly lacking in knowledge and experience, both as an adventurer and as a person. There are still so many things I need to learn.

And Miss Eina has always thought more about me than anyone else, despite the half-baked adventurer that I am.

"You help me realize so many things." Miss Eina knows me better than I know myself. As much as my goddess, even. That's something I can believe in. "I'm glad I came to talk to you, Miss Eina."

I try to put my feelings into words and give her a smile.

Behind her glasses, I can see her emerald eyes shoot open before she also breaks into a big smile. After sharing a quiet moment together, we both start laughing.

"So, something new...Hmm, what should I do?"

"There's no need to force it. Once you find something that piques your interest, go ahead and take a look."

In the meantime, we're supposed to acclimate to our new statuses and work on our coordination as a party. And avoid setting a new goal for the time being.

Settling on that plan, we emerge from the consultation box. Not many people are in the Guild Headquarters since so many adventurers are in the Dungeon during the afternoon, so the place feels more spacious than usual.

Miss Eina watches in amusement as I immediately start racking my brain about what to do next, when—

"!"

"Bell? What is it?"

My gaze immediately turns to the window when I hear a certain sound.

"...A whistle? No, this is..."

It's a sound I've never heard once in Orario.

It isn't loud enough for Miss Eina to hear it. Only a first-tier adventurer who has been through several level-ups could possibly catch this faint, deep note.

A Guild employee bursts through the lobby entrance. As soon as he whispers something to the receptionist at the counter, everyone starts moving at once.

The few adventurers hanging around are also on the move. Sensing something, they dash out of the headquarters with a destination in mind.

"What's happening...? Things suddenly got really busy..."

I'm stunned by the abrupt shift. Miss Eina murmurs, "Ahhh, the School District has come back."

—The School District?

It's an unfamiliar phrase...or actually, I think I heard it once before.

Was it Lai and the other kids who told me the first time I visited the orphanage on Daedalus Street?

"Why don't you go have a look?"

"Huh?"

"The School District returning to port is like a festival for Orario. I'm sure the top of the city wall has been opened to the public."

R-returning to port?

What does that have to do with the top of the city wall? Miss Eina smiles as I obviously have trouble understanding the connection.

"I need to go over there as well to give a proper welcome."

Her smile seems a little awkward, almost revealing the swirl of emotions in her heart.

The top of the city wall where Ms. Aiz and I trained so many times before is on the northwestern side, which was only accessible because Ms. Aiz knew an unlocked way in.

The section of the city wall that the Guild has currently opened to the public is on the southwest side.

"I can see it! It's coming into view!"

"It's been three years!"

From the Guild Headquarters in the northwest, Miss Eina and I walk south together before climbing the long stairs up to the top of the giant wall. As we ascend, we hear the chorus of shouts coming from above.

All sorts of people line the wall's walkway, including regular townsfolk, adventurers, Guild employees, merchants, and even travelers. I'm stunned by the size of the crowd, but we somehow manage to make it to the outer edge.

"There it is…!"

In front of me, dozens of people are pointing farther to the southwest.

Beyond the big harbor and a giant, brackish lake lies the big, wide ocean that goes on and on to the horizon. And on that horizon sits an enormous silhouette, big enough that anyone can spot it clearly from this distance.

"A floating city?!"

Thanks to the enhanced vision of an adventurer, I can make out some details. The gleam of metal in the sunlight. A grand, imposing form consisting of three stacked discs. And atop those discs sits a dense collection of what are unmistakably buildings, plus a giant tower.

And extending out from the inorganic structure are what looks like blue plumage, or possibly wings, almost giving the impression that a town was built on the back of a sea dragon.

A town?

A city?

Or a country?

Is it…a *ship*?!

"That ship is called the Hringhorni. It is far and away the world's largest ship." Miss Eina gazes at it warmly like a second home as I watch in stunned silence.

That's when the realization suddenly hits me.

The sound I heard wasn't a whistle, it was a ship's foghorn. A giant, magic-stone foghorn!

"Its official name is the Maritime Academy for Scholarship Special Administrative District—commonly shortened to the School District."

At the same time she says that, the excitement on the wall boils over.

"The School District's baaaaaaaaaaaaaaack!!!"

The Labyrinth City welcomes the gargantuan ship home with cheers.

My eyes are wide open and the flush of excitement burns my cheeks.

This is just how adventurers are.

The thrill of the unknown…

My heart races as I lay eyes on a new world I've never seen before.

CHAPTER 2
SCHOOL HEAVEN AND HELL

Meren is a port town built on the shore of a lake about three kirlos southwest of Orario. Connected to the sea through Lolog Lake, Meren is Orario's bridge to the world's oceans situated on the westernmost edge of the continent.

Every day, countless ships from distant lands enter port, disgorging countless people, creatures, and items destined for the city that many consider the center of the world. And what flows into Meren are magic-stone products bound for barges setting out to sea. Orario has a monopoly on the production of magic-stone items, and most trade is conducted not overland, but by sea.

Considering that, it might not be an exaggeration to say ships from all around the world gather here.

As for me, this isn't my first time coming to Meren, but every time I'm here, it feels like visiting a foreign country.

The distinct smell of fresh and salt water mixing in Lolog Lake is supposed to be a lot milder than that of a saltwater lake, but I grew up in a mountain village, so I can't help but find it fairly strong.

The lively main avenue feels like a bazaar, and many of the shops are filled with the bounty of the sea. The streets are packed with suntanned fishermen and visitors from faraway islands, deserts, and all sorts of other places. Everything brings home the feeling that this is a port town.

It is easy to forget in Orario, cut off from the rest of the world by giant walls, but the city is surprisingly close to the sea.

Ordinarily, I would be staring, dazzled by these scenes like a country bumpkin. But this time, things are a little different.

"Whoaaa!"

With masterful navigation, the giant ship enters Lolog Lake through a channel. A smaller ship (a galleon still over forty meders long) that just left the docks quickly turns back as the giant ship sails into the harbor with blue sails fluttering in the breeze like a majestic sea dragon.

It's so tall my neck hurts looking up at it. This one ship is filling the entire western half of the harbor where hundreds of ships would normally dock.

An explosion of cheers fills the bay as I stare in slack-jawed awe.

"Welcome back!"

"Tell us about your adventures!!!"

"Welcome to Meren!"

People are holding hands and dancing for joy under the blue skies. The moment the ship enters the brackish lake, the constant cheers crescendo.

There are so many people lining the port, it almost looks like the whole population of Meren is out. An enormous number of humans and demi-humans are waving flags or their hands, and some are even playing instruments.

Several children run past, jumping around as I stand dumbstruck in the middle of the crowd.

"This is amazing…It really is like a festival."

"That's not far from the truth. The School District returns to Orario once every three years, and it's easily one of the city's biggest events," Miss Eina explains.

After going up onto the wall in Orario and seeing the ship in the distance, Miss Eina suggested going to the port. Or more accurately, she saw my eyes gleaming like a curious child's and graciously invited me to join her with a knowing smile, which is how I ended up here in Meren.

The inspection at Orario's city gates is incredibly strict—especially for deities and followers of familias considered key assets—so it would normally be impossible to leave without filling out incredibly time-consuming and tedious paperwork. But the return of the School District is apparently a special occasion.

I don't really understand, but for the duration of the School District's stay, the southwestern gate that connects the city to Meren—and only that gate—is kept open. Adventurers still have to undergo a check by *Ganesha Familia*'s guards, but I was let through without much hassle today because I'm helping out a certain Guild employee.

We came here together with a stream of Orario's residents flowing out of the gate.

"Umm…so what exactly is the School District?"

"Hmm. Put simply…it's a school that travels all around the world. The biggest school in the mortal realm."

Even after the massive ship finishes docking, the cheers are still going strong. When the crowd finally starts to move, we go with the flow and begin walking toward the giant school.

"The School District is a traveling educational institution supported by the Guild. It accepts children ages six to eighteen who wish to study there, picking them up from all over the world."

"The whole world? Why does it do that?"

"First of all, that's the desire of their sponsor, the Guild. A great many people already gather in Orario, but that isn't enough. For the sake of running the city…and more than anything, for the sake of achieving the Three Great Quests, the Guild is always looking for more talent."

When I expose my ignorance, Miss Eina sounds almost happy. She holds up her index finger and launches into a new lesson. It's like she's enjoying the chance to take care of a child who stopped needing her help.

"Also, it is the divine will…or I suppose it's the passion of the deities who guide the School District."

"Eh? Deities…? More than one…? Does that mean the ship is…"

"Yes. The School District is managed by multiple familias. Sort of a union of familias."

A familia union. My eyes shoot open. At the same time, it doesn't really make much sense to me.

I know about Dungeon-focused and mercantile familias, and I have heard about academic ones that charge a fee in exchange for teaching regular folk who aren't a part of any familia, particularly children. Apparently it's common for them to look for promising children in their classes and invite them into their familia.

From what I've heard, academic familias are closely tied to the regions they are located in, which is why cities and countries love having an academy nearby, since it means a big pool of talent. However, it's difficult to gather enough skilled instructors to properly run an academic familia. Any newly established familia trying to break into the market is likely to fail.

Maybe it's just my bias as a country bumpkin born in a village without much around, but I've always felt like school is something usually reserved for the wealthy or nobility. Still, with academic familias, as long as you have some money to start, you can be given an opportunity to learn.

Unfortunately, there aren't any familias like that in Orario—hold on.

Do I have it flipped?

They must need a lot of people to run this giant school. Does that mean the School District is just where all of Orario's academic familias are…?

"Race, status, wealth, and family are not factors here. Only the desire to study is necessary," Miss Eina says as she watches the children streaming past us. "The spirit of exploration, the desire to keep chasing and learn what you can become. That is the only requirement to become a student at the School District."

Connections and pedigree aren't important. And no amount of money will help. Only those who carry the spirit of a student, willing to acknowledge their lack of knowledge, can pass through its gates.

Miss Eina seems proud as she talks about it.

"…Wow, Miss Eina. You know a lot about the School District."

"Hee-hee, I was a student there once."

"Eh?! R-really?"

When I get that unexpected response, I twitch and my voice cracks. The people around us all look at me, and I start to blush, but also…I know so little about Miss Eina despite how much she's done for me, and that makes me feel a bit guilty and ashamed…

But interesting. The reason she knows so much isn't just because she's a member of the Guild. A great many things she learned in the classrooms of that giant school ship have, through Miss Eina, helped us adventurers countless times.

That thought makes me feel oddly grateful to the School District and also sparks my interest.

I'm already an adventurer, so I can't become a student now, but…I do wonder what sort of place the School District is.

"Right, as a former student…I was asked to handle most of the formalities for the School District's return, but…"

"…Miss Eina?"

That's when I notice that even though she looks proud, her expression also makes it seem like she's deeply troubled by something. I study her expression until I notice the flow of people stops.

We've reached the western side of the harbor. Or, more accurately, we've reached the giant shipyard.

The crowd is pushing close to see the docked School District from up close. There are lots of other Guild employees and members of *Ganesha Familia* directing the flow of traffic. Apparently, no residents of Orario, whether adventurers or just regular townsfolk or even deities, are allowed to get near that giant ship.

"I'm home, Meren!"

"We're baaaaack!"

"This is my first time! Meren! And Orario!"

The cheers from the people are still ringing, and from the outer railing sixty meders up—the ship's gunwales—a visible crowd of boys and girls have gathered, waving back.

They are wearing similar uniforms, and it feels like there are a lot of them close to my age. I guess they're students at the School District?

"………"

Looking up at the students, Miss Eina screws up her emerald eyes, and she looks almost like she's in pain.

No, it's more…is she wavering about something?

I feel uncomfortable, but still, I marshal my courage to say something—

"—Mgh?!"

Before I can, a hand stretches out from the crowd behind me, covers my mouth, and pulls me back into the crowd.

"...Sorry, Bell, I have work to do now, so I should...huh? Bell? Beeeell?"

"Fghhhh?!"

One hand covers my mouth, and another grabs my shoulder as we force our way through the sea of people.

Walking backward through the crowd, trying my best to stay upright after I almost trip, I am finally released as we emerge from the crowd of people.

"Puhaa?! L-Lord Hermes?!"

"Aaaah, Bell! To think I would meet you here! This must be fate!"

He flicks the brim of his trademark winged cap as a sort of greeting. I'm taken aback seeing him gesturing so enthusiastically.

"From the looks of it, you saw the School District from the city, and spurred by the unknown like a true adventurer, you found yourself all the way out here?"

"Ugh...! Y-Yes, sir, that's right..."

The reason I didn't immediately shake free is because I sensed his divine presence, and since the person questioning me is a god, I simply confess. I am still really flustered as I ask my most immediate question.

"Lord Hermes, why are you...?"

"The School District's finally back, so of course I'm going to come out and see it for myself. Every god and goddess with a familia is here," he whispers into my ear, wrapping his arm around my shoulder. "See, look over there in the crowd, and up there on the rooftops...You can see deities and adventurers here and there, right?"

"Ah, I do..."

Looking where he pointed, I can see deities who are presumably patron gods and goddesses, and also followers. They're all looking at the School District and whispering to each other, as if plotting something.

Is the fact that I feel a premonition of some kind of uproar a sign of how much Orario has seeped into my bones?

I have a bad feeling when Lord Hermes answers.

"They're all here to scout for their familias."

"S-scout…? Do you mean the students at the School District? But why…?"

"Because the School District is a treasure trove of talent, obviously!"

Clenching his fist, Lord Hermes says, "Let's find a place to talk," though we don't go very far and just move to the mouth of a side alley between some buildings where we can still see the ship.

"Have you heard how the School District is an educational institution that travels around the world?"

"Ah, yes, sir. Miss Eina told me that…"

"Then that makes it quick. The School District is famous, so it has a tendency to get involved in troublesome things. If there's a request from a town, they'll slay monsters, and at times even intervene in conflicts between countries."

"C-conflicts?"

"'Make thy will a sword, thy knowledge a staff, and thy failures a crown.' If anything, they have a habit of sticking their nose into things without waiting for a request. Practical studies, they call it. Helps the students grow."

All of a sudden, the School District is sounding a lot more dangerous…!

"With all that happening, it's an environment that isn't lacking for experiences, even if it isn't quite to Orario's level. It's standard for the students to be Level Two, and I've heard there are even a few Level Threes sprinkled around, too."

"Level Threes?!"

I've been shocked a lot today, but still, there's no helping this one.

Orario can mess with your perception, but a follower who has leveled up at all is already extraordinary. For reference, a village or town with even one person who's leveled up would have no issue defeating a swarm of monsters that are common up on the surface world.

The shift from quality over quantity after deities descended to the mortal realm created the current age where even a single person who has leveled up can overcome most things. And leveling up twice, reaching Level 3, anywhere outside Orario would make that person overwhelmingly powerful. Many of the Level 3s out in the wider world usually lead whole organizations or are powerful figures. The power of a Level 3 is more than enough to break the mold. It's Orario that's simply absurd as a city, home to hundreds of upper-class adventurers.

So hearing that the School District has Level 2 and Level 3 students even without the den of monsters that is the Dungeon undeniably makes it a treasure trove of talent, even if we're only measuring pure combat strength.

"There are lots of graduates of the School District even among the current upper-class adventurers. *Loki Familia*'s Thousand Elf being the most prominent example."

Thousand Elf…that amber-haired elf…ugh, my head…!

"It is a place for learning. The students pretty much always graduate and proceed down various career paths. Naturally, some of them want to become adventurers. And we gods absolutely love recruiting them! That's the long and short of it."

"I—I see…"

I'm starting to see why they would get heated over that.

I can already imagine Lady Hestia's eyes when she learns about this. I have no doubt she'd want to immediately rush out and start recruiting…

"The regulations aren't just to tamp down on the common folk's enthusiasm. It's also to keep Orario's deities and their familias from making contact with the students."

"I-Is that so?"

"Yes. Thus the rules. Can't have anyone getting the jump on recruiting and internships."

Internships? Recruiting?

He clenches his fist while I cock my head at the unfamiliar words.

"However! Everyone still wants to get dibs on a promising prospect! As the patron of a familia! You understand, don't you?!"

"Y-yes…"

Overwhelmed by his sudden burst of passion, I just barely manage to nod.

Not that it matters much, but I feel really uncomfortable, even though we aren't doing anything I should feel guilty about. Maybe it's because we're talking secretively in the shadows for some strange reason…

"Which means, Bell my boy, we're going to slip inside the School District!"

"Why is that the natural conclusion?!"

Agh, something bad is coming!

"Our familia is always hiring, or rather, we always need people who can make a real difference! We can't afford to be left in the dust when a gold mine like the School District is staring us in the face!"

"That isn't a reason for me to help, though! Wh-why not just get Ms. Asfi to help instead of me?!"

"Asfi is…well, I gave her time off. She's been *constantly* working for so long…"

Ah……

Lord Hermes's gaze drifts to something far away as he answers, and I can't help doing the same with my eyes, staring into the distance.

This is also applicable to Ms. Heith the healer, but in Orario, when people think of the quintessential example of someone who is supremely competent and gets worked to the bone, who always has dead, exhausted eyes…Well, it has to be…

"Or rather, if I hadn't given her some time off, I might have been killed. The truth is, she was supposed to take a break around the Goddess Festival, but…well, *that* happened, right?"

"Urgh…!"

"Asfi was racing across the map, and unfortunately, the timing just wasn't very good."

When he brings up an incident that could sort of be blamed on me, I groan like I bit into a rotten fruit.

And from the sound of it, Ms. Asfi's vacation spurred the rest of his familia to take some time off all at the same time. Basically, there aren't many people to go along with his *request* at the moment.

"I didn't really want to say it, but the reason I'm here all alone without my familia is sort of your fault, isn't it?"

"Urk?!"

"And I did give Hestia a hefty amount of support during the war game, too..."

Uh-oh...!

I'm getting sucked into his pace...!

"By the way, Bell? Did you know that I put in a lot of effort behind the scenes to negotiate with the goddesses who wanted to make Lady Freya pay dearly? That's a big part of why Syr is allowed to stay in Orario...Don't you think it would be fair if *someone* did a little bit to reward me for everything I've done?"

Lord Hermes winks and flashes a smile. I just hang my head in defeat.

It goes without saying that Bell Cranell can't refuse a god's request.

The School District is supposed to be *strictly* off-limits to outsiders.

Other than the students, teachers, deities, and others who belong on the ship, all other factions, groups, and unaffiliated individuals are forbidden from boarding.

The reason is because the School District is a vault of secrets, including its production of orichalcum, among other things.

With its graduates including many mages, alchemists, and other skilled artisans, the School District is equipped with many different systems utilizing its own unique knowledge base. To ensure that none of these are used for evil, the School District is apparently really strict about making sure no information leaks out. For an outsider to set foot on the ship takes a similar amount of paperwork, hassle, and time as getting anywhere with Orario's bureaucracy. No matter how powerful the royalty or great the figure—even a first-tier adventurer from Orario—there are no exceptions…or so Lord Hermes tells me.

Basically, what I'm saying is, sneaking into the School District is extraordinarily difficult.

In port, School District staff and *Ganesha Familia* are equally on guard, so even with invisibility, someone sneaking around will definitely be noticed. All the cargo loaded onto the ship is inspected with a fine-toothed comb. It's virtually impossible to get in from land.

The natural question is what if you go by sea, but that's also difficult. If you get a boat and try to sail close, there is no way it won't be seen, and even if you somehow did reach the giant ship, the idea of trying to climb up that towering hull is dizzying.

I'm Level 5, but sneaking in while carrying a god is really just not reasonable…was the argument I was clinging to, but Lord Hermes just grinned and immediately shot back.

"Then what about from the sky?"

"—UuuugghhhhaaaaaaAAAAAHHHHH?!"

Falling down from impossibly high up, I cry out pathetically as I hold on to Lord Hermes. Staying unnoticed is the last thing on my mind, but fortunately, my shouting is drowned out in the furious rush of wind.

"I was right to borrow a spare Hades Head and Talaria from Asfi's rooooom!"

"You call this 'right'?!"

"Of course it is! We can get in from the sky this way! All we need is for you to control the descent!!!"

"I don't know how to control these at aaaaaaaall!!!"

We're shouting as loud as we can to be heard over the deafening rush of wind as we fall out of the sky. I'm doing my best to control Ms. Asfi's spare Talaria that Lord Hermes made me wear.

Ten minutes ago, he put this magic item I have no clue how to use on me. After he had me wear the suspicious-looking helmet, we became invisible, and I somehow managed to wobble my way up into the sky, reaching the area above the School District without anyone noticing, but—that was where the miracles stopped.

Like fools who flew too close to the sun, Lord Hermes and I are falling from around five hundred meders up!

"Apparently Hestia and Asfi treated themselves to a two-person flight behind our backs! So we should stick a heart-pounding landing of our own, shouldn't we?!"

"This isn't the time for stuff like thaaaaaaaaat!!!!"

Lord Hermes's laughter rings in my ears as I cradle him in my arms and the wind makes a mess of our hair and clothes.

This is different from when I fell down the Great Falls. A primordial terror is welling up from the pit of my stomach, and massive tears are stinging my eyes! They get torn away by the wind as soon as they form, though!

As I grow increasingly more panicked, I could swear the gods and goddesses above are having a great laugh at us. The distance between us and the ship rapidly closes until—

"Gwaaaaaaaaaah!"

We safely crash-land in a corner of the School District where wooden boxes are piled up—a storage area.

Just before we crash, right as I let out an unholy scream, Talaria's four wings unfurl and forcefully brake, but it's simply not enough. Unable to fully kill the momentum, I slam feetfirst into a mountain of boxes with a loud crash.

"...I...I'm alive..."

"Woo, that's a Level Five for ya! Not a single scratch on the package. You really have grown, Bell!"

I did everything I could to make sure Lord Hermes wasn't hurt, and just like he said, I can't see a single scratch on him. If anything, he's quite happy and well.

Pushing myself up from the bed of lumber, I start to smile weakly.

"What was that sound?!"

"I'm sure it's another trespasser from Orario! Hurry!"

PIIIIIIIIIII!

A shrill, piercing whistle is the only warning we get as everything starts moving all around us.

"Eeeep?! I-is that...?!"

"Looks like they noticed us. Well, we did make a pretty big crash-landing."

Of course we did!

Screaming and cradling my head inside my heart, I frantically stand up.

"L-let's escape while we're invisible! If we do, they won't...!"

"Yeah, the truth is, I sneaked in using a Hades Head a while back. The School District's developed magic items that can pierce invisibility magic."

"What?!"

And wait, you've done this before?!

Then *obviously* their defenses will be even higher now! Meanwhile, I can sense people closing in on this place fast!

"Which means, time for a decoy, Bell!"

"I—I have a really bad feeling about this, but what's the plan?!"

"You act as the decoy while I escape! That's the plan!"

"Lord Hermes?! Wait, ah!"

There's no time for me to argue as he pulls the magic item off my head—the one that kept us invisible while falling—and pushes me in the chest.

As I fall off the bed of broken boxes and land with a *thud* on the metal ground, the invisible Lord Hermes says "Sorry!" and "Take care!" before causally leaving me behind! And he makes sure to grab Talaria before throwing my shoes back at me, too!

Lord Hermes!!!

As I lamely cry out in my head, I hear someone shout, "Hey, you!"

Immediately, a boy and girl in the school uniform appear, looming like executioners.

I just manage to get my shoes back on and catch my breath before bursting into a cold sweat upon sighting the new arrivals.

I feel like a thief cornered at the top of a cliff.

But then…

"Were you caught in the explosion?! You aren't injured, are you?!"

"N-no…I'm all right."

"Did you see anyone suspicious?! Do you know where they went?!"

"U-umm…I did. Th-they went that way…"

As I leap to my feet, the human girl charges in with a ferocious look, *worried about me*, and the animal-person boy *considerately* asks me where the trespasser has gone.

I carefully don't meet their gazes and keep my face down, while pointing in the opposite direction from where Lord Hermes went.

"There!"

"What a mess! You should go to the infirmary right away!"

"I'm sure it's *Hermes Familia* again! Coming in from the sky's impossible without Perseus's magic items!"

They are not suspicious of me; in fact, they seem appreciative as they run off in the direction I pointed.

After they disappear from view, this time I slump down weakly.

"I-I'm safe…"

I let out a big sigh in relief.

After staring up at the blue sky while sitting down for a bit, I slowly stand and look down at myself.

"So this is why Lord Hermes made me wear this uniform…"

I'm not wearing my usual everyday clothes or my battle gear. I'm wearing the same school uniform as the students I saw before. The outfit is mostly white, and I'm wearing a burgundy tie that Lord Hermes tied for me. The shirttail is long and split, like the outfit I wore to Lord Apollo's banquet. The pants are sharp and slender, sort of like what the gods call skinny fit…

Well, it fits my body perfectly. Did Lord Hermes…intend for me to wear this from the start? Was this really the plan?

If not, then he wouldn't have prepared this specific uniform in advance, would he have? I wipe the sweat from my brow, but then my breath catches in the back of my throat.

I managed to avoid suspicion somehow, but if I hang around here all alone at the site of the crash, it's going to be too suspicious. If I'm questioned, I have no confidence in being able to talk my way out of it.

I immediately start to leave.

And what I see leaves me awestruck.

"Whoooa…!"

Passing through a narrow path, what appears before me almost makes me forget I'm on a boat—a cluster of white stone buildings with blue roofs. The symmetrical construction is practically a work of art, making them look like churches or cathedrals.

This is the School District, so I guess these buildings are all schoolhouses?

Walking along an empty, stone-paved road, I swing my head all around. The magic-stone lamp at the corner is comparable to Orario's in quality of design, and I guess they are made by students, because "Crafts Department 42nd Term Graduation Project" is engraved in it. The other buildings, the beautiful arch, and a sculpture of a goddess, too!

I'm staring at everything around me in such obvious wonder that if anyone saw me, they would definitely assume I'm not a student.

"If someone told me they took a capital from some country and just plopped it onto this boat…I would probably believe them."

That's just how big and organized the School District is.

I assumed all the buildings would be packed together because of the naturally limited space of a ship, but maybe the construction is why nothing feels cramped or crowded. And not just the architecture. The evergreen trees here and there are pleasant on the eyes. And they're closed at the moment, but there are even buildings that are obviously not schoolhouses and look almost like stores, boutiques like I've never really been in before. It feels like I'm walking through a luxury residential neighborhood.

This is…the School District.

This is all floating on the water!

"Gh…!"

Losing out to the excitement that is building in my chest, I start running.

Just like half a year ago, when I first came to Orario, entranced by the new world around me!

Forgetting my precarious situation, I dash through the street, up the stairs, coming out on a little bit of a high ground. Holding on to the handrail with both hands and leaning out, the world of study in front of me is just so beautiful.

"Amazing...!"

A sea of white buildings and blue roofs spread out before me. I can make out more than fifty elegant schoolhouses. This place looks like a paradise.

Avenues radiate out from the center, dividing up each section. Amid the beautiful white-and-blue buildings, what's particularly eye-catching is a structure that seems to be an arena. Made of valmars from the Dungeon, a material that's also used for weapon and gear manufacturing, this is easily the most imposing building in the otherwise beautiful cityscape.

The green visible in the distance, near the back of the ship...is that a garden?

Based on just what I can currently see, it's easily big enough to hold three of those arenas.

But the most incredible thing is...

The tower in the middle of the ship is the most striking feature.

It obviously isn't Babel, but even so, there is a giant tower piercing the sky.

Like the other schoolhouses, the tower is a beautiful white with a blue roof, more sublime than imposing.

Seeing the city from here, it almost feels like a castle town built around the base of the giant central tower. Even without knowing any better, it isn't hard to imagine that that tower is probably considered the most important point on this giant ship.

But at the same time, it feels familiar.

"This layout...is a lot like Orario."

I think back to the layout I saw from overhead before we crash-landed.

Other than the giant, blue raiment fluttering all around the ship—probably sails—the School District is a perfect circle. The same construction as Orario, surrounded by its giant city walls. Miss Eina said it was financed by the Guild, and between the giant tower in the center and the main streets radiating out from the center…my guess that it was modeled off Orario might not actually be far from the truth.

A small labyrinth city. Orario's little brother.

However, it is a lot cleaner and more elegant than the original. I guess that comes down to the difference between a city of adventurers and a town built for students.

I'm still frozen in awe at the scenery of the School District when I hear someone say, "You're amazing, Nina!"

"You got top marks on the test! You should leave that loser group and come back to the Education Department!"

Just then, my eyes open wide as a clamor reaches my ears.

The stone-paved street facing the promontory.

Girls of all races are chatting as they pass.

"It was just luck. I just guessed right on the range of topics I expected to be covered."

And seeing the girl at the center of the discussion makes my eyes widen further.

Long brown hair tied back with a ribbon near the middle of her back. Ears longer than a human's but not so pointed as an elf's. A half-elf, but as if testament to the noble blood in her veins, a single lock of her hair is jade-colored. Her eyes are emerald. Even from a distance, I can tell her face is well-proportioned and cute.

But more importantly, I can't help seeing *her.*

"…Miss Eina?"

She isn't wearing glasses, and she's not the same height. Her hairstyle and the air around her are different, too. But even so, that name is what comes to my lips.

"———"

There is no way she could have heard my murmur.

But she stops in her tracks, and as if guided by the sea breeze, she turns to look at me.

My red eyes looking down.

Her emerald eyes looking up.

Our eyes meet beneath the vast blue sky.

"*—Emergency broadcast! Emergency broadcast! There are signs of a trespasser in the School District!*"

Just then, shredding the air between us, an earsplitting voice rings out across the entire vicinity.

"*Based on the Alchemy Department's investigation, there are two trespassers! One is a deity and the second is a follower! Judging from the Morals Police report, it is highly likely the latter is wearing a school uniform to pass as a student!*"

The source of the broadcast is speakers attached to the buildings and pillars. The announcer is clearly brimming with determination to bring down the wrath of heaven upon the villain who dares disturb their holy ground, and my face grows paler as her voice jumps.

"*A male human with white hair and red eyes! I repeat, a human with pure white hair like a feral rabbit's, and bloodshot, red eyes like a deviant's!*"

Okay, isn't that slander?! I don't have time to say it out loud, though.

Only the half-elf girl was looking at me before, but more and more people are noticing me, and their gazes feel like a line of spears at the ready, taking aim at me.

"White hair and red eyes..."

"Hey...over there..."

Five seconds while the students walking by murmur.

One second for a bead of sweat to drip from my cheek down to my chin.

Half a second for an extraordinary sensation to build around me.

""""""That's hiiiiiiiiiiim!!!""""""

They start shouting all at once.

The half-elf girl's shoulders jump as the students roar. Meanwhile, I flip around. Sweat starts pouring down my face and back as I sprint away at full speed!

"The target is running!"

"He's moving north from the sixth ward into the ninth! Have the people in the Sky Lounge cut him off!"

"Ask the supervisor for permission to use weapons and magic on school grounds!"

"Stooooop!"

The students give chase, of course. At least twenty of them, by the looks of it.

Though I'm a bit taken aback by the number of my pursuers growing every time I pass through an intersection, my feet never stop moving. The sweat and my heart racing don't stop, either!

I'm growing paler by the second as I quickly turn into a School District–wide fugitive!

"Another Orario adventurer broke in again!"

"It's not like any of us wanted to be recruited by someone who breaks the rules!"

"We'll catch you! Throw you back to Orario! And demand your familia take responsibility!"

I'm basically turning into a criminal here, aren't I?

Even if I manage to escape, if the School District goes to the Guild, I'm still going to end up in jail, right?!

As the pessimism and despair threaten to topple me, suddenly—

"Stoooooop!"

As I turn a corner, a wall of students stands before me.

Did I dive head-first into a swarm?

No—I got lured here?!

"*Balder Class* cut him off according to plan!"

"We cornered him! Detaining him now!"

There's no mistaking it. The students following me stayed close enough to threaten me without getting too close while giving orders to the people around them to create this trap they were corralling me into.

In just a couple of minutes! Their coordination is too crazy!

Perfectly ordered movements—compared to Orario, where it's a struggle to coordinate between familias. I almost want to congratulate them.

Unfortunately, their impressive feat is also the reason I'm in extreme danger right now!

"Hyah!"

So I forcibly perform an about-face—a leap, to be precise.

"Wh—"

"He flew?!"

Kicking off the stone pavement, I twist my body acrobatically, leaping over the roof of the ten-meder-high schoolhouse lining the street, and into the next ward over.

The students who tried to catch me in a pincer from the front and behind watch, stunned, as I disappear behind the building on the other side.

Less than five seconds to land in a street that is fortunately deserted.

After a brief moment of silence, I can hear an explosion of stunned shouts from the other side of the building.

"…F-follow hiiiiim!"

"What is he?!"

"He leaped over a building?!"

Dodging the encirclement with brute force, I've already started running again when the shouts reach my back.

It's the pinnacle of emptiness, but I'm using the tactics for fleeing groups I've built up between the Dungeon, *Apollo Familia*, and *Ishtar Familia*! The story of Bell Cranell, who even manifested the Escape ability, is at heart a story of running away!

That, and the difference in level.

I heard already from Lord Hermes, but the abilities of the students chasing me are indeed similar to those of upper-class adventurers. And their tight coordination is very much a threat.

But I'm Level 5.

As I am now, even brute force is almost shockingly effective—all the more so after going up against Mr. Allen in a contest of speed—so I'm not going to lose in a simple foot chase. That isn't just confidence, it's fact.

A pair of students leaps out from a side road in front of me. I lean forward and pass right beside them. Just that is enough for them to lose sight of me and start looking all around in confusion.

The situation is still bad, but it really does drive home the feeling that I'm a first-tier adventurer now. The current me might be able to make it through the matches with *Apollo Familia* and *Ishtar Familia* by myself.

But…

"That human, do you think he's Bell Cranell?!"

"Rabbit Foot?! The one who made it to Level 5?!"

"White hair and red eyes…there's no mistaking it! It's Record Holder!"

They know it's me?!

This is the fate of an adventurer who becomes famous. I just keep paying the price for that.

There's basically no point in the uniform now. The students suddenly start muttering as they run behind me and alongside me.

"I was so looking forward to meeting him when we came to Orario!"

"I even looked up to him a bit!"

"I misjudged him!"

"What a disappointment!"

"Trespasser!"

"Criminal!"

""""""You're just an adventurer like all the rest!""""""

U-ughhhhhh?!

The angry shouts and denunciations echoing from behind almost inflict enough damage to knock me out! It's sort of like the time I hurt Lai and the other children during the Xenos incident, and in a lot of ways, this is really eating away at me and threatening to take me down. Tears well in my eyes as I somehow manage to keep running.

Actually, how long do I need to keep running?!

Can I just jump into the sea to escape?!

But leaving Lord Hermes and escaping by myself is...?!

I spend a few minutes caught between pangs of conscience and conflict, demonstrating my natural indecisiveness.

Meanwhile, it seems like my pursuers are losing their patience and calling in even more reinforcements, because I can see students leaping from schoolrooms now!

"""""Wait!!!!!"""""

"Eeeeeep?!"

Not good!

There's too many of them! There's no path out!

Students are pouring into the streets and onto the rooftops, chasing me toward the center of the ship! I can't even leap over the side anymore!

I could probably force my way through a point in the encirclement...but if I hurt any students doing that, I really will be criminal scum!

I can't get violent, so the only option I have is to flee into the tower rising from the heart of the School District.

"He ran into Breithablik!"

Running into the tower that's wide open, I dash up the massive stairs without looking back.

Of course, the students barrel in after me, chasing me higher and higher.

On each floor, people who are seemingly students and teachers cry out as they see me race past at a furious speed. In my head, I apologize over and over, and "not good" crosses my lips.

At this rate, I'm going to be cornered!

All I can do is hide someplace...!

Leaving the students back in the distance, I reach the top floor fastest.

Rushing through the empty hall, I push open the ash double doors.

"—Ah."

And, stepping into the room, I see a single god.

"Oh? You are…"

Goddess-like beauty, despite being a male god. Fuller blond hair than Ms. Aiz and smooth white skin. He's slender in a way I've never seen before, which only adds to his delicate beauty. But he is far taller than me. He wears a long, sacred vestment, leaving his right shoulder and arm bare. On his head is a crown of…mistletoe?

I can't see his eyes. They're hidden behind closed eyelids.

And yet, he has clearly seen me.

As I stand in shock before him, there is just one thing I know. He is surely the patron god of something related to light or something sacred.

Turning toward me, even though his eyes don't see me, the god smiles gently.

"Lord Balder!"

A student throws open the door.

The way she enters, just on the cusp of rudeness while maintaining the bare minimum of etiquette, is I guess because she's a student here? Her face is red from rushing around and her voice rings out loudly.

"Has a white-haired human boy come this way?!"

"No? Did something happen, Alisa?"

"He hasn't come up here? Then he must be hiding on one of the lower floors and we missed him…"

The girl wearing an armband around her upper arm suddenly falls into thought before gasping a little and snapping to attention.

"Sorry, Lord Balder, there is a trespasser! We failed to prevent someone from Orario entering…! And the adventurer this time is Bell Cranell, of all people!"

"Is that so?"

"We will assuredly catch him! Please await our report!"

The look on her face practically screams, "I swear on the honor of the School District!" as she turns and quickly leaves the room.

"It's safe now."

"Th-thank you very much…"

I can feel the tension draining from my body as I get up from my hiding place under his desk, where I was holding my breath and listening to their exchange.

When I barged into this room earlier, this god kindly hid me.

"B-but why would you…? Umm…"

"Balder is my name. And you are Bell Cranell. It seems we've gotten the order slightly mixed up, but it is nice to meet you, Orario's newest hope."

"H-hope…? Ah, i-it's a pleasure to meet you, sir!"

An awkward look crosses my face, but Lord Balder smiles and graciously greets me.

I'm a little confused, and I quickly lower my head, but mysteriously, the guilt and tension I felt earlier are gradually fading. It's almost like time flows more slowly around him, or…how do I describe it? His peaceful nature feels calming.

As the tension leaves my body, as if he timed it, Lord Balder answers my previous question.

"The reason I hid you is because right before I received the report that you are a trespasser…I just happened to have a conversation about you."

"—With none other than me!"

"Whoa?! L-Lord Hermes?! You were here the whole time?!"

Lord Hermes appears from beneath one of the stones on the floor beside the carpet, seriously dumbfounding me.

Apparently he was hiding under the floor since before I entered the room.

"After we split up, I happened to reach the bridge, Breithablik here, and got my old friend Balder to hide me!"

"My oh my…you're always like that when it's convenient to you."

Lord Hermes spins his cap on his finger as he steps forward while Lord Balder laughs a little bit, once again the picture of tranquility.

I don't really know their relationship, but…from that exchange, I can at least tell they must have known each other for a long time.

"In addition to trying to scout some students, I wanted to have a private discussion with Balder here. Talk about a godsend!"

"If you had just left a note, I could have made accommodations for a meeting. Every time…you really do push your way in like the wind."

"What else can I do? If I send a note the official way, it just gets pushed back and pushed back and the Guild will say it'll be a month before we can meet. That's just how busy the School District is around this time…and all the more so for the headmaster."

Looking back and forth between them, I fail to keep up with their conversation, but I let out a little "huh" when I hear a certain word.

"H-headmaster…?"

"It's exactly what it sounds like. Balder is the biggest god here… And if you go back further, he's the one who proposed this whole School District."

The one who proposed it…So he's the founding god?!

As I stare at him in obvious shock, Lord Balder's lips curve into a small, awkward smile, even as his eyes remain closed.

"That's a bit misleading. The School District here is merely a union of academic familias. Each patron deity has equal right to speak… However, in events where a single figure needs to be held accountable, I am indeed the god who is ultimately responsible."

From the fact that his personal room is at the top of this central tower, I should have realized he's a god of significant status, but…I tense up again hearing his title.

It's a little late now, but the thought of what awaits us is making me shift nervously.

He's covered for us once, but that doesn't change the fact that I trespassed…!

"So then, what do you think, Balder? Are you willing to listen to my request from before?"

Ignoring my trembling, Lord Hermes asks as if it were nothing.

Request…?

What were they discussing before I came? Lord Balder said he had a discussion about me, but why did I get brought up?

"Hmm…"

As I stand frozen, unable to do anything, Lord Balder looks at me.

My bewilderment lasts just a moment before his eyebrows arch softly.

"Very well—Bell Cranell, would you like to try being a student here in the School District?"

It feels like time has stopped.

I stand still until I finally realize the meaning of his question and shout.

"Ehhhhhhh?!"

"Attend the School District?! Mr. Bell?!"

You've gotten yourself into another *mess!*

That's what Lilly's hysteric shout implies as I reflexively shrink back.

"Just when we were thinking you were late coming back from the Guild…How were you recruited *by* the School District?"

"N-no, I wasn't recruited…it's more the condition of a certain deal, or rather…Lord Hermes apparently brought it up without telling me…"

"Argh! Lord Hermes's antics again?!"

We're in the dining room of Hearthstone Manor with night fast approaching. As I tell everyone about all that happened at the School District, Welf sits beside me looking exasperated, and in front of me, Lilly is groaning with clenched fists like she might hit the table at any moment.

Before I realize it, this is quickly turning into *that* kind of talk, and I want to just curl up into a ball as I give my foolish explanation.

"Bell, just to make sure, you weren't recruited, and you didn't sign up for an internship, right?" Welf asks.

"Umm…I'm sorry, Lord Hermes said those words too, but I don't really know what they mean…"

"Recruiting is formally adding new members to your familia. And an internship is sort of like a trial membership with a familia. Both are tactics for collecting fresh talent, Mr. Bell."

Lilly explains for me, since, as usual, I don't really know much of anything that's not related to the Dungeon.

When it comes to official recruiting, there is apparently a big event for all of Orario's factions on a set day, which is officially sanctioned by the School District.

A representative gets a chance to explain how their familia works and tries to convince students to join. On Orario's side, it's an important chance to bring in fresh blood, and for the School District, it provides their students with many paths to choose from.

Even non-Dungeon familias in Orario are exceptional, often operating on a different level compared to what can be found in other cities and countries. Given that, it makes sense there are lots of students looking to join them. It is a win-win for Orario and the School District, so this has been the arrangement for a long time now.

"It is also possible for certain familias to send a member at the request of the School District to serve as a long-term recruiter. They build a deeper connection with the students and advertise their familia's activities even more. That is what Mr. Welf was asking about."

Oh. Lilly's clarification makes a lot of sense.

The School District allows familias who have a large number of students hoping to join to send a recruiter, so it's a privilege generally reserved for the largest familias.

The internship part is simpler. Allowing a School District student to experience life in an Orario familia just makes sense. It's an opportunity for them to get to know your familia, and from the School District side, it gives their students a chance to gain some experience and avoid some regrets if things turn out differently than expected.

Unlike with a normal job search, entering a familia and receiving Falna from a deity is a big decision—you have to stay with the same familia for a full year, and there are situations like with Lilly where leaving a familia or converting can be difficult. I understand why some would be hesitant to commit right away.

At the same time, the thought that it's a really *nice* solution crosses my mind.

Not to just cite my own experience before meeting Lady Hestia, but it is really considerate and hospitable…and, well, *behaved*. From the moment I felt that way, I became an Orario adventurer, I guess.

Maybe that's just how valuable the students from the School District are, that the fight for them is that intense. It's probably a bit presumptuous to compare them to myself, a hayseed from the countryside.

Anyway, general recruitment and internships are an important link between Orario and the School District. And they don't really apply to me, since I've been invited to be a student, so I confidently tell Welf and Lilly this is something different.

"Why do you need to become a student anyway?" Welf asks. "Can't you just go as an adventurer?"

"That's…I broke into the School District, and it's turned into a big rumor, apparently…It wouldn't be looked on kindly, or be welcomed…and some people might be totally against it…"

"In other words, they already have a bad impression of Rabbit Foot and *Hestia Familia*…" Lilly sighs.

"Ugh…I-I'm sorry, Lilly!"

I reflexively apologize and hang my head in guilt for causing another problem even though I'm supposed to be the familia's leader. And now that I fully understand what the talk about recruiting and stuff was about before, I feel the gravity of my actions all the more.

"I really am sorry…If our familia can't do any recruiting because of me…"

"Ah, that part is fine. Who cares?"

"Eh…wh-who cares?"

"Yes. Lilly spoke with Lady Hestia, and we have already decided that with Ms. Lyu joining, we won't be recruiting from the School District and won't be looking for anyone new for a while."

"R-really?"

"We just became B rank and have earned an unnecessary amount of fame. There's the uproar from the war game and the festival, so it may seem like we are being praised all around…but beneath the surface, other familias, especially more powerful ones, are surely going to give us the cold shoulder."

I blink repeatedly at Lilly's unexpected response.

Apparently, Lilly and our goddess's plan is to say we have no more room after a Level 6 joined our ranks, so we won't be participating in the fight for talent at the School District.

Or more precisely, it's more like, *We'll let you have all the Level 2s and higher, so please don't hate us. Just please also be understanding if anyone does specifically come to us anyway.*

This comes as a surprise to me, since after the uproar about our goddess's debt, there haven't really been any people interested in joining, so I figured we would try to get the recruits we've always wanted after our victory in the war game. But hearing Lilly explain it, I understand now.

Hestia Familia has grown at a dizzying rate, going from a nothing familia at its formation to what it is now, so familias that have been steadily putting in the work to grow gradually probably have a thing or two to say about us. Whether that stems from frustration, disappointment, or a general sense that we're an eyesore.

"At the very least, if we attempt to grow even further, we will assuredly be treated as a dangerous entity. I don't think there will be any conflicts with everyone scared of Mr. Ottar and the others standing behind us, but…rivals can still cause us plenty of headaches. Inside the Dungeon, for example."

We don't want to cause any unnecessary friction or conflict with other familias. That's what Lilly is suggesting.

"The nail that sticks out gets hammered down, was it?"

"Ah. Ms. Lyu."

Ms. Lyu emerges from the kitchen, neatly serving dinner in front of us.

Today, Ms. Lyu and Ms. Mikoto are on cooking duty.

Ms. Lyu, who bluntly admitted that only Ms. Syr was worse than her at cooking (before apologizing guiltily) has taken it upon herself to set the table while Ms. Mikoto handles the cooking. Ms. Haruhime is currently helping out, too.

Trained at The Benevolent Mistress, Ms. Lyu's movements are beautiful, and even though she is just wearing an apron over her normal outfit, she looks so pretty it's captivating.

Ms. Lyu is still working some shifts at The Benevolent Mistress whenever there isn't any familia work going on, like Dungeon exploration. After all, the restaurant is a precious place to her, and she apparently still wants to repay Ms. Mia and Ms. Syr for everything they've done for her. In that sense, it's sort of like having an active waitress adding flair to the dinner table at home.

It's luxurious…or rather, it's so intense, I reflexively sit up properly.

"I've only just joined this familia, but…for another incident to already have started. You really aren't lacking when it comes to topics for discussion."

After setting out Welf's meal, she sets a vegetable bowl with less rice (Ms. Mikoto prepared a vegetarian dinner for Ms. Lyu that is delicious even without meat or fish in it) in front of me.

"I-I'm sorry…"

But she just smiles slightly.

"Not at all. This isn't so much your fault as it is pure happenstance. In a way, this is your fate as a first-tier adventurer…and as the one with the title of Record Holder. Maybe this is just the star you were born under."

Hearing Ms. Lyu, formerly of *Astrea Familia*, entertaining thoughts like that, it doesn't really sound like a joke, and I can't manage a response other than an empty smile.

"That said, what will you do? Is there any precedent of an adventurer becoming a student at the School District?" Ms. Mikoto asks as she and Ms. Haruhime carry the fish and the miso soup Welf has been waiting for out from the kitchen.

"There are plenty of examples of the reverse, but…at least to my knowledge, the opposite has never happened."

Ms. Lyu, the most experienced of all of us, is the first to answer, and Lilly, who was born in Orario, closes her eyes and nods in agreement.

"This is just something Lord Hermes went and set up himself, so it's not like it's a done deal, right?" Welf pointed out.

"That's right! It's not like it gets us anything special, and we don't know what the deities at the School District are planning, either! You should turn it down, Mr. Bell!"

Lilly's response is entirely reasonable.

In fact, if I really do go with it, apparently it'll have to be kept a secret from the Guild. They would never allow a first-tier adventurer to be idle like this, not even a fledgling one like me.

…But…

"…What are you thinking, Master Bell?"

With the table set, Ms. Lyu and Ms. Mikoto have sat down with us, and Ms. Haruhime joins us in her maid outfit, looking at me in open curiosity.

Not just her. Everyone is wondering what I'll do.

Thinking about the deities who are probably talking right now, I stare up at the ceiling.

"I…"

"Haaah…you really just keep bringing more and more trouble, don't you?"

"Hey, come on, Hestia, I explained it already, right? This isn't trouble."

Sitting on a couch, Hestia grumbled while Hermes gesticulated from his seat on the sofa across from her.

"The School District holds a wealth of knowledge gleaned from the whole width of the mortal realm. For Bell, who only knows the small world inside the walls of Orario, this'll be a stimulus unlike anything else he's experienced."

"I'm telling you to quit acting like encouraging his growth is the default choice every time…Don't twist him around with your divine will. It should be fine to just let him do what he wants the way he wants to."

"I just gave him an opportunity. And besides, this is as much for your sake, Hestia, as it is for Bell."

Hermes had been waiting for Hestia as she came back exhausted from her part-time work. In an empty room on the second floor, and a little bit ragged from the exhaustion, she sighed and opted to at least hear Hermes out.

"Bell is Level Five now. And he got there at a speed that's unheard of. Whether anyone pushes him or not, he's a hero candidate now. The Guild already pestered you about it, right?"

"...Yeah. I got called out by Ouranos and given the news. Bell's gonna be given a little bit of time off, but after that, we're expected to do even more Dungeon exploration."

Right after the war game had ended, the old god had spoken with her at the altar beneath the Guild.

He'd thanked her and Bell, who had been run ragged by the incidents with *Freya Familia*, and spoken of his intention that they be rewarded, but he had also made it clear they were expected to continue pressing forward.

With the great familia war as impetus—and in emphatic fashion—*Hestia Familia* had gathered the attention of the world, both inside and outside the city, and it was now bound to the swell of the mortal realm's shifting times.

Without saying as much, that was what the Guild's founding god had told her.

"Bell will assuredly be wrangled into challenging the last of the three great quests given to the Labyrinth City—slaying the Black Dragon."

"........."

"For the sake of that, I want him to not just focus on the Dungeon, but also turn his eyes to the world outside Orario. Broaden his perspective and deepen it, too. Since the dragon of the end is perched outside these city walls."

Hermes was no longer hiding his unstated plan to have Bell become this era's hero. It had been clear he was interested half a year ago, when Bell and the others had run into trouble in the middle floors and a rescue party had been put together.

Hestia looked at him reproachfully.

"The world wishes for a hero."

Hestia knew the true meaning of that statement.

"...And you're saying the starting point of that broadening or whatever is the School District?"

"At the very least, if he goes there, he can learn the state of things in the wider world—learn just what terrible shape the mortal realm is in now. And it's far more efficient than traveling around the world with me."

The air in the room got ever so slightly heavier.

Hestia bit her tongue as Hermes said what he was really thinking, as insurance.

"And more than anything, the other Level Seven. I want Bell to have a connection with him."

Hestia was visibly shocked by this revelation more than anything else that had been said tonight.

"There's another one besides Warlord? And he's in the School District?"

"Yes. I'm hoping he'll be another stimulus for Bell. A man who can be called a modern-day hero."

Hestia had only descended from the heavens relatively recently, so she was unfamiliar with a great deal about the mortal realm.

Finding out there was another absurdity on the level of Ottar came as quite a shock. And a current-day hero at that. If Bell heard that, his eyes would surely light up.

"Also, this time, it might really be Bell's last chance to take a breather."

"......Please don't say something so ominous..."

After a long pause, Hestia managed a world-weary response.

But Hermes was right.

Bell would not be able to escape the quest to slay the dragon that Orario was betting everything on. He would need to learn how to survive while standing at the eye of unavoidable turbulence and upheaval.

Becoming a first-tier adventurer meant being right in the middle of the era.

"Well, it's up to Bell to decide what he wants in the end. I don't want to force him to do something he doesn't want to, either."

Hestia glared at him, knowing this was premeditated.

Before letting Hermes in, she had heard what had happened today from Bell, and she had already asked what he was thinking.

"Umm…I would be lying if I said my heart didn't race a bit when I went there. I talked to Miss Eina too, and she said if I want to try something new, then this is probably the best time."

Alone with Hestia in the hallway, he had nervously revealed his honest feelings.

"If I'm allowed to take a detour…then I would like to try this."

Bell had said that as captain, he would turn it down if it would cause a problem for the familia.

He couldn't just be a child anymore, so what Hestia truly wanted was for him to do what he wanted while he still had the chance. Plus, there weren't really any problems that needed to be tackled at the moment. If anything, she would love for him to proactively take a break and step away from the Dungeon for a bit.

He didn't realize it himself, but Bell Cranell was in the process of becoming a Dungeon junkie. When she had glanced over his profile and seen "Special Skill: Dungeon," she'd stared up at the ceiling and nearly class-changed into a goddess of grief.

And also, the thought of him going to school is…emotional.

That was her perspective as a motherly patron goddess and as a goddess who loved the boy dearly.

It really, really rubbed her the wrong way to agree with Hermes, but it was true that now that Bell was a first-tier adventurer, he needed time to develop.

"The School District…What is Balder saying?"

"He'll let Bell in as a student as part of a deal. In exchange for granting a secret and special exception to enter the school, Bell is going to be placed with some of their problem children. That part, Bell doesn't know, though."

A bit of give-and-take.

After learning that there was an absurdity like Ottar there, she equated the School District a bit with *Freya Familia*, but…she was familiar with Balder's character and that of the other deities there, too.

She could entrust Bell to them knowing that nothing bad would happen.

I'm really lenient with my own kid too, huh.

Or maybe it was just a natural feeling for a deity with a child to take care of.

Her eyes half open as she kept looking at Hermes smiling there, she sighed again and chose to respect her child's will.

"Fine. I'll allow Bell to enter the School District."

When I slip my arms into the uniform, my heart starts racing a bit.

"Ha-ha-ha! It's a good look on you, Bell!"

"Yes, it suits you well."

Lord Hermes and Lord Balder compliment me as my cheeks redden in embarrassment.

It's the morning three days after I was given the offer to enter the School District. With permission from Lady Hestia and Lilly and the rest of the familia, I made my way to the School District. There, I went to Lord Balder's divine room in the central tower—no, to the headmaster's office—and changed into the school's uniform.

The white school uniform is incredibly elegant. I never pay much attention to my clothes, so it's a little hard to relax in it.

But right now, the bigger issue is…

"Ummm, it's a little difficult to see in front of me…is this disguise really going to be okay?"

Brushing aside the brown hair hanging over my eyes again, I look at myself in the mirror.

Standing before the polished mirror is not a white-haired human, but a brown-haired animal person. *Rabbit* ears are sticking out of my brown wig, and a short, fluffy tail is attached to the back of my uniform's pants. And the slightly longer brown hair hangs down just enough that it mostly hides my red eyes.

In the disguise Lord Hermes provided, Bell Cranell has transformed into a hume bunny.

"All the students are wary of you after the incident the other day. I can already see the cold stares if it was announced that Bell Cranell is entering the school. Thus, the grand plan to have you disguise yourself as someone other than Bell Cranell!"

My smile twitches as Lord Hermes snaps his fingers, and I look at myself in the mirror again.

At a glance, there are no outward signs that I'm Bell Cranell. I think. The wig special magic item—technically, curse item—that Ms. Asfi made does a good job of covering up my most distinguishing characteristics. And apparently the curse is extremely light and shouldn't have any negative repercussions.

I don't know how it would work with someone who knows me better, but at least with the students who should only remember me from the chase the other day, it shouldn't fail…I hope.

I know I said I wanted to go to the School District, but I do have some qualms, or maybe I feel guilty about deceiving people to do it. However you want to put it, I'm basically starting to feel a little queasy…

"Starting today, while you are in the School District, your name is Rapi Flemish."

"Rapi Flemish…Y-yes, sir!"

"The story is that you passed the entrance exam in the city of Bella before the School District docked at Orario, but because of family circumstances, you came aboard here in Meren."

I repeat the new name Rapi to myself several times while Lord Balder, seemingly knowing that I am starting to get nervous, puts his finger to his lips with a gentle smile.

"Please be careful to conceal your identity and your strength. If this special arrangement is revealed, I will receive quite the scolding as headmaster."

His face looks as divine as before, but at the same time, there is a trace of playfulness there, too.

I think he's enjoying this…

"Now then, officially, I am pleased to welcome you, Bell. I mean, Rapi. The School District welcomes you to find what you might become."

With Lord Hermes watching, the smiling god pins a badge on my left chest.

It is a crest…The School District's emblem? It has a motif of light and a large ship.

Behind the gleaming badge, my heart trembles in nervousness and excitement.

"Pardon me."

Just then, there's a light knock on the door.

"Come in," Lord Balder says, and the ash doors open as a man walks in.

Gold hair flows down the nape of his neck like a lion's, and his eyes are the same dazzling color. He's tall, and at a glance, he seems slender, but he emanates an unmistakable firmness.

A handsome but not elven face, he is somewhere between masculine and graceful. He looks to be in his late twenties.

Looking at him almost makes me think I want to be like him when I grow up.

I'm sure he could be described as a handsome man, but that doesn't really capture him fully.

A more accurate expression would be…earnest, upright—a knight.

…*He's* strong…

My eyes widen as I clearly sense how powerful this man is.

"This fellow has been made aware of everything. He is a supporter of sorts, a special homeroom teacher for you."

Nodding to Lord Balder and to Lord Hermes as well, the man walks up to me as Lord Balder explains who he is.

A golden spade emblem adorns his left sleeve, his left leather shoe, and the left leg of his slacks.

In the holster at his right hip are multiple sticks of chalk and a wand-like, thin teacher's cane.

The man wearing black clothes that almost look like formalwear—the uniform of a teacher—smiles and holds out his hand.

"My name is Leon Verdenberg. Nice to meet you, Rapi."

I shake his hand in a daze.

Today, I enter the School District, not as Bell Cranell, but as Rapi Flemish.

CHAPTER 3
SCHOOL LIFE IN ANOTHER WORLD

"Good morning, sir!"

"Good morning, sir!"

Voices ring out beneath the blue sky.

On one of the School District's main streets, paved with white stone.

A human and a dwarf carry book bags and some books.

An animal person and an Amazon wear their uniforms in a casual style.

A prum rushes to finish breakfast at a sidewalk café while an elf scolds them for it.

The one thing they all have in common is the uniform they wear and their matching, burgundy neckties.

Even though I've never seen one before, I'm sure this is a classic going-to-school scene. The morning sun shines down on the academic city that boasts a different sort of liveliness from Orario's.

"Good morning, Nym, Intha. Don't be late to lessons today."

"""Yes, sir!"""

Mr. Verdenberg's greeting makes two girls passing by very happy. I can hear the excitement in their voices.

I've seen a similar sort of scene several times now since leaving Lord Balder's office in the central tower.

Boys and girls, humans and demi-humans, everyone calls out to him. Even without asking, I can tell the man beside me is popular.

"Hey, who is that kid? He has a *Balder Class* badge."

"I've never seen him before. The entrance exam hasn't started in Meren, so he shouldn't be a new student."

...And I can also tell perfectly well the girls we passed just now are glancing back and whispering about me.

First-tier adventurer problems. Or maybe they're perks? I'm already very sensitive to people's gazes, but with my senses so enhanced from leveling up, I can hear people perfectly clearly even when they whisper quietly behind me.

It isn't just those girls, either. The students around us are curiously watching the person—the hume-bunny student—walking next to Mr. Verdenberg.

It's a pure and earnest curiosity, not like the support and cheers I felt in Orario when I became an upper-class adventurer.

I think I remember Gramps mentioning that the cute new transfer student being the center of attention is a classic school moment, but… i-is this what he meant?

Since the incident with Wiene and the Xenos, a lot of people have commented about my expression changing or how I've grown, but outside of my role as an adventurer and outside the realm of the Dungeon, I feel this surge of natural timidity, or nervousness, or bashfulness, or something like that, and even I feel kind of disappointed in myself.

I mean, I'm definitely also really nervous about people possibly seeing through my disguise, but…

That plus being thrown into an unknown environment…maybe everyone would feel the same way? More or less?

Anyway, I can't quite calm down, and as my shoulders tense up…

"Nervous?"

"…! Y-yes. Sorry, Mr. Verdenberg…"

I reflexively apologize, but Mr. Verdenberg stops, his gold hair swaying as he looks at me.

"That's a little stiff, *Rapi*. You're a student now, aren't you?"

I am a little startled by the man in front of me who carefully addresses me by *my* name.

"As a new student, let me give you your first pop quiz. 'How does the teacher Leon Verdenberg want to be addressed right now?' Let's hear your best answer."

My cheeks flush at his gentle question.

Feeling a ticklish sensation near my neck…I gather my courage and attempt to answer my first school question.

"…Professor Leon."

"Correct. You have the makings of a model student, Rapi," he says with a warm smile.

Blinking a few times, my face still red, I break into a little chuckle. My shoulders have loosened up. Mr. Verdenberg doesn't fail to see this, and his smile deepens.

I think I understand a little bit of the reason why so many students look up to him.

"Look, Professor Leon's charmed that new kid already!"

"That's the Ultra Page for you…!"

"Professor Leon and a bashful rabbit boy…I could ship that!"

…I think I heard something concerning there, but I do my best to pretend I didn't hear anything. I can feel the Lilly in the back of my mind shouting not to pay it any attention, so I just play along. I'm sure that's the right choice.

"You've received a book bag from Lord Balder, correct?"

"Ah, yes, sir. Along with my uniform."

"Then go through the contents, please. There is a handbook outlining school life. If there is anything you don't understand, including your choices for classes, please don't hesitate to ask."

I keep up as he starts moving again, slipping my book bag over my shoulders. It's thin and square. It's similar to the backpack I used when Lilly wasn't around, and it can fit a lot more inside than it looks like.

"Forgive me, but I'm afraid I'll have to explain things as we move. First of all, your student ID is 4646B3333, and your major is Combat Studies. And, like myself, you are a part of *Balder Class*."

"St-student ID? Combat Studies? *Balder Class*…?"

I listen carefully to his explanation, but half the words don't really mean much to me. Feeling extraordinarily awkward, I make up my mind and ask about the things I don't know.

"Umm, I'm sorry for not understanding a lot of that, but…first of all, what do you mean by *Balder Class*?"

"That is an excellent question. The School District uses a unique system of organization broken into what we call classes."

He doesn't betray any disdain for my utter lack of knowledge despite wanting to enter the School District, and patiently explains the terms he used.

"The students of the School District are here to study, and they will all someday leave this place. The recruiting system is a fine example. Students who have decided the path they will follow go on to join other familias or organizations such as the Guild. Classes are a term of art we use to avoid burdening students with a prior familia on their résumé."

"Ah, I see..."

It's easy to forget as a member of a familia, but most people consider it a very serious choice. Followers who wield physical abilities significantly greater than the average person's are often considered dangerous by the common people, who aren't a part of any familia themselves (though Orario has always been dangerous from its inception, so its residents are used to it, in a way). There are some people who have an extreme reaction to seeing the word familia in a résumé. And when it comes to conversion between familias, there have supposedly even been cases where the transferees are suspected of being spies.

So the School District used the idea of classes instead of familias out of concern for their students' futures.

And also, it might be a bit of an emotional point. For other familias, being able to think of someone as a member of their familia from the start, who just happened to learn a bunch at school first instead of as a convert from a previous familia, makes them feel less like an outsider. It's something small that helps their patron deity and fellow familia members feel closer to them.

So the School District is careful about just being an institution of education and instruction...

As I come to my own sort of conclusion, the professor adds, "The School District is managed through the efforts of a small number of deities, teachers like myself, and many, many students. The gift of Falna is necessary for the sake of that management. Teachers and students alike receive it without exception."

"Not just from Lord Balder, but from the other deities, too?"

"Yes. This sort of system is similar to a nation-level familia. As the representative of the School District, Lord Balder is headmaster, but the various classes are all equal."

That makes it easier for me to grasp the situation.

From what I have seen, there are probably well over a thousand students, so for a single god to manage it all…I briefly imagine the sheer amount of work involved in updating statuses for a thousand people. It would definitely be impossible. So it makes sense that a system like country-level familias with their subordinate deities to divide up the workload would be mandatory, but something like the link Lady Hestia and Ms. Syr have now creates a lingering differential in authority. However, from what he said, each deity and each class has equal rank.

Incidentally, there are ten classes, apparently. *Balder Class*, of course, but also *Idun Class* and *Bragi Class*, among others.

The badge on the right breast of the student uniforms is the sign for which class a student belongs to. It is similar to familia emblems, and the light-and-ship badge on my chest is the emblem for *Balder Class*.

"If it is hard to grasp the class system, you can think of them like familias. Teachers such as myself form the core leaders of each class, and students are much like standard familia members."

I murmur an "oh" as everything falls into place.

And along those lines, that is also probably the difference in strength between teachers and students. If they are entrusted to guide others as instructors, then the teachers must surely be expected to have strength in addition to wisdom and dignity.

"Student IDs exist for the sake of managing the information of students who attend the School District. And your major of Combat Studies…that, I shall explain later."

A chime comes from the central tower that seems to be a warning signal, and the students around us suddenly start to thin out as he enters a nearby building—one of the schoolhouses.

Like other buildings, it is made of white stone with a blue roof, and the interior is perfectly clean. And like a yokel, I of course stare around in wonder.

Walking down a white hall that is different from the castle-like interior of Folkvangr, he stops in front of a door.

"Here we are. The students who will be your classmates are waiting."

Huh?

As my eyes widen, he smiles and encourages me to come in with him. He opens the door and I follow him inside, a step behind—and it is without a doubt a classroom.

"!"

A wide, open space. It almost feels a bit like a theater. Farther into the room are long, mahogany desks set out in a semicircle, as if gathered around the podium and blackboard. The seats are set in ascending circles, creating a bowl with the podium at the bottom. I wouldn't be surprised if this actually is used as a small theater sometimes.

And inside the classroom are tons of students in their seats.

Humans and animal people, elves and dwarves, prums and Amazons. People of every race in their teens and preteens. At least fifty of them, and they're all in the school uniform.

Every single one of them looks at Professor Leon, and at me.

My body starts to tremble, and in a fluster, I follow him to the podium in the front of the classroom.

"Today we will cover the guidance regarding your excursions in Orario. However, before that, allow me to introduce your new classmate. *Rapi*."

He gently calls me by my new name again, and I realize what's going on.

This is an introduction. Right now, this is the beginning of my life as a student. As I realize that, my nervousness swells again. Every pair of eyes in the classroom is looking at me with interest.

It feels like I might be hearing someone saying, 'We've got a weirdo here.' Or is that just my imagination?

I don't know, but my legs are starting to feel wobbly. In the grips of a heart-racing experience completely different from the Dungeon, I steel my resolve.

Breathing in desperately through my nose while making sure not to make a sound, I take a step forward from the podium.

"................Ummm..."

The intense scrutiny almost feels like it'll crush me. Is it just my nerves?

If nothing else, it makes me respect the professor and the other instructors who stand here every day to teach.

With that stupid attempt to escape reality, I finally open my mouth.

"I'm Bel...I'm from Bella! My name is Rapi Flemish! P-please take care of me!"

A sheen of cold sweat drenches the back of my neck as I almost ruin everything by saying my real name, but I somehow manage to get past it and then vigorously lower my head.

That would have been really dangerous if I hadn't heard my fake background from Lord Balder!!!

I can feel the wry chuckle from Professor Leon as I nervously look up—

"Nice to meet you, bud!" An animal boy waves.

"You don't need to be so nervous," a human girl calls out.

"You're a man, right? Act like it!" a red-haired Amazon jokes.

The other students all smile cheerfully as their warm voices fill the air.

I—I guess this is okay...

It was definitely embarrassing, but at the very least, I haven't revealed myself as the trespasser from the other day...

"Rapi passed his entrance exam in Bella when we were there earlier, but due to personal matters was delayed in enrolling. He traveled here to Meren on his own to meet us. As his classmates, I would appreciate it if you would help him, since he is in an unfamiliar place, just like you were when you first enrolled."

""""Yes, Professor!""""

As Professor Leon finishes my introduction, everyone in class answers right away.

"Very well then, Rapi, please take an open seat," he gently encourages me as relief wells inside me.

"Y-Yes, sir!" I respond, my voice cracking a bit.

There are chuckles around the room and my cheeks burn as I move away from the podium. Going up the stairs, I look for a seat as fascinated gazes continue following me.

It's a good thing the wig's hair covers my eyes…I think.

I can feel my eyes darting around desperately, and I'm sure it looks suspicious.

Umm, an open seat…an open seat…

Since I was looking down in embarrassment, I didn't really notice where all the students are sitting. As I wander through the rows of full seats…

"There's a seat over here!"

A girl holds up her hand.

Right in the middle of the classroom. One of the seats right next to the stairs is open.

Grateful for her help, I start moving—but I'm stunned when I stand in front of her.

"You're…"

Slightly pointed ears and long brown hair tied back with a ribbon.

A single jade tuft of hair. And more than anything, those emerald eyes that remind me of *her*.

I remember this girl.

She's the half-elf girl I saw when I first broke into the School District!

"My name is Nina Tulle. Nice to meet you, Rapi."

Tulle?

So then, is she really Miss Eina's…?

"…Was that too presumptuous?"

"Huh? Ah, no, not at all! I-It's nice to meet you, Miss Tulle!"

I manage to stammer a response. Not knowing what to do at the sudden encounter, I frantically sit down in order to cover how flustered I'm feeling.

"Professor Leon said it too, but just say the word if there's something you don't know. I'll be happy to help if I can."

"Th-thank you very much…"

Maybe she's being kind because of how obviously nervous I am, but even after I sit down, she talks to me with a friendly ease.

The badge on her chest is the light and ship. *Balder Class*, just like me.

Her well-proportioned face is eye-catching, but...the way she reminds me of Miss Eina is nagging at the back of my mind.

Even though there is a trace of the elven tendency for propriety, she seems flexible and easygoing more than anything. An affable, adult sort of demeanor. She isn't wearing glasses, but she really seems just like Miss Eina.

I can't just keep staring at her, but she looks a little confused when I keep glancing at her. Even so, she just smiles.

I'm in disguise, our eyes only met the one time, and she doesn't seem to have realized my true identity, but...to think we would meet again like this.

"Don't get the wrong idea just because she's nice, new guy. Nina's a model student and she's like that with everyone."

"Milly! Please don't say strange things like that! Also, Professor Leon's about to start!"

The girl in front of me with blond, braided hair—an elf—smiles back at me, I guess misunderstanding my reaction, but Miss Tulle directs my attention forward.

I—I should be careful. I can't help being curious, but I should focus on the lesson!

"Now then, we touched on it at the all-school meeting the other day, but we have safely made port in Meren. These next few weeks are going to be very important for everyone, but especially for all of you in the Combat Studies Department."

A clear, piercing voice rings out from the podium. When he speaks, I can sense the excited air of the classroom suddenly changing.

"As the name implies, Combat Studies is dedicated to both the practice of martial arts and the attendant mindset and philosophy. Most of you here in this room have expressed a desire for future roles involving combat."

He is addressing the classroom as if rekindling their original resolve, but it also serves as an explanation for me.

Was it Lord Hermes who had me placed in this Department?

Either way, it seems about right. If I was asked what I wanted to learn, what I wanted to improve, my first answer would definitely be combat knowledge and strategy, things with a strong link to exploring the Dungeon.

"Imperial knights, Dizaran marines, court mages of Altena…and adventurers in Orario. There are any number of such routes, and experience in the Dungeon—one of the three great frontiers of the world—is precious for all of them. You may be sure that we instructors also value it greatly."

His words give the impression that visiting Orario is a big event for the School District as well, especially for the Combat Studies Department. I sit up in my seat, inspired by the earnest looks on the students' faces.

"Starting three days from today, students will be given permission to enter Orario. Internships will also be allowed to commence starting that day. But the first task asked of you in the Combat Studies Department is hands-on study in the Dungeon."

Professor Leon pulls a piece of chalk from the holster at his right hip and begins writing on the blackboard.

"Each squad will be asked to explore to a depth appropriate to your status and return with specified drop items of monsters. You will be graded relative to your results in the Dungeon."

The words *squad* and *graded* caught my ear, but for now I set them aside.

A neat Koine that doesn't look handwritten fills the board and a big diagram takes shape, all while the professor continues talking.

"Of course, you will also be expected to present daily reports. I am confident none of you would do so, but you may be sure that the use of drop items purchased from adventurers or any other falsification of your efforts in exploring will be uncovered immediately. As such, I would not recommend attempting it."

"Professor! If someone did do that, what would happen?"

"A good question. There was a student who tried it before, and they underwent three straight days and nights of makeup studies in the Dungeon under my supervision. Upon returning aboveground, they cried tears of joy at how beautiful the sun could look."

There are a few titters around the room as he turns to face us. On the board behind him is a diagram of the floors of the Dungeon and a basic chart of limitations. The ability norms for various floors are set precisely.

Those who are Level 1 with lower abilities can only go down to the fifth floor, while those with higher abilities are progressively allowed down to the ninth floor. Only Level 2 parties are allowed to proceed to the tenth floor, and even then, the deepest anyone is allowed to proceed is the fifteenth floor.

It's set much stricter than the Guild's standards...

I heard from Lord Hermes that the students of the School District are skilled, and most have leveled up at least once. Relatively speaking, this is a fairly strict line. Some might even call it a bit overprotective, but...none of the people in this classroom are adventurers.

Status numbers are crucial in the Dungeon, but experience matters even more. Just how much of the unknown you've experienced, how much you've already been through, could quite literally be the line between life and death.

The way Lilly, a Level 1 supporter, was able to help out even around the tenth floor is a good example, and the opposite is true, too. From what I've heard, it's not exactly rare for an upper-class adventurer who theoretically met the standards to wind up dead in the middle floors.

Thinking of it that way, it's kind of obvious that students who are overwhelmingly lacking experience with the Dungeon shouldn't really be judged by the same standard as adventurers who make their living in it.

The standard is strict, but it is out of concern for the students' safety.

"Instructors will be deployed at every floor during your practical studies. We will of course be watching your movements, but...the Dungeon is big. Remember that we cannot see everything."

"""" . . . !""""

"Irregularities go without saying, but there will likely be trouble with adventurers as well as monsters. If you allow yourselves to be distracted, something unexpected can easily put you into a dangerous situation."

Tension fills the room.

Miss Tulle beside me and the other students all gulp as the professor looks around the room.

"You students of the Combat Studies Department have trained yourselves in body and mind through fieldwork and volunteer combat opportunities. Many of you have leveled up. However, I will be frank with you. For all the various battlefields you have experienced—the Dungeon is *different*."

The room falls completely silent.

The students' tension and their brimming determination are both clear.

After a moment's silence, Professor Leon smiles.

"Remember what I said and embark on your studies in Orario. It will be okay. If you abandon your pride and prepare yourself, you will absolutely be able to do it. You are students of the School District."

""""Yes, sir!""""

What bubbles up after is a faint fervor.

It isn't exactly an esprit de corps, and it's not quite curiosity...I guess you'd call this a determination to learn.

It's a feeling that makes my body tense up.

I want to learn something, to experience something I didn't know before. That sort of vague feeling is why I came to the School District, but since I've been placed in Combat Studies, I will also be participating in the Dungeon practical. I should make sure to remember what I'm hearing. Taking on the Dungeon while hiding that I'm an adventurer is more than a little unusual.

Professor Leon explains the schedule in more detail and writes it all out on the blackboard.

"That is all for the guidance. Ordinarily, this is where I would take questions, but...today we have a new comrade joining us. Let's change tack for today and ask for *his* thoughts."

...Huh?

Things seem to be shifting...?

"Rapi, do you have anything to share?"

"...Y-yes, sir?! Uh...um?"

Still not used to the name, it takes me some time to realize it's me he's calling out to before I reflexively stand up.

He is looking at me from the podium. Everyone's eyes are on me.

My heart *just* stopped hammering before, but now it's off to the races again!

"If I recall correctly, you were hoping to become an adventurer. So please share your thoughts with us on how to make this Dungeon Practical a more fruitful learning experience."

I-I'm more of an actual adventurer than a hopeful, but...

Well, basically, that's the setting they gave me.

I don't have the confidence to convincingly pull off any complex backstories they could have given me, so this was definitely the safest choice. I'm sure that's Professor Leon and Lord Balder's thoughtfulness.

I'm sure that's all it is, but...wh-what should I say?!

"Rapi, here at the School District, it is important to express your thoughts. There is nothing wrong with being mistaken or even entirely off-base. We want you to always be thinking and never stop questioning your own thoughts or those of others."

"...!"

"By doing so repeatedly, we come to know what it means to learn."

I'm shocked by the gaze of a teacher—something altogether different from the gaze of a deity.

He is probably trying to teach me even now. These are the School District's rules, or rather, its way of life. He is holding this first lesson for my sake.

"Something that you consider important is enough. As someone who has set his sights on becoming an adventurer, could you share your thoughts with us?"

He asks in a kind, gentle voice. Standing frozen there, I glance to the side and see Miss Tulle smiling too, silently urging me on.

The students' gazes are still piercing me, but…I clench my fist and my lips move.

"An adventurer must not risk adventure."

That's what I say as I fight back the tremors in my voice that even I can't help but think are pathetic.

The professor's eyes widen a bit. I can tell that Miss Tulle is stunned, too.

Just as it feels like my voice fades away and the room starts to fall silent, all of a sudden, the students start murmuring.

"What do you mean…?"

"An adventurer shouldn't adventure?"

"Isn't that weird? What are you trying to say?"

Catching the exact contents of their murmurs, the sweat starts pouring down my neck—

"—Fantastic." Professor Leon smiles. "Rapi's statement may sound contradictory, but I believe there is a truth to it." The students' gazes leave me and turn back to the podium. "In the Dungeon, recklessness is not a virtue. Quite the opposite. To avoid unnecessary risk is to protect your own life and the lives of your comrades."

""""!""""

"For an adventurer exploring an environment as dangerous as the Dungeon, the judgment to know when to retreat and when to avoid taking unnecessary risks is the most crucial of skills."

The surprised students all begin to have a look of understanding. Everyone in the room is hanging on to the professor's every word.

"If you are going to set foot in the Dungeon, there will be much to learn from adventurers' perspectives in the coming weeks. Thanks to Rapi, we have all gotten a little bit wiser— Ladies and gentlemen, a round of applause!"

The thunderous roar of applause instantly fills the room.

The sound of praise from the other students surrounds me as I stand there in a daze.

The first three students from before, the animal boy, the human girl, and the red-haired Amazon, look at me a little differently from before. Miss Tulle breaks into a gleaming smile and is more enthusiastic with her applause than anyone else.

...This is the School District.

Candid, unreserved opinions, and an indiscriminate, unreserved welcome for thoughtful words.

My chest fills with embarrassment but also with a sense of exaltation I can't really explain. It isn't because what I said was particularly amazing. It's because the professor broke it down for the class, putting it into words that allowed the true meaning to reach them. And with far more skill than I could ever manage.

More than anything, he intentionally set up this opportunity to give the new student a chance to settle into the School District.

I've only just met him, but...I really can't hold a candle to the professor.

People like him are what you call a fine adult.

As the applause dies down...

"Rapi, out of curiosity, are those words something you came up with yourself?" he asks.

I answer honestly, this time actually holding my head high.

"No. It was taught to me by someone special to me."

An adventurer must not risk adventure.

Those are Miss Eina's words. An admonition and a teaching that saved me as a fledgling adventurer when I was prone to getting carried away.

"Is that so? I see..."

Miss Eina was originally a student here, apparently, and the teaching that has taken root in me might very well be the legacy of what she learned here. As I'm thinking that, Professor Leon puts a hand to his chin and nods slightly a few times.

"I would like to expand on this discussion a bit further, but...there is the next course to consider. We should call it here for now. If there is anything that you do not understand, come to me individually."

Taking a pocket watch out of his black instructor's uniform, he then looks at me again.

Or more precisely, at the person next to me.

"Nina, if you don't mind, could I ask you to show Rapi around the school?"

"Of course! I don't have any classes today after this, so it won't be a problem."

"Thank you. Rapi, I will come see you again after classes are over. Please meet me in this classroom."

"Y-yes, sir!"

After neatly clearing the blackboard, Professor Leon dismisses us and leaves the room.

I can't help feeling a little abandoned, but I'm sure he has lessons to teach after this…and I can sort of guess what he was trying to say.

Get involved, make some friends, and do what students do.

"Hey, new kid, what did you do before you came here?"

"U-umm…helping out around the house, working in the fields…"

"A farmer in a big city like Bella? You want to be an adventurer, so do you have any combat experience?"

"U-um, a bit, I guess…?"

"What level are you?"

"…………L-Level One?"

"Why are you saying it like a question? You received a blessing from Lord Balder, didn't you?"

I awkwardly muddle my way through the barrage of questions.

Right after the professor left, five or six students instantly gathered around me.

I appreciate them being curious, but what should I do? I haven't thought at all about Rapi's background…

In order to hide my actual identity, I immediately say the exact opposite of Level 5 and then do my best to blend the truth with some lies as I squirm under the impromptu interrogation.

This unsurprisingly gets a laugh as someone mentions I seem like a weird guy.

I don't disagree…

"But that was amazing, Rapi. Professor Leon was really impressed!"

Miss Tulle praises me cheerfully.

"The moderation not to venture risk…the self-control not to get greedy? I was startled as well."

"Ah, no, that was really just me repeating someone else's…Uh, I mean, I was taught it, too…!"

I hurriedly wave my hands, but even the students who were laughing start nodding along with Miss Tulle.

She probably changed the topic because she saw I was starting to feel cornered.

It's rude to compare them like this…but she's a nice person, just like Miss Eina.

It would be weird if a student suddenly asked if she had a relative who works for the Guild, and I can't be sure, but…seeing her sure brings back memories of when I first came to Orario. The kindness Miss Eina showed me, helping me so many times before I knew the first thing about being an adventurer.

"It wasn't amazing at all. Professor Leon can turn any stupid opinion into the ultimate teaching material is all."

Just then, I hear a laughing voice behind me. Turning around, I get startled.

"Iglin."

At a seat a few rows back from us is a dwarf brushing back his hair just so.

A boy wearing a perfectly fitted and neatly kept uniform. Naturally, since he's a dwarf, he's short and broad-shouldered. He has a bushy, dwarven beard. And there is a rose on his chest…What's that about?

The boy Miss Tulle called Iglin is sneering at me.

"Not only is he unsightly, he's a Level One to boot? I have to wonder what you were thinking, coming to Combat Studies."

"The prerequisites are the same for any new student at the School District, aren't they? Why are you saying that?"

"Because he looks so weak, obviously. Having a complete amateur with us in the Dungeon is just going to be a burden."

Miss Tulle's eyes flare as she gets angry for my sake even as Iglin's sneer never drops, but I can't do anything but stare open-mouthed.

A handsome, unpleasant boy—with a shaggy dwarven beard. This is also probably pretty rude, but his fancy, aristocrat tone doesn't really match his dwarven appearance!

"I feel sorry for whichever squad gets saddled with him. Don't slow us down too much, hume bunny."

"Ah, right, I'll be careful..."

Iglin gracefully stands up from his seat and I just reflexively lower my head like normal, still reeling from the shock. Brushing back his hair elegantly again, he leaves the room.

"D-don't pay attention to him, Rapi! Iglin is always like that with new people."

"I-is that so..."

Miss Tulle hurriedly encourages me, but honestly, more than being hurt by it, I feel weirdly back in my element as an adventurer flustered by an encounter with something entirely unknown.

This is the School District...a melting pot of all sorts of people I've never met...!

As that silly, idle thought crosses my mind, a bell rings. The other students start moving, leaving just me and Miss Tulle.

"...Shall we also get going?"

Quickly changing tack, she flashes a bit of a wry smile. Now that I've finally calmed down, I nod with a bit of a smile of my own.

Leaving the schoolhouse, the sun fills my eyes.

A field of white buildings and blue roofs spreads before me, intersected by wide streets that make it hard to believe we are on the water. With a bit of help from the faint scent of the sea wafting up, the scenery of the School District, framed by gorgeous blue skies above and blue water below, feels almost like a holiday resort.

"One day isn't enough to see all of the School District, so today I'll introduce you to the academic layer."

"Academic layer?"

Drawn in by the beautiful blue-and-white scenery, I parrot what she said.

"Mhmm." She smiles. "The School District can be broadly split into three layers. The control layer, the residential layer, and the academic layer."

"Layer, is it? Is that, umm...sort of like the floors in the Dungeon?"

"Hee-hee. It's a little different, but it's fine to think of them that way in a general sense."

She explains things in an easy-to-grasp way, smiling like a mature older sister.

Apparently, the School District is divided up into three massive discs set atop each other called layers. The control layer, the lowest level, holds the mechanisms and structures that could be called the heart of the ship, along with several laboratories and many large-scale magic-stone devices—including things similar to the elevator in Babel. In the middle is the residential layer where students and teachers live.

And finally...

"The highest of the three layers is the academic layer. That's where we are now. As you can see, there are many schoolhouses and seminar halls and all sorts of places for lessons."

Each layer having its own role is a feature of the School District... or rather, they are all crucial to the Hringhorni being able to continue sailing all around the world and performing its mission. Apparently, there are more than ten thousand people on board, counting the sailors responsible for handling the ship itself, so it makes sense to organize the ship into sections. When I looked out at it from the land, it was undoubtedly a long vessel, but it's also unbelievably tall...

Because of the way the three layers are arranged in a stack, the School District is sometimes jokingly called a short stack of pancakes. Apparently, it's also compared to a clock with the hour hand sticking out, and the back of a majestic dragon, too. There's no end to mortal comparisons for this impossibly large ship.

I can sort of get the clock one. When I came in from the sky with Lord Hermes, there was a really long something sticking out…I guess it's the bow?

As for the back of a majestic dragon, I guess it's probably due to the blue wings set around the outside of the academic layer here.

When I looked out from Orario's city wall with Miss Eina, I almost thought the School District looked like a village built on the back of a dragon, and I guess other people got the same impression.

The sails are fluttering in the tranquil breeze, and it almost feels like they blend into the blue of the skies.

They're glimmering with light, just like magic-stone lamps…no, dimmers? Maybe I should ask later.

I find the beautiful sails entrancing as I walk through the schoolhouse-lined street with Miss Tulle.

"Even just the academic layer feels like a city since there's this many streets. I recommend always keeping the handbook you were given close at hand! There's a map in there! When I first enrolled, I often got lost, too."

"Ah-ha-ha…True, it really is big."

"If you ever don't have a map on you and start feeling lost, look at the signs on the magic-stone streetlamps. They have the street names on them, like 3rd Street, 17th Street, and so on. If you follow the lower numbers, you will always end up at the bridge…at Breithablik, in the center of the ship."

She throws in an anecdote while pointing to the central tower where I met Lord Balder. The tallest building on the academic layer is apparently, and unsurprisingly, a really important location.

"Also, I guess I should mention there is a park at the stern of the ship."

"Ah, so that was a park."

Remembering what I was looking at the other day when I was trespassing…

"Ninaaaa! What are you up to?"

There's a voice from behind us.

We both turn around to see three girls. All animal people, a chienthrope, a raccoon, and a cow.

"Betty, what about your lessons?"

"We're just getting out of third period."

"More importantly, who's he?"

"Is he your man, Nina?!"

Her friends, I guess?

My eyes widen and I fidget a bit as her cheeks redden just a little.

"No! This is Rapi Flemish. Because of a family situation, he just enrolled today."

"Hmph, really…He seems kind of unsteady!"

"Pretty unreliable."

"Ugh?!"

The chienthrope called Betty and the raccoon girl both laugh.

"Hey, you two! Be nice!"

She gets a little upset for my sake, but I don't really mind. Better than getting found out, at least.

Her friends leave with a "Have fun, you two."

This sort of natural banter is part of the charm of school…I think?

"…?"

"What is it, Rapi?"

She is puzzled when my gaze gets drawn away suddenly.

"…I was a little curious this morning, but…are students working at those shops?"

I point at the stylish…I guess, boutique street?

A lot of the buildings are closed off with crystal shutters, but one is open with a small shop running out of it. Inside, behind the counter is an animal girl with a cute apron over her uniform.

"Yes, that's right. Any student in the Business Department who earns enough credits and passes their qualification exam can run a shop."

"A-anyone? That's incredible…"

"I was surprised too the first time I heard that. But being able to open a shop is also dependent on finding a location available to rent, so the norm is to work part-time at a senior classmate's shop first, I think."

From the sound of it, this is also part of the School District's studies.

Practice for students who want to work in a commercial field or join a commercial familia. And inside the walled garden of the School District—with over ten thousand potential customers—it's important to read the market's mood.

"There's a ranking of monthly sales, and you can even win prizes from the gods and goddesses. That's why the people in the Business Department are always fired up. Lots of new things come out every month, so it's a ton of fun for us, too!"

With a bit of a wry smile, I find myself thinking that the School District isn't quite as formal as I first suspected. It's more open-minded than I thought.

Lessons are in session, so there aren't many students working currently, and most of the shops are closed, but come evening, it's bound to get more and more lively. A lot of the shops are for food of various sorts, but there are all sorts of options for accessories and sundries too, apparently. The shop that's currently open is…

"…Jyaga Maru Kun?!"

"Hm? Oh, right. Jyaga Maru Kun originated in Orario, didn't it? It's pretty popular here in the School District, too."

I'm taken aback by the Koine sign that leaped into my eyes.

The feel of the shop, the decorated sign in front—it's so classy! This doesn't feel like a Jyaga Maru Kun at all!

Wow! Goddess was right when she flashed a thumbs-up and told me that Jyaga Maru Kun is a worldwide franchise! Whatever that means!

"Since we're here, do you want to go try it?"

"S-sure…!"

I'm not really hungry yet, but as a resident of the Labyrinth City, I can't help a sudden curiosity.

Like Ms. Aiz, I've been lured in by the Jyaga Maru Kun shop.

"Welcome!"

"Hello, Misa. What will you have, Rapi?"

"Uh, umm…p-please, you go first!"

A bead of sweat pops onto my forehead. I quickly let her go first. The easygoing greeting contrasts with the stylish exterior, and the parchment menu set out on the wall is full of unfamiliar words, so I don't really know what to order.

As Ms. Mikoto always says, when in a foreign place, do as the locals do. I decide to wait for Miss Tulle to order so I can learn by example.

"Hmmm, what to get. It's pre-lunch, so I can't eat too much…All right, I'll have that!"

The girl who guided me so neatly and perfectly puts her slender finger to her chin, and her expression suddenly changes. It may just be my impression, but it's only now that she feels like a regular student, and it's a bit adorable.

I break into a bit of a smile when—

"One Jyaga Maru Kun grande, chocolate-chip caramel icy java with extra coffee, nonfat milk, and chocolate drizzle, please."

…What was that?

I can't believe the magic chant I just heard, but moments after I hear an easygoing "sure thing," something incredible appears.

A crystal container filled with a creamy drink, covered with syrup, and with a Jyaga Maru Kun sticking out of the middle…

………No, this is…

This isn't a Jyaga Maru Kun anymore. The syrup and drink are the main feature…

I feel like if my goddess or Ms. Aiz saw this, they would both declare this as heresy…

Also, didn't you say you couldn't eat much? Are sweets different or something?

The adorable schoolgirl image disappears in a massive case of culture shock…!

"What'll you have?"

"…One hojicha-pepper Jyaga Maru Kun."

Nudged by the girl behind the counter, I pick the shortest spell name, or rather, the most normal-seeming one.

My face tenses as the corner of the worker's mouth turns up a bit as if to say, "Yeah, you get it."

Seriously though, I'm not great with sweets, and I can feel my heart burning already after seeing what Miss Tulle ordered…

"How much for two, Misa?"

"Two hundred ragnars."

I breathe a sigh of relief seeing a normal-shaped Jyaga Maru Kun come out with just some unusual spice on top. Then I watch as Miss Tulle pulls out a cute wallet and takes out two slips of paper.

Is that…paper money?

Paper instead of valis gold coins?

Wait—

"W-wait, Miss Tulle?! I'll pay!"

"But you haven't gotten any ragnars yet, right? Even if you have valis, you have to exchange it at the student bank."

"Eh, ehh…?! I—I don't really understand, but I can't make a woman pay for me!"

More specifically, Master will pummel me if he finds out! I can hear him sentencing me to death for failing like this after all his reeducation, and I can already feel the Caurus Hildr ready to light me up!

"It's fine! Let's go!"

"Uwah?!"

Quickly handing over the paper bills, she takes my hand and starts running before I can argue. The girl behind the counter waves as my cheeks flush from the warmth and softness I feel in my hand.

"This is to celebrate you joining the School District!"

"C-celebrate?"

"Yeah! Let's go to the park to eat!"

The two of us trot through the empty streets together. Her smile is dazzling, more than a match for the clear blue skies.

"Congratulations, Rapi! As classmates, let's both do our best!"

She really does resemble Miss Eina. But she is definitely different, too. Mature, but childish and carefree.

A troubled look crosses my face, but drawn by the kind girl in front of me, I break into a smile, too.

After the two of us have a little welcome party, all alone in the big park, the chime from Breithablik rings twice, and a swarm of students flows from the schoolhouses. A lively energy fills the academic layer.

It's lunchtime, and everyone is hungry.

Schoolchildren with healthy appetites attack their meals like they've been waiting all day for this.

"S-so good…!"

"Right?! Sky Lounge is a top-class cafeteria!"

I'm stunned by the small serving of pasta with a slight mound of jewellike fish eggs atop it.

Sitting beneath a parasol, Miss Tulle blissfully lifts a forkful of noodles from her matching order to her mouth.

We're sitting at a table on an outside terrace that is buzzing with chatting students.

"The shops run by students cost money, but ones managed directly by School District staff and deities are generally free of charge. And among them, Sky Lounge is very popular! So popular that it's almost impossible to get in, even if you don't have classes! We got lucky today!"

I can't believe such delicious food is free, but apparently an actual deity does the cooking for the Sky Lounge. Lunch is limited to fifty meals, and it's first come, first served.

Across the table from me, Miss Tulle's voice is filled with excitement.

Maybe she really likes eating?

Smiling a bit and getting a little fired up myself, I finish my pasta with gusto.

"With this, that's pretty much it for the important points on the academic layer. The tour was a little hurried, but will you be all right?"

"Yes, it was very helpful! Thank you very much, ma'am."

From the terrace, just looking to the side, you can see the academic layer spread out before you. It's a beautiful view, and the wind is chilly but pleasant. It was a really fun tour of the school, including the great food.

Her smile changes, and her eyes focus on me.

"Nina."

"Huh?"

She raises her finger.

"Call me Nina. I'm calling you Rapi, and we're classmates!"

I'm surprised by her response. I guess it's been bothering her a bit.

The School District—maybe it's because it has the feel of a school, but I keep just saying what I'm thinking.

"B-but you've been at the School District longer than me...and it would be rude to be so casual with a senior classmate..."

When I say that, the smile she has had throughout the day turns into something a little sharper.

"...How old are you, Rapi?"

"Oh, umm, fourteen..."

"I'm thirteen."

"Ehhh?!"

No way!

I reflexively leap to my feet, and this time, the younger girl's eyes really do flare.

"Ah, so you have that sort of reaction, too! It's fine, I guess I just look ancient and decrepit!"

"Whaaat?! Th-that's not it!"

She looks so much like Miss Eina that it tricked my eyes...!

Something like this has probably happened a few times before. She closes her eyes and turns away, clearly bothered.

"No, really, I wasn't thinking anything like that at all! I was just surprised. How do I put it...you don't seem childish, and you're more mature than me...and you're so pretty...!"

Desperate to improve her mood, my face turns bright red as I just let what I really think escape my lips.

"...Hmph..."

Opening her eyes, she glances over at me.

And then her eyes crease mischievously, like she's a child who enjoys pranks, and she flashes the same warm smile as before.

"All right, then I'll forgive you."

"Phew..."

"Just call me by my name. No need for formalities."

"...Umm...N-Nina."

"That'll do," she says with a nod and a smile.

I awkwardly scratch my cheek as an almost comfortable sort of ticklishness fills me.

It's currently serving as a cafeteria, but apparently the Sky Lounge is also a break room in the central tower, and the students who have finished eating are just enjoying conversations without getting up to leave.

After becoming classmates in a more concrete way, we clear the dishes from our table and continue to chat underneath the parasol.

"Rapi, sorry if I'm butting in too much, but have you finished registering for courses?"

"Registering...?"

"Mhmm. Choosing the lessons you'll take here at the School District."

Ah, right, I think the professor mentioned that, too...

I grab my book bag from where it's resting on my seat. Checking the inside, I see a guidebook, multiple documents, a quill and other writing implements, plus a scroll with the School District's wax seal closing it.

I'm sure this is what Nina's talking about.

Undoing the seal and unfurling it—there is an overview of courses in neat lettering.

"Whoa?! Are these all courses...?"

"It's the curriculum, to be technical. There are some you can't take in your first year, though..."

I spread it out on the table as Nina begins explaining.

"Broadly speaking, there are two types of courses—required courses and electives. For the Combat Studies Department , Martial Studies and Fieldwork are required, as well as a Combat Volunteer session of some sort. Practical lessons like Fieldwork and such are being replaced by the Dungeon Practical for now, so you don't have to worry about them. So the question is electives," Nina says. "Combat Studies has a high number of practical courses, but if you don't take at least six electives, you won't have enough credits. It would be best to pick subjects that interest you or something that you're good at."

"Umm, incidentally, what happens if you don't have enough of those…credits…?"

"You won't be given the right to graduate, I guess? In the worst case you could be expelled. But anyone who went to the effort to enroll in the School District wouldn't avoid taking classes, so I've never seen it happen…"

I—I see…

So basically, if I don't properly take courses, it won't just end with me looking suspicious. I don't know how long I can be in the School District, but if there's something I can get, then I want to really study too, so I should be serious in my choices.

Umm, what's available is…Magic Theory, Incantation Studies, Magic Development, Spirit Studies, Harmonic Theory, Alchemy, Compounding, Cooking, Elixirs, Smithing, Monster-Taming, Ethnohistory, Ancient History, Modern History, Divine Era Seminar, Eschatology Seminar, Koine, Elvish, Animal-People Dialects, Prummish, Amazonian, Dance, Theater, Performance, Music, Poetry, Swordsmanship, Spearwork, Archery, Ax Mastery, Hand-to-Hand Combat, Staff Fighting, General Combat—how many are there?!

Looking down at the parchment in my hands, my eyes are on the verge of spinning out of control.

"Ugh…?! Wh-what should I take…?!"

"I-if you overthink it, it can be overwhelming. Are there any that piqued your interest?"

"O-ones that interest me...ah, um, what is this 'Theological Synthesis'...?"

"A course related to deities. You can learn the meaning of hieroglyphs and how to read them, but..."

"Eh?! R-really? Then maybe I should try that...!"

"It's a little hard to recommend it...The word is only around one in ten people who take it pass...and even fewer people learn how to properly interpret hieroglyphs."

"One in ten?!"

Hearing her advice, I groan and continue racking my brain.

I could take the History of Heroes course I saw on the list...and then just some sort of course related to martial arts that seems doable would probably be the safest choice. But since I have to hide my identity, I should probably limit the opportunities for revealing information about my status as much as possible...Wh-what do I do?!

My ambiguous desire to study at the School District instead of a clearer goal is coming back to bite me. I can almost feel the smoke rising from my head—

"...Rapi, can I have this for a moment?"

Nina takes the parchment from my hands and picks up a quill pen.

"Do you know the type of weapon you want to use as an adventurer?"

"Eh? Umm...a knife...I think?"

"All right, so in the shortsword section, Swordsmanship should be doable. Is history a tough subject for you?"

"Uh, no, I don't think..."

"All right, then you can take Ancient History and Modern History. Professor Adler is the instructor for those, and he refers back to previous lessons a lot in addition to regular reviews, so it shouldn't be too hard to catch up even if you're starting midway. In the other direction, Divine Era Seminar assumes a lot of prerequisite knowledge, so you should probably avoid that."

"Huh, wha—?"

"If you have any aptitude for magic, then I would recommend Incantation Studies…but that really comes down to you. If you have the leeway for a language course, there's Elvish, which I could help you out with."

Nina is jotting down things as my eyes keep spinning. When she finally gives me the parchment back, there are wavy lines under several of the courses.

"Um, is this…?"

"My recommendations…I guess. Entering this late in the year, courses have already started moving, so it can definitely feel like you're being left behind by everyone else…and, well, it can be hard to catch up."

Nine's cheeks glow a little bashfully.

"Also…I recommended courses I'm taking too, so if we're both taking them together, it should be possible to make it work."

My eyes widen.

"Why would you go so far…?"

When I look up, I see her break into a joyful smile.

"I was the same."

"Really…?"

"When I first enrolled, I didn't understand anything, and I struggled to keep up with lessons, too…but there were lots of people who helped me." She closes her eyes for a moment. "Do you remember Milly, the one in front of me during the guidance hall this morning?"

"Y-yeah. The elf, right?"

"Right. Milly is my senior and she taught me a lot of things. There were times it was difficult and when I wasn't sure what to do, but thanks to her and the others who helped me, I fell in love with the School District, so…" She looks me in the eye again before continuing. "I want to help too, just like them…I know it might be annoying for me to stick my nose into your business, though."

She laughs awkwardly at that.

"Not at all!" I frantically respond. "You've been really, really helpful! Studying isn't my strong point, but…you made me want to do my best!"

That's how I genuinely feel.

Inspired by her passionate, kind reception, all the unease I was feeling fades away. I'm even starting to think I'd like to get to know this place better.

I don't know if what I'm feeling made it through, but her expression brightens, and her ears twitch.

"Then I'm glad! It makes me happy that you would say that!"

"Mhmm! Right, if you have time, could you teach me some about studies? How I should prepare for courses or something, just that much would be enough..."

"—Really?!"

Her face brightens even more hearing that.

"Then should we start now?!"

"Huh? Now?!"

"You're going to have to start going to lessons tomorrow, after all! And preparing for lessons is really, really important!"

"That's true, and I don't really know what to study...if it isn't too much trouble for you, could I ask you for some help?"

"Leave it to me!"

I'm a little surprised, but she's totally right. Exploring in the Dungeon without even any knowledge at all is suicide. Excited by the study party suggestion, Nina has an enchanting smile on her face.

"Go back to the classroom where we had the guidance hall this morning, Rapi! It should be empty for the rest of the day! I'll grab some reference books from the library!"

BAM!!!

My pupils turn to dots as an absurd mountain of books slams down in front of me. Is the desk going to be okay?

"Huh?"

"It's a little on the low side, but this much should be doable!"

"Huh?"

"After five hours of diligent work, you should try some mock tests! I'll make some problems for you to work on."

"Huh?"

As I turn into a broken doll that can only say "huh?" Nina just keeps smiling. An indomitable, innocent smile without a trace of malice or ill will.

My reaction is delayed, but a massive wave of sweat springs out.

"N-Nina? This much is a little rough, or like, impossible, or like, I'm not sure I can cover it all…"

Lunch just ended and we're currently in the room where we had guidance hall this morning.

I arrived first, and what Nina brought in for me turns out to be a pile of a dozen or more thick, heavy books. My face tenses as this incredibly familiar scene plays out in front of me, but the half-elf girl just a single year younger than me cocks her head in confusion.

"Eh? But you took the entrance exam, didn't you? The interview with the deities?"

"I-interview…? Umm, yeah, I met Lord Balder and talked to him, but…"

"Then you'll be fine! Everyone who can enter the School District has the determination to study! The deities would see right through anyone who doesn't and wouldn't let them enroll."

Ah, so that's the actual enrollment system, then…?

Miss Eina did say the requirement for becoming a student was the determination to study. No mortal can lie in the face of a deity, so an interview with them could be considered the perfect and simplest test to see if someone is fit to be a student here. That's why the School District is known as the world's biggest school, because only people who really want to study gather here.

But having a passion for studying and not being terrified by a despair-inducing load of topics aren't the same thing…

"Studying isn't really my forte, either…but if you don't do it, you'll just get nervous, right? So let's do our best."

Scary.

This is the first time I've thought a smile on a younger girl's face is scary.

"It's okay, I'll properly teach you, too!"

It's Miss Eina!

Miss Eina is here!

It's the same as that spartan Dungeon study party!

The Guild's famed merciless instruction: Fairy Break.

Nina and Miss Eina *have* to be sisters!

"All right, shall we?"

Forced to take up a quill, the only path I can take is to buckle down and begin, as a river of cold sweat pours down my back.

"Amazing!"

The sun has completely set beyond the classroom's window.

Right beside me, as I lie collapsed on the desk, nothing but ash, Nina is holding the impromptu test sheet in both hands, her eyes gleaming.

"You got half of the questions on the test right!"

"I-is that really amazing…?"

"It's covering topics you don't know and haven't taken classes on at all, right?! And you still managed to get half of the questions right in such a short amount of time!"

Nina's voice is filled with excitement while mine is dry as the desert.

I wonder…is this because of my experience from Miss Eina's study parties? She would always immediately give me a test after she finished her lessons, too. Also, the questions were less about calculation and analysis and more about memorization for history and stuff. Now that I'm Level 5, maybe my memory has improved, too…Hmm, yeah, probably not.

But as an adventurer, remembering things is very important—when faced with the unknown, delving into the depths of everything you do know for clues is a question of life and death—so I've gotten in the habit of picking up whatever I can notice. And the result is getting about half the questions right, I guess.

"If you can manage this, you should be able to catch up in your lessons quickly! Wait just a minute, I'll go return these books to the library real quick!"

Nina celebrates my progress and picks up the mountain of books easily before leaving the room. It goes without saying, but it really is obvious she has a status…as I'm thinking that, the presence that has been waiting outside the classroom this whole time enters after she leaves.

"Finished?"

"Professor Leon…"

Seeing how exhausted I look, an amused smile crosses his lips.

"I could have said something sooner, but I simply watched since I thought it would be a good experience for you…Then it ended up getting this late. I forgot about Nina's studying habits," he says with a glance out the window at the night sky. "Sorry about that."

I noticed that he came to see me after school like he promised, but I don't blame him. Nina has been working so hard to help me, and I figure him not stopping it means he thought it was a good thing for Rapi Flemish.

"It's fine." I smile awkwardly back.

"How was it? Your first day of school?"

"Well…it was hard to get used to the name Rapi at first, and it took a little bit of time to realize people were talking to me, but I'm used to it now. Other than that…it was fun. I learned a lot about the School District."

"That's good."

He nods magnanimously, and while it's embarrassing, I also decide to bring up some self-reflection I had, too.

"As a student, I was a little pathetic…I was just nervous the whole time."

"But you blended in well."

"I-is that so…? The other students didn't think I was weird…?"

"No, no one noticed you're a first-tier adventurer at all."

"!"

Hearing that, I realize what the professor was getting at, and my eyes widen behind my bangs.

"I imagine you noticed, but in between lessons, I observed your surroundings several times. And every time, there was not a single person who suspected your true strength."

—Because he looks so weak, obviously.

—Pretty unreliable.

Those are the sorts of evaluations I got from other students today. I encountered a lot of students out on the streets and in the hallways. Not a single person suspected I'm actually a first-tier adventurer.

"As you know, there are many students at the School District who have leveled up. Their eyes are not just decorations. They can sense true strength beyond mere appearance. Be it balance, center of gravity, stance, movements, what have you."

Because of the nature of Falna, every fighter knows to never judge a book by its cover. At a minimum, the students here would not use something like age difference or size or an impression of weakness to judge someone with a blessing.

He is also, without saying as much, pointing out that I managed to carry myself in a way that meant they didn't notice my deception.

...And like he said, I've been performing a terrible act the entire day.

By actively suppressing my status, I've been able to keep people from guessing I'm Level 5.

"If I might ask, what was the logic you used?"

"...I took the advice I've received from many different people and did *the opposite*."

Ms. Aiz and Ms. Lyu, and Master, too.

I thought that by going against the best advice of those people who allowed me to get closer to becoming a full-grown adventurer, I would look more inexperienced and green. I didn't think about this very deeply, but that's what I came up with.

I made use of the manners and way of carrying myself that Master taught me—even though they were supposed to be for dates. Turning my back on the spartan teachings he ingrained in me, letting my posture slump, carrying my weight more like a normal person, and being awkward, I managed to create an unreliable sort of feeling for myself.

That was especially effective this time, and it sounds like I managed to deceive the students of the School District.

I'm sure it would be seen through by an experienced upper-class adventurer, or even a second-tier adventurer. And of course, it was easily seen through by the man in front of me.

"Disguising your true strength...that is quite the trick. You really are an adventurer."

I don't think it's as impressive as he makes it sound. I'm just desperate to not let anyone find out.

Though I can't bring myself to say that part out loud.

For some reason, his natural smile, devoid of any openings, makes me feel like all I can do is keep my mouth shut.

"Rapi, earlier today, you said 'an adventurer must not risk adventure.'"

The portable magic-stone lamp on the desk is the only source of light as he suddenly changes the subject.

"Yes, sir..."

"I would like to ask you a question not as an instructor, but out of my own *personal* curiosity..."

I'm a little surprised to hear a bit of a rougher intensity in his voice.

"I believe that there comes a day for everyone when they will have to knowingly take on risk."

"...!!!"

"Regardless of their wishes. Whether they are adventurers or not...What do you think?"

His eyes now are completely different from the instructor's gaze before. They're sharp, almost like blades. But also, how do I explain it? It feels like there's some expectation of me in them, too.

Our eyes lock, and there is a moment's silence.

My eyes have widened, but slowly. Taking my time, I say what I feel.

"...I also think there will come a day when you can't run away from it."

I think back to my duel with the minotaur. My encounter with the Black Goliath on the eighteenth floor. And the rematch with *him* that resulted from meeting the Xenos. The calamity. The deep floors. The war with *Freya Familia*.

As I think back on all the other times I put everything on the line, I continue.

"No matter how much you try to avoid it…even if you keep choosing the safest route, eventually you will have to face it."

I don't want to deny what Miss Eina said. It is an important lesson, admonishing adventurers starved for wealth and hungry for the unknown. But in another sense, in another place, there comes a day when we all have to venture forth.

"In that case, what will you do?"

I already have the answer to that.

"Prepare myself. I am always trying to grow, to be ready for whatever might come."

It's not recklessness and not foolhardiness. Just…someday there will come a time when I'll have to take a risk. I don't know if it will come in a year or in a day, or even a few seconds from now, but to make it through that moment, I have to improve myself. In a lot of different ways.

Always in the frame of mind of searching for the best answer, preparing.

I think everyone we call first-tier adventurers are like that. So that they don't have any regrets. That is the belief I gained after fighting with the swarm of iguaçu on our first expedition.

"I see. So that's your answer?"

It lasts for just a moment. An incredibly small instant. But it feels like his eyes peer into my soul, taking the measure not of Rapi, but of Bell Cranell.

"Have you decided which lessons you will take?"

"Ah…yes, sir."

I just manage to nod at the unexpected question.

"May I see?" he asks while holding out his right hand.

Stunned, I take out the parchment with the courses I decided on with Nina and hand it over to him.

He glances at it for just a moment and then pulls a quill pen from his holster. Then he makes two marks on my registration.

"Modern History and Eschatology Seminar. You should take these two as well."

"Eh...?"

"The promise I made with Lord Balder was to observe throughout the day."

He smiles like a knight, reaching some sort of acceptance, even as I struggle to follow what he's saying.

"You are right, we should prepare. In order to face the end against which we must take a stand."

I take the parchment he hands back to me, still dumbfounded.

Something that we must someday face. Even though my head doesn't fully understand what he is getting at, my heart subconsciously picks up on it.

Looking down at me in my seat, Professor Leon smiles again like an instructor.

"You will be notified officially at a later date, but you will be joining a squad, Rapi."

"A squad...?"

"Yes. As Lord Balder mentioned before, there is something he, and I as well, would like to put in your hands."

There is a clear glint of expectation in his eyes as he says that.

"You will be in the 3rd Squad, together with Nina. Please guide them."

CHAPTER 4

STUDY, REFLECT, EXPERIMENT, ADVANCE

"The School District's orichalcum production is up forty percent over last year's! That's a big haul!"

"Your plan is starting to feel more realistic, Mr. Royman!"

"The School District's reluctant, but the deal made when it was established is still in force! They have no choice!"

Several people joined the discussion in heated voices.

Emerald eyes looked in a daze at the Guild leadership who were currently experiencing what could only be described as euphoria.

Should I really be here...?

That was what Eina thought as she retreated into the uncomfortably plush seat at the table.

She was on the second floor of the Guild Headquarters where the Guild head Royman and the rest of the leadership were gathered in a spacious meeting room.

"...Um, Chief Rehmer? Why was I called to the second floor? Should I really be sitting alongside chiefs and the other high-ranking staff...?"

"You've produced several notable adventurers in a short period of time. Is that not more than sufficient an achievement to merit consideration for promotion?"

"Wha—?! Chief..."

As she whispered to her boss sitting next to her, the animal person who ordinarily never cracked jokes broke into a quiet chuckle, and Eina let out a shameful squeak just like a certain adventurer she was charged with.

In the giant Guild Headquarters with its pantheon-like majesty, the second floor of the building held a special meaning.

Eina and the other Guild employees going about their jobs every day did so on the first floor. The second floor and higher was off-limits to everyone below the level of chief. They could only go upstairs on the summons of Royman or another member of the leadership.

In the Guild Headquarters, the line between the first floor and the second floor was a hard-and-fast barrier expressing the difference in status between employees. At the very least, it was not the sort of place a simple receptionist could just waltz into.

"This meeting marks an important fork in the road for Orario. I thought we should have at least one person with a perspective more in line with how adventurers see things. And the topic concerns the School District as well."

Chief Rehmer watched the continuing discussion while speaking softly so that just Eina could hear.

"You graduated from the School District. That makes you a perfect fit for consultation."

"If that's what you want, Misha graduated from the School District, too..."

"Frot wouldn't have worked. There's a distinct chance she might've thrown this whole meeting into chaos."

Eina's last argument was shut down in a rather blunt manner.

The cabriole-legged chair she was sitting in creaked slightly, as if reflecting her state of mind.

I was given permission to attend, but...I could swear the Guild chief glared at me as if telling me not to speak out of turn...

Eina could already feel traces of anxiety growing as she shifted her gaze.

There were ten people on each side of the long, ebony table, and at the head of it sat Royman, just opening his mouth to speak, his good mood showing on his face.

"With this, there should be no problem. We will finally be able to set to work on the plan connecting the depths of the Dungeon with the surface!"

Eina looked over the documents in her hand again as the meeting heated up. The contents were a design calling for the creation of a shaft into the Dungeon and the construction of a large-scale elevator.

In other words, a shortcut for adventurers.

"When the Shaft plan is complete, exploration efficiency will go up dramatically. And by extension, it will provide a tremendous boon to *Loki Familia*'s expedition, allow the retrieval of even more valuable resources, and contribute significantly to the growth of Finn and the rest of them!"

Royman's euphoric statement was not wrong.

Dungeon exploration and the expeditions carried out by upper-class adventurers all began at the first floor, and it took significant time, effort, and money in order to reach whatever floor their goal was at.

It was entirely possible that a familia, even one like *Loki Familia*, wanting to explore the fifty-first floor would use up a significant amount of their supplies, exhaust themselves, and not achieve much if they had to pass through fifty floors to get to the starting line. The current expedition system was a gamble where even a single irregularity could be the difference between success and failure for any familia. It was very inefficient.

But if this plan came to fruition, that massive amount of required labor could be dramatically reduced. And an increase in adventurers' exploration efficiency would pay out significant dividends for the Labyrinth City.

Transforming something high risk, high return into something low risk, high return. That was a prospect that Royman and the rest of the Guild leadership who ran the city were keen to advance.

"All the orichalcum the School District produced will be used for the giant shaft! We won't have to use adamantite or any other alloy to make up for volume! With that, we don't have to worry about any damn monsters breaking it! If we just avoid areas where floor bosses are born, there is no chance of anything happening!"

And that was where the School District came in.

The School District's Alchemy Department was a world-leader in rare metals work, including the manufacture of orichalcum.

Achieving repeated breakthroughs as it traveled the world and gathered materials and talent, it was unmatchable in its production of valuable metals, providing an impressive stream of orichalcum—including master ingots, which were pieces of orichalcum refined to the limit.

It was impossible to create a giant shaft that would not be broken by the Dungeon without the orichalcum provided by the School District's alchemists.

"If we bring this plan to fruition, it will be a feat comparable to the raising of Babel! If the adventurers' growth is accelerated, then Orario's dearest wish will be achieved before long! A new age will soon be upon us!"

""""Oooooooooooooh!""""

A roiling fervor filled the room.

The higher-ups of the Guild could practically see the vast wealth and unprecedented fame that awaited them.

Royman's argument was certainly simple to understand. There were surely many upper-class adventurers who would agree if they heard about this plan. But even so, it was impossible to shake the tentative *in theory* that loomed over the entire discussion.

Eina glanced to her side. Rehmer stayed quiet, as if none of this was his concern. She took that to mean she could do what she liked.

"So then, I move to adopt the—"

"Apologies, sir. May I make a comment?"

Unable to hold it back, Eina summoned her courage and raised her hand.

Royman glared at her with an extremely suspicious and distasteful gaze, displeased she had ruined his momentum.

"What is it, Tulle?"

"The Shaft plan is certainly an alluring and revolutionary proposition. However, might it not need a little more consideration from a safety perspective?"

"Get to the point."

"...Linking the surface to the Dungeon, which has killed so many adventurers, and connecting directly to the lower floors and deep floors that are the source of irregulars that even upper-class adventurers cannot always cope with is…a scary thought."

The general presumption was that the Dungeon was just barely made manageable by the combination of the lid on the labyrinth—Babel—and Ouranos's prayers. Even if they managed to make an unbreakable orichalcum shaft, in the event that anything went wrong and the interior of the shaft were compromised, there would be terrible consequences.

Creating a shaft also created a risk of monsters spilling back out onto the surface.

"There is a real chance that the Dungeon might do something terrifying in reaction to having something foreign inserted into it."

"We have already debated that issue countless times! And our conclusion after all those debates is that there will not be a problem! Lord Ouranos has been consulted as well! And while you wouldn't know about it, we even have a model case to show that the Dungeon won't necessarily go wild in reaction to external interference!"

The information was confidential, even inside the Guild, so a low-level employee like Eina couldn't possibly have known about it, but the knowledge of the existence of Knossos had been a significant factor in the push for the Shaft plan.

Even with a neighboring massive, man-made labyrinth connecting to multiple floors, the Dungeon remained silent. That was why the higher-ups had decided the addition of another artificial object into the Dungeon would not provoke an incident. In fact, the orichalcum doors found throughout Knossos would almost all be stripped down with the help of *Goibniu Familia* and reused for the Shaft plan. It could be said that the massive amount of resources in Knossos was practically a prerequisite for making this plan a reality.

I don't know what exactly he means by a model case, but…

Between the incident with the armed monsters and adventurers' rumors, Eina had a faint idea that there was something connecting Daedalus Street and the Dungeon, so she quickly changed her approach with a grimace.

"Another concern is that with the establishment of the shaft, adventurers will lose significant opportunities to gain experience on various floors. A shortcut might also lead to a loss of experience in explor—"

"Access to the shaft can simply be limited by familia ranks! What problem could there be in differentiating normal exploration and mission-related expeditions?! And frankly, the thing we should be supporting is surpassing the seventy-first-floor record set by Zeus and Hera!"

Royman was of course entirely comfortable in a battle of words. And unlike Eina, who was joining this discussion for the first time today, he had debated this countless times already. He could counter her concerns without breaking stride.

"We don't intend to connect the shaft directly down to the deepest floors right away! First the upper levels, then the middle levels and the Under Resort! Progressing almost too cautiously and carefully through each floor and watching for any developments!"

"........."

From the moment creating a shaft that led into the Dungeon was part of the discussion, the words *cautiously* and *carefully* more or less went out the window, but the subject shifted quickly out from under Eina. Royman's face turned red in anger, as if he understood the thoughts behind the emerald eyes silently watching him.

"The plan is to have *Ganesha Familia* always guarding the shaft and elevator! That will mean that security aboveground will be shorthanded, so we are also urgently looking for a familia fit to act as the city guard! Tulle, all of you advisers need to continue raising adventurers and cultivating the city's combat abilities!"

Eina made one final comment, not as an employee of the Guild but as a graduate of the School District.

"The plan also calls for taking all the currently available orichalcum for construction, which is to begin immediately. But the master ingots are also used to reinforce Hringhorni's hull and are the School District's treasure and its pride...Even if the Guild is financing them, excessive and unreasonable demands will surely invite opposition. Especially from impressionable students—"

"Enough! Silence, Tulle! This plan is the work of the century! You have no right to criticize it after walking into this discussion for the first time today!"

Eina's insistent arguments had finally worn through the last reserves of his patience, and Royman snapped back with a shout.

Others around the table snipped at her about how a new attendee should not be talking out of turn, too. As Eina closed her mouth, Rehmer next to her was the only one who sighed at the prospect of the Shaft plan. At the same time, it also seemed to be an apology to Eina.

"More than anything, this is Lord Ouranos's divine will! There is no reversing it now!"

He was right. That was the biggest problem.

In the end, no matter how many issues and faults a newcomer like Eina might point out, with the Guild's patron god having already given his sign-off, there was no stopping the Shaft plan anymore.

If an all-knowing god has allowed it, then perhaps I'm being overly worried and there shouldn't be any problem. But would the Dungeon really not react at all to a giant shaft being dug right into it?

Eina's lingering concern refused to go away. That was just how terrifying she found the Dungeon, which had swallowed up and stolen away so many of the adventurers that had been in her care.

But either way, the motion to begin construction on the shaft was approved.

Royman fixed Eina with a smug, self-satisfied look as he stamped the seal of approval on the parchment. The various leaders of the Guild cheered and shook hands.

The path to glory and riches…or a pitfall into the underworld.

This was a turning point in Orario's thousand-year history, the first step into the next stage of its existence.

Why did Lord Ouranos allow this to go forward…?

"Is this really right, Ouranos? Allowing the Shaft plan?"

A voice echoed from a crystal sitting on an armrest—an oculus.

In the underground altar beneath the Guild, the Chamber of Prayers, Fels spoke with a tinge of admonition.

"This will make Royman even more insolent. And it invites suspicion and discontent from all sides. The School District will surely oppose the plan."

There was a tone of "this isn't like you" lurking in Fels's prophetic declaration. Coincidentally, this was almost the same exact moment Eina was having similar doubts in the meeting room.

"I chose to observe and prepare for the potential trial that awaits… instead of the difficulties that might occur."

"Oh?"

"However many means we get will never be enough."

"To hear a god such as you say that only raises more concerns."

There was a resigned regret emanating from the depths of the crystal.

Even saying that, though, Fels did not try to probe further. Even if it was not enough to be satisfied, it felt sort of like receiving an oracle. There was only the sound of movement from the crystal as Fels trusted in the god's words and began working.

"What about you?" Ouranos asked.

Fels's voice was ever so slightly more animated than normal, like a child who had just been given a toy.

"It's excellent. Thanks to Knossos, I've unexpectedly gotten my hands on an enormous atelier. I'm already making progress on my research."

In the southeast of the city, far from the Guild's underground altar, Fels was busy setting up various facilities inside of Knossos, beneath Daedalus Street.

"My research requires a massive amount of space. I'm grateful for getting this whole sealed-off floor to myself, Ouranos. I know it can't have been easy to placate Royman."

The labyrinth that had tormented Bell, Wiene, and the others had changed completely.

Only a single magic-stone lamp had been set up so far, lighting a large, gloomy space. A mountain of books was piled along the wall's edge, and a single snowy owl perched on a pillar. The space was filled with magic gauges imported from Altena and a massive number of flasks. And there was multiple cylinders filled with mysterious, multicolored liquid.

It was the shady laboratory every villain dreamed of. The prototypical mage's lair.

"Heh-heh-heh, I'm going to renovate it even more. My mage's blood is racing...!"

Completely conquered after the incident with the Xenos, Knossos was now under Guild management. Or more accurately, it was under Ouranos's control, and the old god had granted the legendary Sage full access to everything it had to offer.

The benefits of controlling this former hotbed of evil were immeasurable.

First, the sheer scale and depth of the place, which connected directly into the Dungeon's middle floors. And then, the hidden complex that was used to create magic items such as Jura's whip. All of it was supremely useful, and it was like Fels had inherited a massive fortune.

As both a secret base and source of materials, Daedalus's thousand-year legacy that connected right into the Dungeon was ideal. Fels planned to work on a production plant to create medicinal herbs and an elixir spring next. The mage was also considering inviting Asfi in the future to enlist her help with research. Her patron god had already pledged her ceaseless service, which would begin once she was back from her time off.

"I never had anything like this while I was alive. There wasn't even one like it in my vexing homeland."

"You are not dead yet."

"Ha-ha, what are you saying when I've completely lost my skin and flesh? I'm already halfway there."

Though Fels was just bones now, the mad mage's sagely nature was really showing, going so far as cracking a rather wicked joke.

Fels was in the process of turning Knossos into something other than just a second entrance to the Dungeon. The mage was making a personal base.

"How is it *coming?"*

"The knowledge and theory are in my head…in my soul. For equipment, I should be able to compensate using the remnant spirit magic. I'll make something that equals Altena's underground palace."

Fels was planning to use everything in what came next.

If Lyu were here, she would abhor it, but the mage was even going to use the technology left by the Evils.

"The School District has returned, too. If I can just restock the materials I requested from Leon—ancient dolupha, stellas alluvium, and elpis sparkle—then all the requirements should be met. There should be plenty in the School District."

The giant ship that sailed all around the mortal realm was both a massive source of resources and a critical factor of its own.

Yes.

All for the sake of machia.

"…I am already in the process of production."

The mage stopped in front of a certain structure.

An extremely large flask filled with liquids injected from five different cylinders. And inside was a jewel gleaming with a sorcerous, crimson glow, floating in the liquid.

"Will you make it in time?"

"I won't promise it right away. But whatever the cost, I will have it for the Black Dragon hunt…no, for the promised time."

Because the times are already changing—

The black-robed mage's murmur was swallowed by the darkness.

It's day two after I (temporarily) enrolled in the School District.

Because an empty room in the residential layer apparently wasn't ready yet, I stayed overnight in Professor Leon's staff office. Today is the true beginning of my school life.

That's right—classes are actually starting.

I meet Nina in the center of the academic layer in front of Breithablik, and we head to our lessons.

My first course is Ancient History—

"Everyone!!! What time is it?!"

""""*Aoharu time!*""""

—or at least, it was supposed to be, but for some reason, the lights in the classroom are dimmed, and standing in the spotlight centered on the podium at the front of the room is a stunningly beautiful blond-haired goddess all fired up first thing in the morning.

"I can't hear you! Youthful in body and spirit! Never slacking on lessons! Let's Aoharu!"

""""*Aoharuuuuu!!!*""""

The voltage in the classroom rockets up as the gorgeous goddess winks.

My expression is straight as I glance at the girl beside me who is suddenly very interested in the floor.

"Miss Nina?"

"Argh…! Every once in a while, the deities stop in and take over a class…! If it was Professor Adler, it would be more normal! Of all the people it could be, it just had to be Lady Idun…!"

I instinctively revert to a more polite tone as Nina covers her face with both hands and the tips of her ears go bright red. I feel bad for her, but it's also kind of cute.

The goddess with long, wavy hair—Lady Idun, I'm guessing—is apparently beloved by many students, and people just sort of get sucked into her innocent, youthful performance. Finally, after getting the room all fired up, she says, "All right, let's get to the lesson," and the lights turn back to normal. A regular lesson seems to finally be starting. What was the point of getting all fired up, then?

"Just before the era of deities, there were frequent, terrible famines in the northeast of the continent. What was the underlying cause? Who should I get to answer? How about…the new student, Rapi! Who I'm sure has done some rock-solid, Aoharu prep!"

"Eh?! Ummm…!"

As I stand up and start to panic, Nina whispers the answer to me.

"The roaming dragon problem, Rapi."

"Th-the roaming dragon problem."

"Correct! Hopefully you'll be able to answer by yourself next time!"

Of course, Lady Idun sees through it all and flashes a childlike smile. The other students have a little laugh as I sit back down with a red face and share a smile with Nina.

The lesson is difficult.

Copying the notes the goddess makes on tiptoe on the blackboard is an entirely new experience for me and a lot of work, but also, there are many differences between the reality that the all-knowing goddess teaches us and the history passed down by mortals, and she constantly highlights the discrepancies with questions from the perspective of a divine being. While Nina and the others aggressively ask questions throughout the lesson, it takes everything I have not to fall behind.

"Let's start today's lesson using the materials brought back from the Combat Studies Department 's fieldwork."

After the course is over, there is a short break, and then the next class.

This is Eschatology Seminar, the course Professor Leon recommended. Professor Adler, a monocled dwarf, arrives and projects various pictures in the darkened room using a magical projector that the School District's Alchemy Department made in collaboration with Altena.

"———"

What greets my eyes are burned towns and a devastated elven village.

Neighborhoods destroyed and countless refugees.

"As you all know, there have been powerful monsters coming from the Valley of Dragons in recent years. There is no end to the damage caused by the various dragons slipping through the barrier the School District set up. If any of you are considering Orario for your future path, be sure never to forget the tragedy that is even now occurring elsewhere in the world."

I'm still frozen by the gruesome images as half of his words pass in one ear and out the other, and I have to ask Nina:

"…Did you see things like that before you came here, too?"

"Yes…I've seen it before. Not being able to do anything, forced to watch so many people suffer…it was terrible." Sadness fills her eyes. "It was at the School District that I first learned this is the current state of the wider world."

I also had no idea.

Until Professor Leon recommended this course, until I entered the School District, I didn't know anything at all about the outside world. I was totally focused on coming to Orario and making my way through life as an adventurer. For the first time, I've been forced to face the reality of the mortal realm.

As the world's troubles suddenly start to feel a lot closer and immediate, the dwarf instructor's final, grave message rings out.

—The world yearns for a hero.

"Are you ready, Rapi?"

"J-just a second!"

I frantically answer Nina's question from the other side of the door as I get dressed in a deserted changing room.

After making sure there are no issues with the rabbit-tail pants and rabbit-eared wig that Lord Balder and Lord Hermes provided me, I fidget with the brown hair in front of my face a bunch, and only then do I finally open the door.

"Oooh! The battle uniform looks good on you!"

Seeing me, Nina breaks into a smile and happily presses her hands together.

A red-and-white top and pants. The material is thin, light, flexible, and in terms of defensive capability, it is a match for the battle clothes that adventurers use. This is the battle uniform provided for students in the Combat Studies Department .

I can't help laughing a little when I notice there's even a knife holster for me. Lord Hermes must have provided that.

As it so happens, I've brought hardly anything with me to avoid being discovered, but the Hestia Knife is always in my book bag, so I have it that at least—

Nina is wearing a similar red-and-white battle uniform, but unlike the boys' uniform, hers has a skirt. She is carrying a rod on her back. I guess she has a backline position.

"By the way…what level are you, Nina?"

"Me? I'm Level Two."

"L-Level Two…!"

I don't have any proof they're related, but still, finding out someone in Miss Eina's family has the strength of an upper-class adventurer…I don't know if I should call it a shock or a terror or what. In any case, it's a weird feeling.

Nina looks a little oddly at me as I almost tumble backward, and we go through the magic-stone-lamplit passage and come out beneath the blue sky.

There is a large, reddish-brown-clay sort of field and stands surrounding it on all four sides. This is one of the arenas built of valmars in a corner of the academic layer.

"That's everyone. Then we can begin General Combat."

Students all in battle uniforms are gathered around Professor Leon, who is wearing his usual instructor outfit.

This is also a full-fledged lesson, one for so-called applied skill. Unlike written courses where you study at a desk, the key here is hands-on practice and training your body.

Students in Combat Studies are required to take a minimum of three applied-skill courses in a year. At Nina's recommendation, I chose Swordsmanship, Hand-to-Hand Combat, and General Combat.

Like the name implies, it's a course for learning how to approach combat as a whole rather than instruction on specific techniques.

"The Dungeon Practical is approaching, so today I'll have you work on your fundamentals with anti-monster combat. After that, you will divide into squads and conduct a debrief. Take care not to slack off."

While Professor Leon explains the day's lesson to everyone, I am once again feeling nervous.

Students of all races are gathered here, and they all have the same demeanor as Nina…It's the attitude of someone with real strength who has leveled up. They might just be able to leave a mark on one of the mid-tier factions in Orario—

"Sir, may I?"

"What is it, Kate?"

"Since it's his first time, let's get a look at the new guy's strength!"

"—Eh?!"

My shoulders twitch at getting suddenly pulled into the discussion without any warning.

Right away, more and more voices start ringing out.

"I want to know, too!" "He must have something, joining Combat Studies this late in the year, right?" "I'm curious as well."

My eyes shoot open behind my wig while only a single person tries to stop them.

"Wait! What are you thinking, making him prove his strength? If you're going to put Rapi in danger, then I'm against it!" Nina shouts.

"We're in Combat Studies; danger is in the description, right?"

"He looks pretty weak, so I get being worried, but you don't have to be *that* overprotective, right, Nina?"

"St-still…!"

When another boy and girl point out what department we're in, Nina is at a loss for words. The overprotective charge was pretty on the mark, and it's probably because she's seen my pathetic reactions several times now that she's a bit more worried than she needs to be. She mentioned how she couldn't leave me alone, too.

But what do I do? I don't know what they'll have me do, but I can't let them see through my disguise, so if I can avoid it, I would love to…!

"He's Level One, right? Nina'll get annoying if it's a spar…"

"Hey, new kid, can you use magic?"

"Huh? Oh, yes!"

I immediately answer the question. And at pretty much the same time, Professor Leon speaks up, too.

"Rapi, you only just received a blessing from Lord Balder, so you wouldn't have developed any magic yet, right?"

"Huh? No, I have..."

His reaction feels strange, but I answer naturally.

He has the faintest trace of what looks like a strained smile on his face, like he's at a loss.

"You can do magic?!"

"Say so sooner! If we see that, we can get a feel for your strength easy!"

"If you can use magic, then even at Level One, you might be useful in the rear!"

...Ugh!

Seeing their sudden excitement, I realize what I've done all too late.

Magic is considered a trump card. It's so important that it takes up a big section of your status, and having useful magic or not can often make the difference between being sought after by parties and being totally unwanted.

Nina looks at me in surprise, and the other students who were half joking around before are now genuinely curious. There's no way I can avoid getting tested anymore!

The professor was trying to give me a way out earlier.

"Hmph, even though you're a human...What element is your magic? And what type?"

As I start panicking, Iglin brushes back his hair and steps forward, his crisp, perfect battle uniform rustling.

"Eh, ah, that's...i-it's fire..."

My cheek spasms as I answer meekly. I'm not really in a position where I can just say, *Sorry, I was lying.* Really, they probably wouldn't forgive me if that was all I could say for myself.

"Offensive type, huh? I'll make a barrier, so hit me as hard as you can."

He smirks and moves away, stopping in the middle of the field and turning to face me with his hands outstretched. After a short cast, a wall of earthen-colored light appears.

"There it is! Iglin's classic Rockwall!"

"I've got a feeling this'll go badly for him again!"

"He never learns..."

"Hey newbie, hurry it up!"

"Don't worry, Iglin's tougher than his barrier, so just let him have it!"

A pincer attack from the boys and girls in our class, urging me on.

Pushed a step forward from the group, drenched in sweat, I look down at the palm of my hand.

Even if they tell me to give it all I've got…

"Oooooooooooooooooooooooo, Argonaut, activate! Chaaaaaarge! Gong! Gong! Gong! Full-charge! Firebooooooooooooooooooooooooooolt!!!"

"Guaaaaaaaaaaaaah?! I loooost!"

"Iglin went flying!"

"That power! He's like a first-tier adventurer!"

"No, he has *to be a first-tier adventurer!"*

""""It's Bell Cranell, the intruder!!!""""

……No way, nuh-uh, there's no chance!

If I get serious, it'll be so, *so* bad in so many different ways!

I have to hold back as much as possible to not get caught!

I hold out a trembling hand, pointing it at Iglin and his barrier.

As long as I tamp down on the power and Mind as much as possible…I just have to make sure he isn't injured…!

"Hey, hurry up and cast already! You gonna do this or not?!"

"…C-cast?!"

The sudden complaint about my apparent stalling sends me into a panic.

R-right. Magic normally needs an incantation!

If I just use Firebolt, it'll definitely look suspicious!

Faced with yet *another* pitfall, my head is on the verge of melting down. I don't have the capacity to pay attention to Nina's anxious gaze as my nerves and the pressure make the world start spinning.

My sweat pours and pours for a few seconds as the situation quickly surpasses my ability to keep up, and then I say the fake incantation I've desperately thought up.

"…*B-Blasphemous Burn*!"

It's pathetic, but I borrowed Welf's chant.

And that isn't good.

While I was desperately searching for a fire-y sort of incantation, I slipped up, failed to charge as little as possible, and lost control of my magic.

Agh—

I feel the magic slipping its leash and bursting out in search of an exit.

Experiencing the greatest failure for the first time, I see my friend's face in the back of my mind for a moment.

This is what Welf is always—

The next instant, an explosion rocks the field.

"I-Ignis Fatuus?!"

"No way!"

"Rapi?!"

Iglin behind his barrier, the gallery, and Nina all shout in shock or concern at the explosion that erupts around me.

After the smoke from that tremendous blast clears…I'm splayed on the ground, singed and smoking as I stare up at the blue sky.

…Am I really a first-tier adventurer…?

Nina rushes over as I, having accomplished the inglorious and never-before-seen feat of backfiring a spell with no incantation, wish silently to disappear into the wide and open sky.

On that day, Rapi Flemish received the title of scrub for triggering an Ignis Fatuus in a fit of panic…

"Now then, Rapi will be joining *Balder Class* 3rd Squad."

"No way!!!"

The students I'm supposed to form a party with are not particularly excited to have me on their team.

Around the time the General Combat lesson ends, Professor Leon makes his announcement while I'm still singed, even after some treatment by Nina's healing magic. The moment they hear that, three students erupt in furious resistance.

"Why do I have to be in a squad with a scrub like him?! He managed an Ignis Fatuus on a trial shot. It wasn't even in combat! He's just going to drag us all down!"

The loudest of them is the dwarf Iglin, who's forgotten to brush back his hair for once.

Yep, that's right…

"We're already a four-person cell…we don't need baggage… maybe emergency rations, or a human shield…" mutters a dark elf girl wearing a mask that seems to be armor on the lower half of her face.

Wait, what are you *saying*?!

"Ahhh! Another trial from Fianna! Jealous of my talent, the goddess has set another obstacle in my path!"

And finally, a small prum boy—girl? No, I think boy—smiles, brimming with self-confidence. He's immediately treating me as an ordeal he needs to overcome…

"R-really, Professor? Rapi is in our squad…?"

"Yes. As the squad leader, your burden will likely increase some, but you can rely on Rapi. He should be able to support you, Nina."

And lastly, Nina stands up after finishing the healing, a look of surprise on her face.

"I'm surprised…But I also sort of guessed it. You intended this from the start when you had me show Rapi around."

That is how it feels to me, too.

Most likely, he and Lord Balder intended this. But…

"…Umm, I'm sorry, Nina. This squad that everyone keeps talking about…"

I can guess it's essentially a formation for combat.

My half-elf classmate, who holds out her hand and helps me to my feet, summarizes it for me. "In the Combat Studies Department , whenever we leave the school for Fieldwork or Combat Volunteer opportunities, we work in four-person cells. Though there are occasionally times when it goes up to five because of the number of people involved…"

There are only as many classes as there are deities in the School District, so classes are divided into squads. Members of squads are only drawn from the same classes, which makes it simpler logistically, as squads receive status updates as a group.

As part of the curriculum, the deities and instructors usually shift people around to fill vacancies and create well-adjusted teams, but…

"…I'm sorry if I end up causing more issues, Nina…"

"You're fine! If anything, it's a relief having you in my squad. If you were in another one, I would probably be worried about how you were doing."

Nina's single lock of jade hair sways as she smiles, and I can't help an awkward, strained smile.

Nina really is nice. She's just like Miss Eina in that way, too.

"But…" I follow her slightly troubled gaze as she trails off.

She is looking at Iglin and the other party members, who are still arguing with Professor Leon.

"The worst party's breaking new records in suck. Good luuuck."

"If you drop any lower, you might have to stay back a year."

"Don't call us that! Dammit!"

The chime marking the end of the lesson rings, and some of the students leaving the arena laugh as they pass the 3rd Squad.

Blinking at the phrase "worst party," I glance over at Nina, who doesn't look super happy.

This party…Does the 3rd Squad have some issues…?

As that thought crosses my mind, Iglin concludes he won't be able to change Professor Leon's mind and stomps over to me to stick his fat finger at my face.

"You're just a supporter!"

Yes, sir, no arguments here, sir…

The middle of the short stack of pancakes is the residential layer.

In between the control layer and the academic layer, the residential layer is a vast, open space with multiple columns that also serve as elevators holding the ceiling up. In place of sunlight that can't easily reach here, there are multiple large magic-stone lights embedded in the ceiling. The lights' intensity shifts depending on what time of day it is, and it reminds me of the eighteenth floor safe point. Of course, in front of me isn't the wide open and natural space of the Dungeon, but a forest of buildings made of stone and metal.

Unlike the academic layer expanding in a circle around Breithablik in the center—sort of like Orario—the residential layer is a patchwork of instructor- and student-living areas.

All the student dormitories and schoolhouses are lined up at regular intervals. What's interesting is that every dormitory is slightly different in appearance, and some of the buildings are almost artistic or oddly shaped.

The open room I've been assigned is in the third student dormitory, and the shared room in that dormitory is also where the 3rd Squad is currently meeting, since Nina somehow managed to call everyone together.

"Introductions? Kind of late for that, isn't it? I'm Iglin."

Iglin comments with his sharp tongue, as per usual.

He is shorter than me, an appropriately dwarven 150 celches with stocky legs. As the rose on his chest suggests, he acts like an aristocrat, but his body is solid and toned. His hair is a lighter brown than Nina's, and he is making no effort to hide his distaste for these proceedings.

"Legi...dark elf..."

And Legi is still wearing that mask, even though we're indoors.

Dark skin and red hair, around 160 celches tall, she's a little taller than Nina. Not very talkative and hard to read, her uniform also sports a skirt. At the moment, she's hugging her knees and reading a book that looks like some sort of holy tome. I can't really look in her direction, but my impression as I try to keep the heat from rising to my cheeks is that she is an odd child with a unique manner of speaking.

"And last is me! Christia Elvia! Call me Chris! A slumbering lion not yet known to the world! My status iiiis...Level Two!"

The cheerful prum boy—girl? No, he's a boy...I think—introduces himself. He *is* wearing a boy's uniform. Because of his race, it's no surprise that he's the shortest member of the squad. His blue hair is neatly combed back, and unlike most prums who tend to be a bit more self-deprecating, he's brimming with confidence.

"Wait, Level Two?! Even though you're a prum?!"

"Mhmm, ahhh, that's it, that's the reaction! I am the sort of once-in-a-generation talent who will surpass Braver! The School District's famed superstar! Eh-heh-heh!"

He's the same as Lilly after she made it back from the expedition?!

Chris closes his eyes, puffs out his chest, and puts his fists on his lap as his face gleams at my shock.

It's a bit of a delicate topic, but because of their almost universal lack of physical strength, prums are widely known as the weakest race. There are certainly first-tier adventurers like Mr. Finn and Mr. Alfrik and his brothers, but among adventurers, prums are definitely underrepresented in the ranks of people who have leveled up. And yet, he reached Level 2 in the outside world, without the Dungeon...I don't know if the School District is simply that amazing or if it's due to Chris's innate talent. Incidentally, Iglin and Legi are also Level 2, so everyone in the 3rd Squad has leveled up once.

"More importantly, scrub, don't go doing anything unnecessary during the Dungeon Practical! Just hide behind your half-elf mommy!"

Ignoring Chris as if he got over his showmanship long ago, Iglin hits me with a sharp warning. Nina's thin eyebrows arch.

"Iglin, stop treating Rapi like a burden. We're comrades in this squad, so be a little—"

"Who's a comrade?! He is literally a burden! What if he just self-destructs in the Dungeon out of nowhere?!"

I feel sorry for Nina, but I can't really say anything...

I slump a bit, feeling like I really messed up. All of a sudden, Legi, still casually reading her book, starts mumbling.

"It's too late to start getting all chummy...Our squad is crap..."

"Th-that's why we have to talk more...! And don't say things like that, Legi!" Nina blushes and admonishes the dark elf.

"Don't worry, everyone! I will blaze a trail for us! Just follow me without fear!"

And Chris is just going off on his own before we even decide on anything.

"Umm…earlier they said something about 'worst party'…what did they mean?"

Out of curiosity, I ask the question at the forefront of my mind, only to see Nina, Iglin, and even Legi's moods all darken at once. Chris is the only one unaffected, and he's still beaming, confident as ever.

Iglin answers bitterly.

"Exactly what it sounds like! We're the absolute bottom of the barrel, lowest of the low in *Balder Class* and the entire Combat Studies Department ! Because they're holding me back…!"

"Don't know why…they don't break up our squad…and you're… the one holding *me* back…"

"Please stop fighting! Just look at the aura of light welling up from me! *Gleeeam*!"

…I know I'm in no position to pass judgment, but is this really going to be all right?

While the three of them all persevere in their unique, unbending debate, I glance silently over at Nina.

The kind, warm girl lets out a deep, heavy sigh. This is the first time I've seen her do that…

Time flies by quickly once my school life starts in earnest. With help from Nina, I manage to quickly get up to speed in the lectures. My days consist of review and prep work before breakfast, courses in the morning and afternoon, then more review and prep with Nina in the evening.

Since I'm dumber and worse at studying than the other students, all I can do is make up for it with sheer time and effort.

With Ms. Aiz's early-morning training and the baptisms in Folkvangr under my belt, I'm used to waking up early. Going to sleep later than everyone else, waking up early, and even in my sleep, I never stop thinking about my studies. To think I would be relying on the innate toughness of a first-tier adventurer's body here of all places. I really can't begin to repay Nina for volunteering to help me with all this self-study.

But the thing that worries me more than the studying is the 3rd Squad's relationship.

Even though I tried to talk to them several times during the applied learning courses, I can't seem to find a way to improve their coordination.

No matter how much Nina tries to bring them together too, they just unabashedly declare they'll work by themselves, and Professor Leon simply watches us from afar, not intervening.

And on the fourth day of my school life, the Dungeon Practical has finally come.

"Oooooh!!! Amazing!!!! All of Orario is welcoming me!"

That is Chris's reaction the moment he passes through the city's southwest gate.

The School District and the Labyrinth City. With both sides giving permission, the students setting foot inside the great city walls are met with a shower of flower petals. In the distance, I can hear what I think might be a marching band. It's almost like an out-of-season festival, as the city welcomes in students with a bright future ahead of them.

...What is this?

"Wow! To think Orario was this gorgeous! It's my first time here, but it's amazing, isn't it, Rapi?!" Nina exclaims.

"It sure is..."

Wearing my red-and-white battle uniform, I smile weakly and manage a half-hearted response.

"Hmm?" Nina cocks her head.

When I first came to Orario, I was just as excited and called everything amazing too, but I think it wasn't quite this presentable. It was much more like an adventurer's city...At the very least, it wasn't a place that felt like it was in the middle of a days-long festival.

I can see fashionable sweets stores offering special nougats and honey-drizzled treats. Cafés have rare books set out on tables. Southwest Main Street is currently lined with the sorts of shops that students would probably like. It's nothing like what I remember. Glancing down side streets, I spot stylish back alleys extending into the distance, and I'm struck by a terrifying question: Is this really Orario?

The familias go without saying, but the city as a whole is eager to entice the School District's students, or so I'm told...I guess this is their attempt to make a good impression?

Some students are already buying things...Maybe some shops are appealing to the students to turn a profit?

If Lilly were here, I'm sure she could have taught me more, but...

"The brats from the School District are back again, huh?"

"The Dungeon's gonna be a mess again this year."

...I overhear the grumbles of a few adventurers watching us from a distance.

While Nina and the others look around excitedly at all the new and interesting sights, I am gripped by nebulous unease.

"Students participating in the Dungeon Practical have to fill out forms at the Guild Headquarters...Rapi, can I ask you to take care of that?"

"Huh? I don't mind, but...what about you?"

"I...forgot to prepare some items, so I want to go to a store here in Orario first."

"Then I'll come along! A future hero should show his face at the Guild! Let's go, Rapi!"

It's a little strange seeing Nina so inarticulate, but Iglin and Legi want to check out some weapon and gear shops too, so the squad splits in two with the plan to meet up in front of Babel later.

My heart races as I try to avoid being recognized—particularly by any acquaintances—and we take care of the formalities at the Guild Headquarters and obtain permission. Ms. Misha is the one who takes care of it at the counter, but she doesn't recognize me at all and just cheers us on by saying "Good luck, everyone!" and beaming with a big smile.

After rejoining the group without any issue, we head into Babel.

Then we begin the long descent down the stairs into the labyrinth. Our Dungeon Practical is starting...

When you enter the Dungeon, there is always a moment when you can feel the air change. That's the sign you've left the surface world behind.

It's something that becomes less distinct with time and experience, fading a little every time you go into the Dungeon, but it's different for students. For most of them, this is their first time setting foot here. As much potential as they might have, they still get nervous when faced with the unknown. Their eyes dart around the empty passage; they worry about monsters that might start crawling out of the walls without warning. I watch the students out of the corner of my eye as I adjust the big backpack on my shoulders.

"Don't do anything unnecessary, scrub! Just pick up the drop items!"

"Yes, got it..."

The Dungeon's first floor. The beginner's road.

Iglin skewers me with a sharp order while the other squads start moving. Ever since the Ignis Fatuus incident, Iglin has never let it go.

Nina is a little tense, and the other three are at ease. Also, what is this formation? Three people abreast in a line out front...

I'm bringing up the tail end of the party and Nina is in between, so it's technically a T-formation, but...

The 3rd Squad is clearly different from the other squads that are advancing cautiously. I don't know if I should call it bold or complacent, but it certainly feels like this is their natural state. I don't know how they fight yet, but this lack of tension could be considered one of the 3rd Squad's strengths.

Professor Leon asked me to guide this squad, but…

Of course I want to live up to his expectations, but can I really do that while also not revealing myself?

Up front, I see Iglin with a hammer hanging from his back. Legi has twin shortswords at her hips. And Chris is taking practice swings with a two-handed sword as long as he is tall. Nina carries a staff and appears to be the party healer.

Setting aside questions of level, with a healer in our party, we have an overwhelming advantage in clearing the first floor of the Dungeon.

There won't be any *mistakes*, I don't think, but…

I've been watching the party from behind this whole time, and I might be the most nervous one of us all.

"Gobaa!"

"UOOOOOOOO!"

Once we take a couple of turns into the labyrinth and leave the main corridor behind, some monsters finally appear. It's a swarm of goblins and kobolds!

With our first encounter, the party shifts into combat position and Iglin steps forward.

"Watch and learn, scrub! Gaze upon my intelligent fighting style!"

"Ah, yes! Please let me see!"

Iglin reaches out to grab the weapon on his back as if to show me how it is done.

And the instant he grabs the hammer—he transforms.

"—Uoooooooooooooooh! Let's do thiiiiiiiis! I'll murder them aaall!!!"

"What?!"

Iglin lets loose a thundering war cry that is the polar opposite of his usual tone and demeanor. The shock in my voice probably matches how the monsters are feeling.

The dwarf charges forward, his battle uniform stretching as his rippling muscles bulge underneath with every wild swing of his hammer. Goblins and kobolds screech as pandemonium descends and they are knocked aside and shattered. Iglin brings his hammer down over and over and over, as if to declare, *I'm not done yet!!!*

Where's the intelligence here?!

"Wh-what is happening?!"

"Iglin's personality changes when he holds a hammer..."

"You're kidding, right?!"

Nina sounds like she's nursing a headache as she explains.

In a way, this makes him feel a lot more dwarven, but then what was that aristocratic, gentlemanly persona he was maintaining until now?!

"Not bad, Iglin! But I am the true hero!"

"I'm going, too."

In a moment, Chris and Legi move too, as if set off by Iglin's performance.

From this point, it's all downhill.

"Ughhhh...?!"

From my position at the very back as supporter, I groan like a squashed frog as I watch the unspeakable scene unfolding before my eyes.

"Don't charge ahead on your own, Iglin! Legi, Chris, you shouldn't go that far, either!"

Nina's voice rings out, but no one is listening!

Iglin charges into a group of killer ants by himself, while Legi leaps over his head in search of another hunting ground. Then Chris charges forward too, like he's competing with them, yelling, "I'll open a path!"

One in the back and three in the front is already bad enough, but spreading out so much that no one can hear directions from the party leader?! Are you kidding me?!

And they're all attackers other than Nina?!

This isn't a party, it's just four solo fighters!

"Is...is this really your first time on this floor? Or in the Dungeon, rather?"

"Mhmm, it is...So even in the Dungeon, it ends up like this..."

I immediately correct myself, but Nina sounds gloomy, like she's seen this happen before.

Currently, we are on the seventh floor.

Reaching the seventh floor on their first day, on their first venture into the Dungeon! These are the upper levels and everyone is Level 2, but still, setting seven new personal bests in just half a day? And doing it without any experience with these floors?! They're scary!

It's something a skilled adventurer would never even think to try, and I'm almost swooning watching it happen.

"They are always like this during Fieldwork and our Combat Volunteer sessions. Everyone charges ahead alone, but they're strong, so they manage to make it work...but it causes lots of problems. I was hoping we might be able to work together in the most dangerous and deadly Dungeon, but..."

The way Nina says *hope* with the look of a lost child on her face speaks volumes about how much she's struggled and how hard she's worked until now.

She sounds like she's all out of resigned sighs, even. After staring at her for a moment, I look forward again.

"Outta the way, elf! You too, prum! You wanna get smashed?!"

"I hate dwarves..."

"Never fear, you two! I will defeat all the enemies myself!"

The rest of the party push on without us, leaving only the echoes of their voices as they advance deeper in the labyrinth.

Leaving us behind, the echoes of their voices reach us from deeper in the labyrinth.

As we stand in the middle of a passage filled with monster corpses, not even keeping up with the magic-stone collection, Nina and I have no idea what we should do.

"Why don't we work together? Because these barbarians just get in the way, obviously!"

In the evening, we return from the Dungeon.

After getting berated by adventurers and other students for disrupting the passage, Nina and I spent most of the day apologizing and dealing with all the monster corpses (or rather, that was all we could do). We only managed to catch up with the other three back in the dormitory.

We meet up in our home clothes, borrow a corner of a cafeteria, and finally sit down to discuss what happened.

"Always getting into my space, making it so I can't properly swing my family's heirloom hammer!"

"The only barbarian getting in the way is you...Your body is so big. I can't cut down monsters cleanly when you're around."

"I'm an amazing prum, so of course I have to be at the front leading the charge!"

...It's painfully clear they don't have much coordination, but I'm starting to get a headache from this constant bickering.

They tolerate going into the Dungeon as a squad because it's an ironclad rule of the School District, but that's it. If we run into any monsters, they just start fighting by themselves.

Trust, faith, thoughtfulness.

They are fatally lacking in those core qualities, which is unacceptable for a functioning party where you're supposed to be able to trust that the others will watch your back.

...It's a bit extreme, but...

Probably a strange thought to have, but seeing them just reminds me how amazing Lilly and Welf and everyone else are.

Even for adventurers, it's natural to have some amount of discord in a party. Everyone has their own quirks, their own personalities, their own plans. Adventurers and supporters are always being asked to figure out how to blend all that together to improve their coordination. This experience is a painful reminder of just how blessed *Hestia Familia* is.

"Because of you, I'm losing out on study time! Scrub! Write the report and turn it in for me!"

"Eh?!"

"Iglin!"

I'm dumbfounded as Iglin pushes his homework onto me, and even Nina gets angry. But Iglin doesn't care at all.

"He can't do anything but gather magic stones and drop items! He's getting a passing grade thanks to our work! The least he can do is make himself useful!"

His tone practically screams, *If anything, he should be grateful to be in the same squad as me.* Overawed by the sheer audacity, I can't say anything. And it is true that I haven't been able to contribute much.

Iglin storms off before Nina has time to stop him.

"I'm…done. Turn it in, please."

"I'm not done yet! So help me out with the report again please, Nina!"

Legi puts her paper on top of the one Iglin pushed onto me, while Chris is on the floor begging Nina for help. Nina tries to chase after the two who have already left, but Chris hangs on to her like an anchor, and she gives up with a defeated shrug.

The worst party…

From an adventurer's perspective, that label might actually be too generous…but I finally understand why the other kids called it that, and I can't help thinking things are looking grim.

"Pardon me, Professor…Oh, Lord Balder?"

I just managed to finish writing my report before it was time for bed. Nina offered to come with me, but I told her it would be fine. And so I walk to Professor Leon's office alone, only to unexpectedly stumble into a god.

"It's been three days, hasn't it, Rapi? How has your time at the School District been?"

"Umm…I've been struggling to get used to everything."

Lord Balder is sitting at a table with Professor Leon, enjoying tea—or was he waiting for me to come by?—and with an awkward smile, I tell him the truth.

"But as much work as it is…I'm also excited to experience so many new things."

And that's the truth.

The studies are certainly difficult, but I've discovered that it's a lot of fun to learn things I don't know. All the more so when it is a subject I'm interested in. Interacting with the instructors who know so much, discovering new ways of fighting, visiting the great library and arenas and all the other facilities...The School District is a place where you can improve yourself however much you want if you have a mind to. It is perfect for what Miss Eina said about remembering my original motivation.

Even the battles for limited cafeteria space during lunch are amazing, and compared to my normal life with my familia, every day brings something new and different.

As Lady Idun might put it, this is probably that Aoharu feeling she's always talking about.

"Is that so?" Lord Balder asks with a smile, his eyes still closed.

"Ah, Professor Leon. Here are our reports..."

"Thank you, Rapi. I'll glance over the details later, but please tell Iglin to come see me first thing tomorrow morning."

Busted...

With a single glance, he saw right through my extra writing. I feel a bit nervous, and all I can say is "Yes, sir..."

"You went into the Dungeon for the first time today. How was the 3rd Squad?"

"Umm...th-they are quite unique...?"

As I choose my words carefully to answer Professor Leon's question, Lord Balder puts a finger to his mouth and chuckles quietly.

"...Professor Leon. Lord Balder. Why did you place me in their squad?"

I ask the question that has been on my mind.

"Because the way they are now, the Dungeon Practical will totally crush them."

The answer came surprisingly easy...

I'm a little stunned to hear his blunt assessment.

Because, vaguely, I was thinking the exact same thing.

"Other than Nina, the members of the 3rd Squad were all previously in different squads, but after causing issues, they were transferred around and now are gathered together," Lord Balder explains.

"...So they're problem children?"

This time, Professor Leon answers my question.

"At the very least, they are treated that way by other students. From an instructor's perspective, they have praiseworthy strengths, but even bearing that in mind, they lack the spirit of cooperation and are too unbalanced."

I sensed it, too. They aren't coordinating at all, but at the same time, that means they made it through several floors of the Dungeon on individual strength alone.

That strength stands out even among other Level 2s. But…as powerful as they are, sooner or later, they will lose their lives in the Dungeon. Just as so many other upper-class adventurers have before them.

"Were I or another instructor to accompany them during their trips into the Dungeon, it would essentially be giving them special treatment, and it wouldn't help them grow, either. And frankly, we are always shorthanded this time of year."

Lots of instructors are stationed in the Dungeon during the practical exam. But considering the scale of the Dungeon, they can only cover the main routes. They simply don't have the numbers to spread out any farther, especially if they want to protect the students from any irregularities that might occur.

And from the sound of it, there have been issues with certain adventurers holding grudges against the elite students of the School District and ganging up on them or otherwise causing problems…

"Breaking up the 3rd Squad and placing the members in other teams would cause problems elsewhere like before. We dearly want to limit complications in the Dungeon as much as possible. And just when we were wondering how we could possibly handle this situation…You came to the School District, Rapi—or rather, Bell Cranell," Professor Leon explains.

"!"

"When Hermes sounded me out about letting you enroll, the truth is, there was a condition for allowing you to come here. In exchange for providing you with the School District experience, we want you to watch out for the 3rd Squad."

It all makes more sense when Lord Balder explains the deal Lord Hermes struck.

I haven't paid any money or anything in order to enroll in the School District. I've just been blessed with an opportunity at no cost to myself. I felt bad about it, but knowing there's a condition like this makes me feel better.

Now this feels like a quest.

The reward—enrollment in the School District—was paid upfront, and in exchange, I need to live up to their expectations.

"What do you think? Can you keep the 3rd Squad safe?"

"Ah, yes. If it gets truly dangerous, I can let loose. I won't let anyone die."

On that point, there wouldn't be any problems. I feel confident enough to just say it outright. As long as we stay in the middle levels, I can absolutely protect them.

Professor Leon seems to approve of my reassuring response.

"I'm sorry to trouble you when we've already just made a request of you, but could we ask one more thing of you?"

"What is it?"

"It's not just the others. Nina also has what could be called a problem."

I'm more than a little stunned by that unexpected turn.

Nina is so friendly, liked by everyone, and has done so much to help me. What kind of trouble could she be having...?

"If I might, could I request you support her as well?"

"...May I ask what Nina's issue is?"

"If possible, I'd like you to ask her about her worries as a classmate and friend rather than hear them from us."

That makes sense.

It isn't that they're ignoring her problem. They just believe it would be best for her to get guidance from someone with a perspective closer to her own.

"Right now is a particularly delicate moment for her. The doubt that troubles Nina is mixing with everything else, and if we adults were to take a false step, she might lose a great deal."

"When I heard about you from Hermes, I thought that you, who knew both strength and weakness, might be the right person for the job with your down-to-earth perspective," Lord Balder says, adding on to Professor Leon's explanation. "I discussed it with Leon as well. As a student, and as an adventurer, perhaps you would be able to guide her."

I stumble a little bit at his statement and put my hand on my head. I don't think I'm that great of a person. But I also don't feel like I should say it's impossible for me.

I want to repay her for helping me so much already.

That's all. As a friend from school, that should be enough.

"...I understand. I will do what I can."

"Thank you," Professor Leon says.

"I'm in your debt," Lord Balder says apologetically.

Feeling bashful, I smile at both of them.

"Ordinarily, it might be good to take a breather and have a field trip, but...that is sort of the bulk of the School District's curriculum. I'm a little doubtful it would have much effect here."

"Field trip...?"

"It would be a small excursion focused on introducing students to new environments to expand their horizons and giving them an opportunity to gain experience."

While we are chatting, the dormitory's bedtime draws near.

There are prefects from each class—sort of like candidates for promotion to leadership in a familia—who will put me under strict supervision if I break the rules. I should probably get going before I make them mad.

"Rapi, one final question, if I may?"

Just before I leave the room, Professor Leon calls out to me.

"Where do you think the 3rd Squad will *stop*?"

Turning around, I think about what floors are associated with which grades, and I answer.

"The twelfth floor, I think."

"Dammit?!"

Iglin's annoyed voice rings out from within a swarm of imps.

The Dungeon's twelfth floor is covered in a white mist. Reaching the last of the upper levels, the 3rd Squad, yet again, finds itself in a difficult struggle.

"Take the dragon down already!"

"Can't...tired."

"Even as superstrong as I am, I think we're outmatched! Sorry, everyone!"

Surrounded by a huge number of imps, our party is staring down a small dragon measuring four meders and lurking deeper in the mists.

"OOOOOOOOOOOOOOOOOOOOOO!!!"

The infant dragon is a rare monster on the upper floors. Our unusual opponent roars, shaking the 3rd Squad and the ground alike. Its long tail, covered in sturdy scales, suddenly lashes out, knocking over several dead trees and a couple imps in the process. The three frontliners manage to leap away from the swipe, but their movement is clearly less sharp than earlier.

"Swaying stem, breath of white. Sing of flowers, and of the pristine hill—Magia Kris!"

What looks like a pure white flower petal is actually a fragment of white magic that envelops the vanguard. This is Nina's healing magic. Standing in the back lines with her staff thrust forward, she is supporting the three of them, but it's just not enough.

With their stamina returning, they should be able to escape the dragon's follow-up attack, but they are visibly still exhausted.

"...Nina, we should retreat. This battle is..."

"...Yeah."

Hanging back as a supporter, I give Nina my advice, and for a moment, she looks pained, but she quickly collects herself as squad leader.

"Everyone, fall back! Head for the room in the south we decided on before! Quickly!"

"What?! Who asked you?! I can still...!"

The dwarf immediately tries to argue, but he never gets a chance to finish his sentence. He's the one who put himself in the most danger and fought the longest out in front, and he knows better than anyone. If they continue fighting like this, there is a chance of a *mistake* happening.

If another swarm of monsters appears in this room, for example—

"Bghoooo!"

"Whoa! Orcs! They're hideous! I don't want to fight them!"

"…A tactical retreat. There's no choice."

Seeing four orcs approaching like a wall, Chris and Legi quickly switch to flight mode. Iglin curses but follows suit.

We could use some magic.

Looking around, I calculate the distance between us and the enemy. I reach into my backpack while running, to snuff out the one-in-a-million chance. Moving away from Nina, I match speed with Legi, who is chasing after us.

"Miss Legi! Can you prepare your magic?!"

"…No time…for incantation."

"I have some traps ready! Around the third dead tree up there! Can you do it?"

I smile weakly as I run alongside, holding *them* in my gloved hands. Taking my meaning, the dark elf girl murmurs.

"…I'll do it."

She immediately accelerates to pull ahead.

Stopping at the base of the third dead tree that I pointed out, she kneels and begins chanting.

Once I've confirmed that, I glance back at the swarm of monsters chasing us and scatter a hail of purple moth poison grenades.

Before going to the Dungeon, I bought them at a shop. Lilly used these often when we were exploring the upper floors, and just like the name suggests, they're containers filled with toxic powder made of Purple Moth Scales.

"Geha, gaha?!"

"Ugeeee?!"

That alone won't be enough to stop that big swarm from coming after us, but it does buy us time, just like I promised.

"*Dark Mine*! ...Done."

A magic circle grows as Legi puts her hand to the ground and then starts running again. I also hurry—while making sure to limit myself to around what a Level 1's top speed would be—dodging the area around the dead tree while following close behind Nina and the others.

Moments later, just as the orcs swat aside the imps and begin a wild chase—

"*Boom.*"

"*OOOOOOOOOO?!*"

Legi recites the spell key and triggers her mine spell, allowing the 3rd Squad to shake off the monsters.

"Dammit!"

Iglin slams his broken helmet onto the ground.

The crash echoes in the quiet room. No one says anything. Everyone, even Nina, is completely out of breath.

"That's already the fourth try! I couldn't finish that dragon off this time, either...!"

It's already the fourth day since the Dungeon Practical began.

It's already our third time taking on the eleventh and twelfth floors, and the 3rd Squad still hasn't gotten past the infant dragon that the School District set as a grade requirement. Without the required drop item, we can't go past this floor.

After reaching the seventh floor on the very first day, the 3rd Squad's glorious charge has completely petered out.

"Other than the scrub, we're all Level 2! If we go by the Guild's standards, we should be able to beat that shitty dragon easy, right?!"

Even though we retreated, we still can't let down our guard. Holding the hammer in one hand, the rougher Iglin is on full display, cursing and shouting with abandon.

"Other than those asshole elites in the 7th Squad, we were the first to reach the twelfth floor…! So how have all the other squads passed us?!"

The reason is…incredibly simple. It's because we aren't working as a party. The 3rd Squad is terribly inefficient.

Even following the main route and taking the shortest path possible, twelve floors' worth of distance is a long way to go. Considering all the combat that happens along the way, it takes a huge toll on stamina. And the 3rd Squad relies purely on individual strength to progress through the floors, so our stamina and Mind are sapped at a much higher rate than all the other parties'.

The reason why the 3rd Squad can't defeat the infant dragon and the other monsters around it, even though they are Level 2, is because they 're dead tired by the time they reach it.

This time, we restocked when we reached the twelfth floor like Nina suggested, but even then…

It is true that magic can help recover stamina, and you can use items to make up the difference in depleted Mind. But the infant dragon is a rare monster—there usually aren't even five of them on this entire floor, which is massive. That's the reason they are considered the bosses of the upper levels where there isn't a proper floor boss: they're tough foes.

And what happens when the other School District students are after the same dragon?

The hunt becomes a race.

As we struggle in that race, searching everywhere for the dragon, the stamina we go out of our way to recover just gets depleted again…and we end up like this.

Monster parties can start happening at the tenth floor and down. That's also generally where the number of enemies and number of total fights a party has to endure starts to noticeably increase.

It was also a stroke of bad luck that imps happened to be near the infant dragon.

Nina's magic is more suited for healing and support. Moving her up to the front line just because she's Level 2 isn't a good plan…

Giving up her support and recovery would be a dangerous move for this party. We're already out of magic potions, and if we put any more strain on her, our ability to get back to the surface starts to become questionable.

Everything is going badly.

If it were just a question of making it through the twelfth floor, then the 3rd Squad could do it easily enough. But defeating an infant dragon now, in this situation, dramatically increases the difficulty.

An adventurer who has spent months or years getting used to Dungeon-diving might be able to manage the fatigue better, but they are the ultimate beginners. This is their fourth day ever in the Dungeon. In a sense, being able to almost completely clear the upper levels in just four days marks them out as absurdly talented students. Almost too talented. Unfortunately, the Dungeon will still absolutely torment anyone this inefficient and uncoordinated, even if they are Level 2.

But when I try to say that as gently as I can while carefully choosing my words, Iglin just shouts back, *"Tell me something I don't know!"* I'm sorry…!

"…We should leave for today. We're out of items, and it will be dangerous to push our luck."

Infant dragons can appear on the eleventh floor, too, so it has turned into a big mess of squads competing to catch their prey. The 3rd Squad came down to the twelfth floor in a final desperate bid, so when they hear Nina's suggestion to turn back, they scowl, fall silent, and hang their heads.

There isn't really anything to discuss, and their silent acknowledgment is about to decide their course, when…

"…Nina, sorry. But can you wait just a little bit longer?"

"Eh?"

Apologizing in the back of my mind, I speak up.

"I think the 3rd Squad can keep going a little more."

It's just instinct, but I feel like it has to be *here*. When they're almost completely burned out. They haven't hit their absolute limit yet, but they are reaching the end of their rope. If it's not now, the 3rd Squad will never be able to change.

They've already leveled up, and because they can brute-force some things, they've been ignoring teamwork and trying to handle everything alone. So in a situation like this where they *can't* force it, if they can see that there's a different way—if they taste success after repeated setbacks and experience firsthand the almost unbelievable effects of teamwork, they should be able to learn. Then they can use it again next time. Then they can turn it into a weapon.

This should be more than possible for the students of the School District.

I'm sure this is...knowledge and wisdom.

When I was alone with Ms. Lyu in the deep levels, that was the moment I had to use every method and opportunity at my disposal to become stronger just to survive. If I can recreate that here, even a little, then they can do it, too.

Right now, I feel like precisely because they have their backs against the wall, they have the opportunity to truly grow as a party.

Though, the truth is, *we can keep going* is one of the most dangerous things to say in the Dungeon...

"If it's this party, it doesn't count as adventuring just yet...We're still okay."

I smile as my bangs cover one of my eyes.

Nina, Iglin, Legi, Chris...All of their eyes open wide.

Recalling Miss Eina's words, I tell them without beating around the bush that they still haven't crossed that line yet.

They made it all the way here with their individual strength. If they can work together...the 3rd Squad can go even farther. I know it. Professor Leon and Lord Balder know it, too. That's why they hesitated to disband this squad.

"Wh-what are you talking about?! Nothing we've tried has worked right!"

"Umm, I've been watching everyone's movements these past four days, and I have a plan..."

The past four days, standing at the back as a supporter, I've been studying the 3rd Squad closely.

My usual position is in the vanguard. At most, I occasionally switch with Ms. Mikoto and reposition to the middle of the party, so seeing a party from the rear has been a new experience for me. But because of that, there are a lot of things I've realized.

"We could really use his attack right now."

"If she just shifts a little there, it would really lower Chris's burden."

And *"What would I do if I was in the vanguard right now?"*

While thinking about all those things, I started to learn a lot more about our party. I don't think I would feel that way watching *Hestia Familia*, even if I hung back all the way in the rear. That's just how skilled *Hestia Familia* is.

But because 3rd Squad is made up of students who still have much to learn, there's plenty to point out.

"This isn't a game! Who's gonna trust some scrub's plan?! If it blows up in our face, who knows what'll happen?!"

But Iglin rejects it vehemently, still gripping his hammer.

...There isn't really a good argument I can make. I've been acting as a supporter the whole time, so I haven't contributed much during combat. I haven't earned enough trust to be proposing a plan.

That is a clear failure on my part. If Lilly were here, she would sigh about me not following through and closing the deal.

As I struggle to think of what to do...

"Tell me your plan," says Legi, who has been silent thus far. "I'm listening."

Everyone is shocked.

"Wh-what are you even saying?!"

Iglin lurches to shoot down the very idea, but Legi responds calmly from behind her black mask.

"His directions while we ran...were good. Better than a dwarf's stupid shouting..."

While Iglin reels from that stinging comment, Chris looks back and forth between all of us, and then for some reason puts his fists at his hips and puffs out his chest.

"I'm okay with it, too! Since Rapi's ears and tail are fluffy! I'm sure it will be a good plan!"

That doesn't really have anything to do with it, and my ears and tail are just a disguise, but for some reason, Chris is willing to trust me, too. As the shock multiplies, Nina's eyes meet mine and she watches me—as if remembering all she has seen of Rapi Flemish up until today—and slowly, she smiles.

"I want to hear your plan, too."

Three to one, not counting myself. We've decided by majority vote. Iglin is just silent.

After growling, he gives up and points his finger at me.

"If it's a bad plan, I'm not havin' any part of it!"

Parties are a difficult thing. I finally realize this, after Lilly and Welf and everyone else has been supporting me this whole time. But now that I'm being trusted, because they put some faith in me, I want to live up to it.

Biting back a smile, I nod back.

"So, what is it, Rapi?"

"Mm, it's nothing too difficult…"

We naturally form a circle as we gather to talk. I've only done this a handful of times with Lilly, but…

"How about we do a little hunting?"

"Use the terrain to your advantage."

This is one of the first fundamental tactics that Miss Eina taught me in her lectures. And the fundamentals are what we're falling back on.

"Hey, is this really going to be okay…?" Iglin grumbles hoarsely in the mists.

I keep my *maybe* to myself. Maybe it would have been better if I went out? But this is where the prep is needed most, and I couldn't convince them to let a Level 1 supporter take such an important role. I just have to trust them.

Finally, as if answering our silent prayers…tremors shake the room.

"OOOOOOOOOOOOOOOOOOO!!!"

An infant dragon tears through the passage and flies straight into our room. And in front of it are a half-elf and a prum!

"We caught one!"

"As expected of me! Perfection, even as a decoy!"

Nina and Chris are acting as lures, running toward us and shouting.

What I asked Nina and Chris especially to do was to scout. It's impressive he can fight on the front lines as a prum, but this time I wanted to make use of his prum's uniquely powerful vision and search for the infant dragon in the mists that are the characteristic feature for this floor. I already knew that a prum's vision works perfectly well on this fog-covered floor. Meanwhile, securing a safe escape route was definitely a job for the sharp squad leader, Nina. Working together, the two of them found a dragon and lured it here.

Of course, there are orcs and imps and other monsters following behind the dragon, and our party's still in rough shape. If we fight the monsters head-on, we'll just get overwhelmed again, but—

"*Dark Mine*!"

"GRAAAAAAAAAAAAAA?!"

Legi has already laid mines all around this room.

While Nina and Chris were out fishing, she laid a field of magic explosives everywhere. Every time the orcs and imps step on a hidden magic circle, a dark burst of color erupts, scattering the enemies one after the other. The infant dragon won't go down that easily, but it triggers a mine that leaves its left front leg out of commission.

Nina and Chris split to the left and right like we planned, moving to a safer part of the room. There isn't anything special happening. We just took a little time and prepared the battlefield to our advantage.

"Ooorrrraaa!"

"OOOOOOOOO?!"

Iglin is furiously smashing into the monsters that evaded the mines, and the infant dragon roars as if trying to summon support, but it's pointless.

The walls of the room are already broken. The labyrinth prioritizes regenerating itself, so no new enemies will be born from the walls for now. There won't be a monster party. This is the reason I stayed back in this room.

While Legi was setting the mines, Iglin and I went around breaking the walls of the labyrinth. We've turned this room into our personal hunting ground.

Set traps, lure the prey in, and finish it. A very simple plan.

It was impossible when everyone was just acting independently, but with coordination, there are plenty of ways to make it work.

It just comes down to experience.

I'm just regurgitating everything I saw, everything I learned on my way to becoming a first-tier adventurer. Even if I can't teach them how to fight like Ms. Aiz or the others, I should at least be able to give them an introduction!

"Surround it!"

All that's left is a single dragon.

Instead of mist, black embers dance in the air as the 3rd Squad attacks from four sides, continually pushing the suffering infant dragon to the limit.

And…

"Oooorrrrrrrriyaaaaaaaaa!"

With the others' support, Iglin uses a dead tree as a diving board, leaping up into the air and slamming his hammer down on the dragon's back.

"Gaaaaa?!"

A fatal blow pierces its scales and its spine, reaching the enemy's magic stone.

The infant dragon's throat swells as it cries out and rears back, and then a massive cloud of ash swirls.

Please…!

We all watch with bated breath, praying as we look at the infant dragon's explosion…

With a thud, a sharp infant dragon fang falls to the ground.

"Th-there it iiiiiis! The infant dragon drop! We did iiiiiit!"

"Y-yeaaaaaaaaaaaaaah!!!"

Chris raises his hands and shouts "Hooray!"

And then Iglin cheers too, and Legi pulls her mask down with her finger and flashes a sweet smile.

And finally, as I stand there in a daze, Nina rushes over to me.

"Incredible, Rapi! It all went just like how you planned!"

"Y-yeah, it worked well…Ah, sorry for making you take a dangerous job."

"No, not at all!"

She's more excited than I've ever seen, grabbing both of my hands and swinging them excitedly. I smile bashfully as Iglin grabs the fang and he and the others run over to us.

"Not bad, scrub! I mean, Rapi!"

"Ah, no, you all were incredible, I just…"

"Don't give me that modesty nonsense! You're a Dungeon geek, aren't you?! Everything you said was right on the money! That's why you entered the School District at this weird-ass time, isn't it?! I know it!"

"Ah, ah-ha-ha…"

Iglin laughs and slaps my back over and over.

I'm actually an active adventurer, so he's not exactly right, but not quite wrong, either.

"Rapi, you're a lucky rabbit! I'll let you be my guardian beast from now on!"

"Th-thank you?"

"Yay."

"Y-yay?"

Chris and Legi are praising me too, in their own odd way. As the 3rd Squad celebrates for once, I thank them again.

"Thank you for trusting me as a classmate, Iglin, Legi, Chris…"

"Not classmates. Friends," Iglin suddenly says, correcting me.

"Huh?"

"I said we're friends! So there's no need for that polite crap!"

"Same for me! From now on, you are a friend parenthesis servant!"

"Me…too."

They all have smiles on their faces, and before I know it, I'm smiling, too. It's a mysterious thing—it feels like the distance between us has shrunk suddenly.

A success that we can share as comrades. The longer we suffer together, the greater the joy at the end.

This is the Dungeon. This is the thrill of working as a party.

Even though I didn't plan it, it brought me back to my roots, too, and I can feel my heart racing in joy.

"...Nina."

"...Yeah."

Finally, I turn to Nina. She can tell what I'm getting at.

Nodding, she steps forward with an earnest look on her face.

"Hey, everyone. This really made me realize this is the Dungeon. If we don't all work together, I don't think we'll be able to go any further."

The students who previously never listened to their squad leader are now lending her an eye and an ear.

"So I want to keep working together with you. So that this squad stops being called just the leftovers...What about you?"

"I guess there's no helping it." The answer she gets still isn't fully honest, but Iglin continues, saying, "For the sake of my dream, it would be a problem to not have enough credits...So I'll lend you my strength."

"It's weird. This feels way more fun than when I fight alone! Let's try it again next time, too!"

"The dwarf and prum...so simple. But okay."

I'm relieved by their answers, while Nina just looks ecstatic. I think she's tearing up just a little bit.

The required drop item is now secure in the bottom of my backpack, so we carefully leave the Dungeon.

Once we're aboveground, the sun has already sunk past the walls. In the afterglow of our success, the evening light feels gentle and almost warm.

Our squad is all smiles as we head, not back to the School District, but to the Guild Headquarters.

"...Hey, do we really need to do this? We can exchange magic stones at Babel, too..."

"Today is a celebration! We made it all the way through the upper floors! A tiny little exchange spot is unbefitting of our triumphant return! We should hold our heads high and go to the Guild Headquarters!"

With his hammer hanging at his back, Iglin is back in gentleman mode. I grimace a little, and Nina's face is a little overcast.

"But..."

"You're the one who said we should get on the same page! Time for *you* to read the mood!"

Nina can't say anything when Iglin and Chris are like this, so she simply falls silent.

I agreed because I like to get what information I can from the Guild boards before and after venturing into the Dungeon—though I am a little scared of running into someone I know—but I'm surprised to see Nina so unenthusiastic.

Of course, the reason soon becomes clearer.

After we arrive at the Guild Headquarters and finish the exchange without issue in a corner of the lobby—

"...Is that you, Nina?"

"!"

As Nina quickly tries to leave the lobby, a voice calls out to her. It is none other than Miss Eina.

"...You're Nina, right? It's me, Eina! Do you recognize me?!"

Her matching emerald eyes open wide behind her glasses, and Nina gasps. And then she looks away and starts running.

"W-wait, Nina!"

Ignoring Miss Eina, she runs outside.

The rest of us are dumbstruck, and I look between Nina, who ran away, and Miss Eina, who looks hurt. With a heavy heart, I turn around and go.

I'm Rapi right now, so I can't say anything. Apologizing in my heart, I chase after my classmate who is behaving oddly.

"Nina, wait! What is it?!"

"Hah, hah…!"

Running into the main street and weaving through the crowd, I give her some space but also don't let her slip away completely. When she finally stops in the northwest of the plaza in Central Park, I rush over and find her standing in front of the fountain, holding her chest.

"…Sorry, it's nothing."

"B-but…"

"It's really okay…I'm just pathetic is all…"

She stares at her feet, and for the first time since I met her, there's gloom in her expression.

Shrouded by the dark red twilight, I can't think of anything to say to her.

"…Sorry, Rapi…I'll just go back first."

With that, she wanders toward the main street leading to Meren, disappearing into the crowd of people.

A bunch of curious gazes start to focus on me as I stand here in my school battle uniform, but I just gaze back in the direction we came from.

"…This may be meddling too much, but…"

I've been helped so much by these two who I'm certain are sisters. So I make up my mind. After retracing my steps a little, I apologize to the others and leave my backpack and other stuff with them, and I get their permission to take a little free time off.

"Haaah…"

Around when the evening sun completely disappears and stars fill the sky, I spot her exiting the Guild Headquarters from the back with a sigh.

"Miss Eina."

"Huh…? B-Bell?"

I feel bad for ambushing her like this, and her eyes widen when she sees me. Right now, I'm not wearing my wig, and I've taken off the School District battle uniform, too. My disguise is inside a bag I grabbed.

After I left the others, I made my way to a back alley on Adventurers Way, made sure no one was watching, and slipped into the underground store Witch's Hideaway. The same magic shop I used during the Daedalus Street skirmish, and while running away with Ms. Syr during our date.

It would be bad if rumors spread about a School District student going into *Hestia Familia*'s home…and that was the only place I could think to use instead. The owner Ms. Lenoa greeted me with a tired, "You again?" After apologizing profusely, I changed into the clothes I bought with my share of the loot I'd gotten from Iglin and the others. Then I came back to the Guild as Bell instead of Rapi.

"Wh-why are you here? And is it just me, or do you look more dressed up than normal…?"

"Ah, ah-ha-ha…"

I'm not sure how to feel hearing that the clothes I just randomly picked out are nicer than my usual ones, but I cut right to the chase.

"The truth is, I was in the Guild Headquarters earlier, and I saw you…and a girl who looked a lot like you…"

I feel guilty about lying, but even that much is enough to darken Miss Eina's expression, which just makes me feel even worse.

"It made me so curious…that I waited for your shift to end…I wanted to ask you about it, if you don't mind."

I know I'm butting into their personal lives, but even so, I can't just ignore it. I don't want to leave Nina or Miss Eina like this.

Miss Eina looks a little unsure, but she looks me in the eye and nods slightly.

"That girl, her name is Nina…She's my younger sister."

Miss Eina said it would be inappropriate for her to eat with an adventurer while in her Guild employee uniform, so we first headed over to her home where she got changed, and then we went to a chic little restaurant in a neighborhood on the north side of the city.

It has expensive glass windows instead of the usual shutters and feels safe enough for the upper crust of society to pay it a visit over an adventurer's bar.

Once we're seated at a small table, Miss Eina starts talking over dinner.

"She's six years younger…and honestly, I only have one memory of her."

"Eh…? Wh-what do you mean?"

That is a bit of a large gap in age, but why only one memory…?

"Soon after she was born, I went to the School District."

"!"

"Our mother is frail. Our father was always working so hard to get the medicine she needed, but…even as a child, I wanted to do something for her, too. I actually wanted to start working immediately, but Mother said if I was going to do that, then she wanted me to at least go to the School District first…"

Hearing about her family situation for the first time is more than a little shocking.

Miss Eina entered the School District when she was just six years old. When Nina was born, she set off alone and entered the world of scholars.

She scoffs at herself a little when she explains the reason she chose to work at the Guild after graduating was initially because the pay was high, so she could send more back to her parents.

"I almost never went back home, and I doubt Nina remembers me at all. If anything, other than the general idea that she has an older sister at all, she might consider me a complete stranger."

"Th-that's…"

"…Sorry for dumping all this on you. But that's just how distant we've been. I can only just barely remember her as a baby…and when I finally managed to visit home again, Nina had already left to enroll in the School District herself."

I'm just stunned by the story of how long the two of them have been apart and how much distance separated them.

I'm sure Nina went to the School District for the same reason as Miss Eina. Being far away from your family because you care about them and want to help…Maybe it's a fairly commonplace story in the mortal realm now, but I can't help finding it a bit awful.

"I did write letters. To my parents, of course, but also to Nina while she studied at the School District. I wrote her saying that it might be strange, but I am her sister and that she could always talk to me if something was bothering her. When I got a letter back, the writing was awkward, but I was so happy…"

Miss Eina was smiling throughout her story, but now her expression darkens.

"Then at some point, she stopped returning my letters…I thought maybe she was busy, or maybe it had become a bother, or maybe… she hated me acting like an older sister even though she had never really met me and I had never done anything for her…So I stopped writing to her, too," she confesses sadly. "My parents said that none of that is true, that Nina cares about me, but…I was scared. So this year, when the School District came back…I found it hard to just be happy. If I'm being honest, I was a little scared. Because Nina was on that ship."

…So that's it…

The pained look I saw in her eyes whenever she talked about the School District and back when we were in Meren, that was all because she was thinking about Nina.

"…So, when I saw her today, it felt more like I was meeting her for the first time."

"Eh? …B-but you immediately recognized Miss Nin…er, your sister right away, didn't you? You called out to her yourself…"

"I could tell. She was wearing the School District uniform…and she looks just like our mother."

Miss Eina's smile returns for a brief moment, as if she's remembering what happened earlier today.

She mentioned that Nina looks just like their mother…but to me, they both look incredibly similar. I think almost everyone would recognize them as sisters.

"But it seems like Nina doesn't want to meet me..."

"...!"

"She ran away...so I guess she really does hate me." Miss Eina forces herself to say it like a joke.

But now I'm all caught up. With that, I feel like I understand a little bit of their relationship. Professor Leon said that Nina has a worry weighing on her, too. Is that at least somewhat related to Miss Eina's problem?

He said I should ask her directly, but...can I really do that? At the very least, I don't think I should force her to spill everything. It sort of feels like what Nina is dealing with is even more complex than Miss Eina's concerns. And it isn't clear to me whether I should be sticking my nose into their problems. I'm going to have to think this over carefully.

But even so—

"Miss Eina, I don't think...no, I'm sure that your sister doesn't hate you."

"Eh?"

"I don't think she would make such a pained face after seeing someone she hated."

If nothing else, I can share what I noticed while watching both of them in that moment. Nina's speechless face when Miss Eina called out and her fragile expression lit by the setting sun as she ran away... Neither of those looked like hate to me.

As I stare deep into her eyes, which are just like Nina's, I reassure Miss Eina as best as I can.

Miss Eina freezes for a moment as if in shock...and then she starts to tear up as she smiles, forgetting her sadness for a moment.

"Thank you, Bell..."

"Ah, n-no...if anything, I should apologize...butting into your personal life as an outsider..."

"No, not at all. I'm...glad."

Coming back to my senses, I reflexively apologize, but Miss Eina gently shakes her head. Seeing her smile gently with flushed cheeks, I can't help but find it charming, giant fool that I am.

Before long, I feel bashful and can't stop smiling nervously. Miss Eina giggles a little and covers her mouth. Then, with amazing timing that's got to be either intentional or just a fun extra for putting on such a heartwarming show, the waiter pours a pretty, amber liquid into Miss Eina's empty glass. Since I have to go back to the School District after this, I am drinking juice.

We thank him and raise our glasses in a toast—

THUD!

There's a dull noise from beside us, where we're sitting by the window.

There shouldn't be anything other than a window facing the street here…I glance over to check and see—

"""BE—LL—LL."""

My goddess and Lilly are pressing their faces up against the glass, staring at me with dead eyes.

"Whoaaaaaaaaa?!"

"Kyaaaaaaaaaah?!"

Miss Eina and I almost fall out of our seats with a shout.

Looking closer, I can see Welf and Ms. Mikoto and just about everyone in *Hestia Familia* outside the window. In my head, I shout, "*Why?!?!*"

Goddess and Lilly stop pressing their faces against the glass and run around to the entrance, burst through the wait staff who try to stop them, and tear through the restaurant!

"What are you doing, Beeeeeeeeell?"

"G-Goddess?! Why are you here?!"

"Answer the question first please, Mr. Bell. Aren't you supposed to be dealing with your *quest* right now?"

"L-Lilly, I had something I needed to ask Miss Eina, so I just slipped out is all…!"

I can't stop trembling as the intense pressure feels like it'll drag me down into the abyss. Even though I'm not doing anything bad, I still feel like I have to explain myself—especially when their eyes flare! That's terrifying!

"“Who would believe that?!?!”"

Immediately, a thunderous shout slams into me! My ears!!!

“Look at you, aaall dressed up. You were planning to seduce him, weren’t you, Little Miss Adviser Girl?!”

“I—I would never do that, Goddess Hestia! It would just be inappropriate for me to be here in my Guild uniform, so I had to change clothes…!”

“You most certainly did seduce him! That teary-eyed, womanly affectation…You were trying to take pure and innocent Mr. Bell home with you! Lilly sees through you!!!”

“That isn’t true at all, Ms. Erde!”

Miss Eina’s face is bright red as she also gets interrogated, and I have no idea what’s going on anymore!

Please, can someone explain the situation to me?!

“Sir Bell…a secret note from Lady Syr was delivered to the home by a stone-faced Lady Hörn…”

Ms. Mikoto explains, having followed our goddess and Lilly into the restaurant with the rest of the familia.

“It urged us to hurry, saying that there were signs of an enchantress near the white rabbit Sir Hegni was tailing…and it came with a map attached.”

“What?!”

“Sent to us, or rather, to Lady Hestia, because the einherjar might let you escape…”

I was tailed?! By Mr. Hegni?! How?! I didn’t notice any suspicious gazes at all! Is he an expert in not scaring pets or something?!

It shouldn’t be possible to infiltrate Hringhorni, so…has he been watching me the whole time I’ve been in Orario?! What is Ms. Syr *doing*?!

Picking up where Ms. Mikoto left off, the battered Welf’s addition is so crazy I don’t know what to say.

“That girl from the bar was caught and restrained at The Benevolent Mistress, apparently. And it was hard to hold down the goddess’s attendant when she started rampaging after completing her lady's order...It looked like she was forcing her way into the kitchen to grab a knife when we managed to subdue her, but..."

"Gh...?!"

My heart freezes over.

Even though I wasn't there, I can totally see it playing out in my head!

Does that mean Ms. Hörn is after my life again?!

As my face grows pale, Ms. Haruhime keeps looking back and forth in a panic between our goddess and Lilly, who are arguing with Miss Eina, and it looks like she's the only person who isn't upset.

Or rather, Ms. Lyu is looking at me with a blank expression—she's the scariest of them all!

"You've been cycling through women ever since you left home, haven't you, Bell?!"

"I have not! I've been studying!"

"No, you can't be sure, Lady Hestia! Lord Hermes might have given Mr. Bell some bad ideas!"

"Please believe me, Lilly?!"

"More importantly, Bell, you haven't answered my confession yet."

""""Huuuuuuuuuuuuuuuuuuuuuuuuuh?!""""

"Kiiiiiiiiiiiiiiii?!"

Goddess, Lilly, and Miss Eina shout, and I shriek in a weird voice!

Why did you say that now of all times, Ms. Lyuuuuuuuuuuu?!

"B-Bell, is that true?! Th-that she confessed to you...Wait, there was something like that during the war game, wasn't there...?"

"Right, that was broadcast to Orario through the divine mirror... Wait, Lady Lyu?! Why did you suddenly slump to the ground?!"

"Your face is like the most ripened of strawberries?!"

"The whole city...in front of everyone...my confession of love... they heard everything...eternal shame...save me, Alize..."

"Don't self-destruct after you add oil to the fire, you clown!"

"What is going on, Beeeeell?!"

"Please do explain, Mr. Bell! We won't let you go until you tell us everything! Or rather, come back home at once!"

"Sorry, Bell…I really should have stopped them…I'm sorry for being trash…"

Miss Eina moves closer and then stops as if remembering something; Ms. Mikoto is horrified, having seen the elf suddenly collapse; Ms. Haruhime is flustered by the redness of the elf who looks like she might burst into flames any moment; Ms. Lyu is covering her face and kneeling while still trying to mumble something; Welf shouts angrily, and Goddess and Lilly both unleash their wrath. And also, though I must be imagining it, I swear I can hear Mr. Hegni apologizing.

This is absolute chaos, and I want to just give up and faint.

First, though…I apologize to the staff of the shop with all my might for causing them so much trouble, and then make a note never to show my face here again.

"Rapi!"

It's the middle of the night, just as the date is about to change, when I finally manage to get back to the School District after that unmitigated disaster. Ordinarily, the gangway to the control layer that connects the ship to the port would be closed at this time of night, but for some reason, it's still open. And standing in front of it is Nina, looking worried.

After going back to Ms. Lenoa's store, I'm back in my disguise, and I hide my exhaustion with a smile as Nina rushes over to me.

"Where did you go?! I was so worried when you never came back!"

"I'm really sorry…A few things happened in Orario…"

"…Because of me? Because I made you worry…"

"N-no! It really isn't that! It's not your fault at all!"

I thought she'd be angry, but instead, she looks so sad, and I frantically reassure her it isn't her fault. It was my own decision to go see Miss Eina, and if anything, I'm the one who's been doing questionable things, poking around in other people's lives. So even though I didn't do anything wrong, per se, I still have to take responsibility for everything that's happened…!

Anyway, I just wanted to let her know there's no reason at all for her to worry, but Nina senses something is off.

"…Liar…"

The look on her face is a little sulky, a little reproachful, and also a little happy.

"…After the trouble I caused you and everyone else, I guess we're even."

"R-really? I don't really feel like that happened…but I guess if you're willing to call it even, that would be nice?"

Putting a hand to my head, I just blurt out what I'm thinking, and this time, Nina giggles gently. Seeing her finally crack a smile, I feel relieved.

"Let's get back to the dormitory…Tomorrow is a day off from the Dungeon Practical, but there's still training to do."

"Ah, about that, but…could I go for an internship tomorrow, Nina?"

With everything that happened tonight, I'm under strict orders from Lady Hestia to come back to the familia at once. As far as the School District is concerned, internships in Orario are something students sign up for on their own. As long as you inform the instructors and get permission, you can go whenever. I've heard a few students in the Combat Studies major have already done several internships.

While it isn't ideal to miss the 3rd Squad's training, my request shouldn't be too unnatural—but Nina is clearly shaken.

"R-Rapi…you've already decided the path you want to take?"

"Eh? Ah, mhmm, I wanted to be an adventurer, so, I guess…"

When I fall back on the background that Professor Leon gave me, Nina…looks down and murmurs, "Right…"

"…Nina?"

"…! S-sorry. I'll go start the elevator up! I'm sure Alisa is going to be really angry!"

She gasps, quickly puts on a smile, and starts climbing the gangway.

I can hear the sound of waves. The sound of the wide seas carries across the brackish lake.

I watch quietly as she disappears into the control layer.

"Mmm, the springtime of youth!"

"…Lady Idun?"

"Sweetness and bitterness are the polka dots adorning life! Now, say it with me: Aoharu."

"…A-Aoharu?"

Copying the beaming, blond goddess who appeared from the other end of the gangway, I hold a hand up toward the starry sky.

I'm sure she negotiated with Lord Balder to keep the gangway down for Nina and me. I seriously consider what Aoharu is supposed to be while feeling deeply grateful for the goddess's mercy.

Ultimately, I still have to write multiple paragraphs of self-reflection and a formal apology…

"Incoming! One o'clock!"

Lilly's sharp warning rings out.

Hearing the hum of insect wings in the bark-clad labyrinth, she focuses the entire party's unwavering battle spirit in a single direction.

"I'll get the gun libellulas. Welf, take the deadly hornets!"

"Got it!"

We split the vanguard, with me taking the swarm of gun libellulas that have a long-range attack, while Welf, gleaming with the telltale glow of a level boost, tackles the deadly hornets that just appeared.

I'm wearing battle clothes, my Goliath Scarf, and the new armor Welf forged for me. My gear is like an adventurer's instead of a student's for the first time in a while now. The School District battle uniform isn't bad, but this really does feel more natural. I can feel something thrumming inside me as I let loose with my Level 5 status.

Not using Firebolt, I just immediately get close and disassemble the swarm of gun libellulas spinning through the air like tops.

Before, if I pushed forward without thinking to reach enemies taking potshots at us from a distance, it could potentially leave Lilly or Ms. Haruhime exposed, but now—

"Haruhime, duck."

"Y-yes!"

—Now we have the ultimate floating guard, Ms. Lyu!

As a swarm of mad beetles attempts to flank the party, she passes through them like the wind, and with what seems like just a simple touch with her new Alvs Iustitia, an almost deafening chain reaction of ash explosions takes them all down.

We're currently in a full-on melee. Seeing a battle-hardened adventurer effortlessly reposition and displaying such incredible skill in targeting monsters' cores so none of them can sneakily grab a magic stone without us noticing, I realize all over again exactly what it means to be Level 6.

And, as if collecting on the instruction she gave Ms. Haruhime moments earlier, Ms. Lyu throws the smaller of her two swords.

The blade slips just over where Ms. Haruhime ducked in her Goliath Robe, seemingly whiffing, only to slam into a crack in the bark of a monster that just appeared moments ago, piercing its chest.

"Gishaaaa?!"

The moment the lizardman was born, it was already crumbling into ash.

When facing monsters in the Dungeon, what is the optimal way of dealing with them?

When that question came up in discussions in the familia before, Ms. Lyu's simple answer as she swept the home was, "The moment right before or right after they are born from the walls."

And it's certainly true monsters are uniquely vulnerable in that moment.

They can't do anything while they're being born, but sensing a monster's presence right as they are about to emerge from the wall is an incredible feat. There's no way we can do it. Not the current us, at least. Maybe Ms. Mikoto with her skill could just barely put it into practice during the chaos of combat.

Ms. Lyu, who innately has a level of perception comparable to

Ms. Mikoto's skill, is unmistakably the strongest person in *Hestia Familia*!

Thanks to her, our party has gotten way more stable!

Now we can prevent any flanking or back attacks targeting Lilly or Ms. Haruhime. And a perfect defense ironically frees us up to focus on attacking. The vanguard can just focus on the enemies in front of them without worrying about anything else, making the force of the party's advance even more destructive.

Glancing at the utterly reliable Ms. Lyu, her sky-blue gaze meets mine, and she immediately looks away. I can see the blush spreading even above her mask, reaching the tips of her pointed ears. Embarrassment scorches my body too, and I feel just a little bit dizzy.

We're currently on the twenty-second floor, in the Colossal Tree Labyrinth.

As expected, I received permission to do an internship, so I reverted to being Bell and returned to Hearthstone Manor, where I underwent a thorough interrogation that left no stones unturned by our goddess, who had been waiting all night.

After a long, muddled series of questions and answers that left us both red-faced and confused, Goddess was wheezing as she said we'd continue again tonight before she left for her job. When will I be able to strengthen my resolve enough to answer Ms. Lyu…?

But either way, since I didn't have any plans for the day, I decided to go with everyone else into the Dungeon. And now here we are.

It hasn't even been four months since the first time I set foot on this floor, has it? *Hestia Familia* has already grown enough to be able to easily explore down below the twentieth floor on our own.

"Mr. Bell! Ms. Lyu! Focus! We're in combat right now! That Aoharu sickly sweet eyes-meeting stuff belongs in school, not on the battlefield!"

"S-sorry."

"Sorry!"

Immediately noticing our delayed reactions, Lilly shoots us a stern warning. Is Aoharu a new term making the rounds or something?

I want to cry a little bit at messing up bad enough to make our strategist angry even though we're a Level 5 and a Level 6. Still, the party manages to deal with the whole wave of monsters that just appeared.

"...?"

Which is when, even though we are in combat, I look back.

"Oy! Where are you looking, Bell?!"

"...Sir Bell?"

Welf beside me shouts, and Ms. Mikoto, who is a little distance back behind me, looks confused. Ms. Lyu, who was attacking monsters to the side, also glances over as if noticing something.

I immediately apologize and tear into the enemies in front of us with Welf.

After splitting a sword stag in two, we tear into the large mammoth fool, finishing the fight without any issues.

"...Umm, Ms. Mikoto, may I?"

After the long fight ended, we could finally take a little breather.

Once I finished gathering up magic stones and drop items with everyone, I approached Ms. Mikoto, who is refilling water bottles.

"Yes?"

"In that last fight, since Ms. Lyu was staying back in the middle guard, I was thinking it might be okay for you to move up to the vanguard, maybe..."

In order to improve our coordination and our situational awareness, I share my thoughts.

"That position was fine, but if you moved up to the vanguard, I could push even farther forward, and I think I would have been able to focus all the forward enemies' attention on me. And then the party would effectively be a bit safer...I think."

"I see, that's true...Sorry, I hadn't considered it that far ahead."

"Ah, no, I'm not blaming you at all...! Sorry for saying something so pompous-sounding!"

Before Ms. Lyu joined, as an all-rounder, Ms. Mikoto was the familia's anchor. Using her skill, she always protected the back lines. Her focus being more defense-oriented is, if anything, proof of how much she has done all this time, so maybe it's a bit rude to say it.

I end up just apologizing lamely over and over.

At times like this, I can't help but feel that I'm not really suited to being a leader…and Lilly looks dumbfounded watching me.

"Lilly…? What is it?"

"…Nothing, you just took the words right out of Lilly's mouth…"

"Eh?! I-I'm sorry."

"You don't need to apologize. And the part about focusing the enemies' attention is something Lilly couldn't say, having not experienced fighting on the front line…"

She stares at me, examining me from head to toe.

"Mr. Bell…have you gotten kind of smarter?"

…?

My eyes swirl at her unexpected question.

"I think so, too. Today you seem to feel somewhat more intelligent, or…"

"I-intelligent…"

"Ha-ha, that's becoming a first-tier adventurer for you."

"R-really…?"

Ms. Haruhime and Welf's comments don't quite feel right.

The idea that your brain can go faster because of leveling up… Well, there might be a little something to that, but…

As I cock my head, Ms. Lyu, watching from a little distance, points out the biggest change.

"You're gaining a broader perspective."

Her quiet, clear voice draws everyone's gaze.

"Bell, you've more or less mastered combat on an individual level. When we fell into the deep floors, you instinctually knew how to lure enemies and cover your blind spots. That sort of thing."

…Not to get too self-conscious, but I can agree with that statement.

It felt like my whole world opened up when Ms. Aiz's and Ms. Lyu's teachings clicked together. If that's what she means, then that weapon is definitely in my arsenal now. After being trained by Mr. Alfrik and his brothers in Folkvangr, my awareness of my blind spots is sharper than ever.

"Your field of vision is expanding to include not just yourself, but the whole party," Ms. Lyu continues.

"The perspective from the back lines, then, Lady Lyu?"

"Wh-whoa, wait a minute. Then my whole reason for being here is...!"

"That is not quite right, but not quite wrong, either. But do not worry, Lilliluka. Your perspective and his field of view are different things."

Lyu answers like the reliable eldest sister of a family, reassuring Lilly and answering Ms. Mikoto at the same time.

"If I had to give it a specific name, I would call it tactical awareness."

"Tactical awareness..."

"A commander like you, Lilliluka, surveys the entire battle, guiding the party as a whole, while Bell responds to the ever-changing tactical situation and chooses, or perhaps shares, the moves the party should take."

At a high level, Lilly's vision encompasses everything, whereas my field of vision is more focused.

Being able to deal with things that Lilly can't immediately respond to with people in the vanguard and the formation's center is undoubtedly a strength. It should decrease the burden on the commander and allow a swifter and more granular response—or so Ms. Lyu explains.

"Increasing our reaction speed and ability to wipe out the enemies is useful for the party. It is also valuable for people in similar positions to be able to share the same perspective. The commander can take those movements in from the back and build upon them to unlock more strategic options, giving us more flexibility."

Hearing that, Welf and Ms. Mikoto murmur in understanding.

It's true. I've always prioritized just charging in from the front as an attacker up until now. With Ms. Lyu in the party, the stability has increased, giving me an opportunity to catch my breath and take stock of the battle.

Most likely, this concept of field of vision is something Ms. Lyu has refined ever since her time in *Astrea Familia*. The ability to make tactical decisions on the front line without having to wait for detailed instructions or directions from the rear. A lubricant for the party, the ability to direct. Maybe someone in *Astrea Familia* taught it to her once as well.

"I'm sure this growth of yours is from studying at the School District."

"!"

"I thought your time in the School District would be a good opportunity for you to get some rest, but…you turned even that into material for growth," Ms. Lyu says with a smile.

I'm a little embarrassed being praised so openly, but I'm also happy.

The time I'm spending at the School District is not being wasted. Maybe even my ability to direct the 3rd Squad's hunt was thanks to my new experience as a supporter and also the fruits of my combat lessons.

I'm pleased to be allowed to study at the School District, and I'm proud that Nina and the others are being praised by extension as well.

"Now that we've reaffirmed our coordination with Bell, should we start heading back? It's a long way."

"Yes, we've gotten quite a lot of magic stones and drop items, too! The take really is better when we have our lucky rabbit!"

"Ha-ha-ha…!"

And after a few more battles, we leave the Colossal Tree Labyrinth.

I'd like to get back home before Goddess returns from work. Mr. Alfrik and his brothers are watching Hearthstone Manor today—while also guarding against anyone after Ms. Haruhime—so I'm a little bit worried. And I have to get back to the School District before it gets too late.

As I enjoy a satisfying sort of exhaustion that comes with living a busy double life of an adventurer and a student, I hear a shout.

"You…! School District brats! Don't get cocky!"

"Can you not be a little more refined?! Adventurers really are all ruffians!"

When we reach the Cave Labyrinth on the thirteenth floor, we can hear loud shouts.

Looking at the source of the noise, there is a dangerous mood in the air as a squad from the School District and a group of adventurers face off.

There's signs of a pass parade. Or maybe it's just the remains of a struggle for the same prey? Either way, it definitely isn't a peaceful argument, and seeing the adventurers ready to reach for their weapons, my legs move by themselves.

"Um, did something happen?"

"Huh?! You can just butt out a—R-Rabbit Foot?!"

"The first-tier adventurer?!"

Intimidated, the human adventurer recoils when he sees my face, and the others also cower like they've just spotted a monster from the deep floors. You know, that's not a very nice reaction…

They just mutter, "I-it's nothing" and immediately leave, not noticing or caring about how I feel.

Left behind are me and a few stunned students from the Combat Studies Department .

I don't know them, but the badge on their chest is of a lyre and a book…*Bragi Class*, I guess?

"Record Holder!"

"Bell Cranell! The rogue who broke into the School District!"

"You think you saved us?!"

"But you did actually save us, so we'll at least express our gratitude!"

"""""Thank you for saving us! Bleh!"""""

The squad of four says their thanks and then spits on the ground in unison.

Watching them march off with military precision, I almost want to cry. I really need to make sure Nina and them don't find out who I really am…

"School District students, huh? They really hate you."

"I mean, it is my own fault…so there's really no helping it."

"I can't tell if they're grateful or not…"

I meet back up with Welf and the others, who were watching from the side. My shoulders slump in disappointment.

"It looks like they were in a dispute," Ms. Haruhime comments. "Did something happen?"

"The moralistic School District students are just bickering with adventurers, most of whom are outlaws...It is a common scene when the School District returns. Aboveground and in the Dungeon."

"The morals and etiquette the School District teaches are pretty antithetical to how adventurers act..."

"Anyway, it's not exactly rare."

Ms. Lyu, Lilly, and Welf just answer as if it's just a natural scene when the School District comes back. Ms. Mikoto and I, who have only been in Orario for a relatively short time, and Ms. Haruhime, who lived just within the small world of the Pleasure Quarter, are a bit surprised.

But I guess they're right.

From what I've heard, the relationship between violent adventurers and the School District students is not great...?

"Cocky brats...just you wait..."

Glancing down the passage the adventurers went down, I think I hear some kind of suspicious mutter, and I get a bad feeling...

CHAPTER 5
MY DREAM

"Nrrgh..."

Nina had been groaning since morning.

She was sitting at a desk in a mostly empty self-study room with lots of textbooks and references spread out around her.

"Hello, Nina."

"Ah, Milly."

The three-years-older elf girl called out to her.

Miliria, who had given Nina permission to shorten her name, was in *Balder Class* 7th Squad, which, unlike the worst party, was one of the top squads in the Combat Studies Department .

A true elite was concerned about her for some reason.

"It's rare to see a model student like you groaning at a desk like that. Was there something you were having trouble with?"

"Ah, no, it's not that. I just wanted to make some notes for Rapi."

"Rapi? That new kid?"

Nina broke into a smile as Miliria looked puzzled.

"Yes! He's really incredible! Even though he doesn't really have any knowledge to start from, he is always trying so hard to keep up with lessons! And he keeps up with my studying, too...he's the first person I've met like that!"

"Th-that's incredible..."

Nina understood well that her method of studying was about quantity more than quality. Even students who were admitted into the School District, those who had the will to learn, trembled at the almost murderous amount of studying she did. There had never been another student who could keep up with how much she studied, and she had been told more than once that her method was inefficient.

So seeing Rapi, who blindly and faithfully did his best to keep up, was stunning, fresh, and more than anything...moving.

If anything, there were times he slept even later and woke up even earlier than Nina, covering even more subjects than she did. Knowing just how much Nina actually studied, the elf girl's expression froze, and she updated her evaluation of Rapi.

"I started wanting to support Rapi. I had the idea of making notes for him to make the lessons a little bit easier to follow..."

This was not the first time she had made these sorts of preparation and review notes covering key points. Not to pat her own back, but she could definitely see that the notes she made had been helping Rapi somewhat keep up with the lessons.

At first, it had just been because Leon had asked her to help him some as a new student. But now, knowing his character, she was proactively spending more time with him.

It's a little different from just getting along with a normal friend, though...

Maybe it was more like a set of gears aligning together? Whatever it was, though, Nina and Rapi had a good affinity for each other.

Also...I feel like he reminds me of Father.

His eyes were hard to see behind the hair, but the feeling when he smiled bashfully and the way he always hurried to try to help people were just like her beloved father.

It wasn't just because of that, but Nina, who was naturally amiable and a bit of a busybody, had decided of her own volition to support Rapi.

"What do you think of him, Milly?"

"I don't really know him well enough to have much of an opinion. It hasn't even been ten days since he enrolled."

"That's right! It's only been that long! And yet he managed to bring everyone in the 3rd Squad together! The 3rd Squad! The worst party! The squad I could never convince to work together and made me want to hide in the bathroom and cry!"

"N-Nina...should you really be that blunt?"

Iglin and the others would never admit it, but Rapi was the pillar holding up the 3rd Squad.

He demonstrated such an impressive level of judgment inside the labyrinth that he was called a Dungeon geek, and even Nina, the squad's leader, had started relying on his opinions.

He never tried to put himself in the limelight, and often he seemed to just be watching them, but whenever they were struggling, he always shared some wisdom. Thanks to that, the 3rd Squad was currently in the running with a handful of other squads for top marks.

Rapi Flemish. He really was a mysterious person. Bashful and shy with a tendency to be timid and an inability to turn people down. But he was always working hard, kind to others, and had a strong heart.

Nina knew that her eyes were shining as she talked about Rapi. And watching her, Miliria suddenly started giggling.

"Looks like you're crazy about that rabbit."

"It feels like you are trying to imply something..."

"That's just your imagination."

There was an event after classes that day that just further supported Nina's view.

"Hey, Combat Studies guys! Can I ask you something?"

After Professor Leon had finished announcements and while the students in Combat Studies were preparing to go into the Dungeon, two human boys from the Smithing Department ran into the room carrying a sword.

"We were interning with *Goibniu Familia* and failed again! We can't pass no matter what we make!"

"At this rate, we won't be able to join! We failed last time we were in Orario, too!"

The burly boys put the weapon on the table in grief and were looking to Nina and the others for help.

The students from Combat Studies gathered in a circle to see what was going on and began the School District standard airing of opinions.

"It looks like a solid magitech weapon to me..."

"Yeah, if anything, isn't this kinda ace? I'd love the chance to use it."

"Hmph. I can make better weapons myself."

"Who asked you, Iglin?! Weird-ass dwarves can just pipe down!"

As the classroom grew louder, Iglin snorted and picked up the sword, producing a blade of light. There was a stunned squeak from somewhere in the room. Rapi.

"Wh-what is that sword…?"

"It's just a magitech weapon…Ah, right, this is your first time seeing one, isn't it? I'm the only one in the 3rd Squad who uses magitech gear, and I don't use it in the Dungeon."

"It's an invention produced from the combined efforts of the School District's Smithing and Alchemy departments. It absorbs the magical energy of its user, increasing the weapon's reach and power."

Nina and Iglin, who smoothly swung the blade a bit, explained what it was for Rapi.

There were almost three celches of magic light enveloping the sword. It almost looked like an armor of light. In addition to the weapon's natural strength, it also increased in power with the force of the magic power put into it.

Rapi was speechless seeing his first magitech weapon.

"There aren't many magitech weapons going around in Orario, and I'm sure it's not worthless! It would even work just fine on Dungeon monsters!"

"But still, Lord Goibniu won't accept it…and he won't say anything about why."

The Combat Studies students couldn't find an answer among themselves either as the Smithing students grumbled.

"Rapi, was there something you wanted to say?"

"Eh?!"

"Your mouth is itching to say something, so just say it! You're my guardian beast, so have some confidence in yourself!"

For some reason, Chris's chest swelled with pride while Rapi struggled with whether to say something. Everyone's gazes turned to him, and he recoiled a bit before nervously beginning…

"Umm, that…this magitech part…is probably easily broken, right…?"

"Hmm? Hey, watch your mouth, new kid."

"The instructors can all vouch for their strength. There hasn't been any magitech gear broken during the Dungeon Practical this year."

The Smithing students glared at Rapi, hitting him with their complaints as he recoiled again.

"Ah, no, I didn't mean like that...!" He tried to put his thoughts together and carefully picked his words. "This magitech bit is probably a magic item, or a magic-stone device that is worked into the weapon, right...?"

"Yeah, you got it. It's a fundamentally different structure from normal weapons."

"So would it be correct to say its durability is compromised by having to fit and protect that mechanism...?"

"...Compared to a normal weapon, yes. But only just barely."

"Yes, I'm sure it's just a little bit. I'm sure, but...in the Dungeon, that little bit is scary."

The smithing students started listening intently as Rapi continued.

"When a weapon breaks in the Dungeon, it's like losing a limb...is something I've heard before."

"...!"

"Even if you bring multiple weapons while exploring, there is a limit...so I think Orario adventurers probably value weapons that can last longer."

Orario's blacksmiths were almost universally highly skilled, and their weapons' durability and other abilities were all top-class. So given that, sacrificing durability in order to add magitech functions was a fatal trade-off in Orario's market. That was what Rapi was getting at.

The School District's magitech weapons were high-quality and capable of enduring real combat, but the slightest difference in longevity could be the line between life and death in the Dungeon.

The students, Nina included, were all stunned by the realization.

"For mages who don't really get into close-range fights that much, this magitech bit would be good, I think...but no matter how amazing a weapon is, if it is less durable than a normal weapon, I think it will be hard for an adventurer to choose it...yeah."

Time froze as the students listened to Rapi speaking almost with the voice of an actual adventurer, and then he slipped back into a nervous student's voice to finish.

"...I see. So Orario's adventurers care more about durability—the ability to keep fighting—over absolute peak output. Right, that makes sense, since consecutive battles are the norm in the Dungeon!"

"Yeah, when you get into the deeper floors, or when you're in the middle of an expedition, you can't always maintain your weapons perfectly. And a magitech weapon needs more careful maintenance than a normal weapon, too..."

"Even if you bring a blacksmith along with you, you need a dedicated facility to really give it the attention it needs."

"If nothing else, it would be hard to pick as your main weapon! So we have to consider the people using the weapon and not just the weapon's abilities!"

All of a sudden, the students began talking again, like fish in water.

The Smithing students in particular patted Rapi on the back over and over and thanked him for giving them some hope.

After he shared his thoughts, excitement filled the air as all the students gained a brand-new perspective.

"...Rapi, you should have a little more confidence and share your opinion more!"

"Eh...? N-Nina?"

"Professor Leon said it before, right? Sharing opinions is important! Thanks to you, we've all gotten just a little bit wiser! That's really impressive!"

Nina was pleased by the scene and went over to Rapi, telling him to speak up more. And the rest of the 3rd Squad was in agreement.

"If you mess up, we'll correct you as many times as we have to. Don't be afraid of mistakes!"

"Yeah, this is...the School District..."

"Well done, Rapi. As expected of my guardian beast! My intelligence is going to start shooting up!"

With Iglin, Legi, and Chris saying it too, the boy who had been stupefied at first nodded happily and said, "O-okay!"

Rapi really is incredible…

The excitement did not fade as Nina left the room with a smile on her face to change into her battle uniform for the Dungeon Practical.

Even though he usually felt like a little brother who needed to be taken care of, there were times he would show a more reliable side, like a dependable older brother.

That was Rapi's charm. And that was why Nina couldn't take her eyes off him.

She often found herself looking for him, and when she saw him, her face would light up and she would run over to him.

Sometimes I feel like an older sister watching a kid brother grow, and sometimes he feels like such a reliable older brother.

Thinking back on how she was behaving, she had a bit of a bitter smile.

…Even though I can't say a single word to my real sister.

Her expression darkened as she left the schoolhouse, just in time to run into some friends.

"Nina! Going to the Dungeon now?"

"Ah…yes. Are you studying, Betty?"

"That's right. Cramming for the exam!"

It was the three girls that Rapi had met on the first day.

They were holding textbooks in their arms and looking exhausted as the real exam loomed before them.

When their eyes met, the girls spoke up, as if making up their mind.

"Nina, you should take the Guild exam with us."

"………"

"You worked so hard. It would be a waste not to. Why not come back to the Education Department ?"

"…But I only got a C on the Guild practice exam…"

"My grades are even worse than yours! And five years ago, there was the Miracle of Frot! She passed even though she got a Z on the practice exam! I'm sure you can do it, Nina!"

Her friends all encouraged her.

Looking down, Nina forced herself to smile and apologized.

"...I'm sorry, everyone. I've given up already. I'm in Combat Studies now...good luck."

With that, she left.

She could feel the lonely gazes of her friends on her back as she turned at the next corner. Leaning against the wall in a deserted alley, she fought with all her might against the emotions filling her breast.

"...I'm sure Rapi has already decided on the path he's going to take..." She murmured quietly.

Even though he had entered after her, he already had a goal, or maybe even a dream. And in that moment, that fact made her feel unbearably, hopelessly miserable.

"........."

She looked up at a dazzlingly clear sky. But the beautiful blue had no answers for her.

After coming back to the School District from *Hestia Familia*, the days went by swimmingly for me and the 3rd Squad.

Thanks to experiencing both hard times and a sense of accomplishment together in the Dungeon, everyone's awareness has increased. While on the ship, we work together on coordination, and in the Dungeon, we progress at a solid pace, even managing to safely reach the fourteenth floor. I haven't probed too deeply into the issue with Nina that Professor Leon asked me to help with, but everyone in the squad is doing their best to work together now, at least.

The morning of my tenth day of school life, the seventh day of the Dungeon Practical, arrives.

"Today's the day! Let's go to the fifteenth floor!"

The 3rd Squad is fired up to finally set foot onto the deepest floor that the School District has allowed for student exploration.

No one has any arguments against Iglin's shout.

Gathered in front of the School District's main entrance as it undergoes an overhaul in the giant dockyard, we all nod and set out for Orario.

Passing through the southwest gate of the city like always, we go to the Guild Headquarters to take care of the paperwork. No one pushes Nina about her situation anymore as she waits outside the Guild. We're just waiting for her to tell us more as we finish the paperwork for today. I see Miss Eina looking around at the students in the lobby, but I can't say anything to her right now. I feel bad for her as I go to the Guild's big noticeboard.

"Any useful information?"

"No, it's mostly just quests."

Iglin leans on the backpack I'm carrying as he checks in with me.

Rapi Flemish is currently the 3rd Squad's supporter and resident Dungeon geek—no combat ability whatsoever, but a useful source of information and insights. If I wanted to put it nicely, then I guess it's a position sort of like Lilly's. Not that I would ever claim to be on her level.

"…Hmm?"

I make a point of checking the information for the floors three above and below our target floor at a minimum. That is the standard Lilly set for herself, and I'm copying that as the 3rd Squad's supporter. And while performing that routine check, I cock my head at something.

"What is it?"

"Nothing, I'm just a little curious about this Monster Rex information…"

The floor boss of the middle levels, Goliath, has an approximately two-week interval, and when I see the report on it, something feels off.

The board says that the next interval should be two days from now, but…

It was fourteen days ago when the last big banquet after the war game was held…

Mr. Bors and the others returned to the eighteenth floor after that.

Given its role as a safe point, the people in Rivira are the ones who usually slay Goliath. They should have taken care of it this time too since pretty much every familia left the Dungeon and waited aboveground until the great familia war was over. So Goliath, which was born on the seventeenth floor, should have been left alone for a while.

So the earliest someone could have defeated it was Mr. Bors and them fourteen days ago, which is at odds with the report saying it happened twelve days ago. If it said one day left until the interval, people would be cautious, since it would be hard to say when exactly it would come, but two days is right on the cusp of what would make people exploring the middle levels let their guard down.

"Why are you looking at information about a floor boss that shows up on the eighteenth floor? Our goal is the fifteenth floor, isn't it? You think we would accidentally end up going that far?"

"No, of course not, but..."

Iglin leaves before he can hear me finish muttering, "just to be sure."

I glance back at the board again as he walks away.

I have heard stories about the residents of Rivira being lazy and not bothering with the hassle of sending a message after defeating Goliath, and that causing confusion, but...

There were a few examples where a party left thinking Goliath was on the eighteenth floor, only to find out the people in Rivira had defeated it three days prior. Maybe this is also just one of those situations.

But there are informants who get a reward from the Guild for going back and forth to the eighteenth floor for up-to-date information about Goliath, too...

Maybe it's just me...but I should make a mental note just in case.

"Hah."

Seeing the hume-bunny student leaving the noticeboard, several men smirked.

They were the contacts who had provided the information this time. They were upper-class adventurers nursing a grudge from a few days ago. They'd gotten into an argument with some of the School District students only to have Bell Cranell himself get in their way and not get a chance to vent.

"Let's see how much you piss yourselves when you hear that howl."

They sneered while looking down on the well-behaved little children wandering around the lobby.

"HOOOOOOOOOOOOOOO!"

"Nina, hellhounds from the side!"

"Legi, Chris! Don't let them get off a breath attack!"

"Roger!" "Leave it to me!"

I'm carefully searching for enemies from behind Nina, and when my alert goes up, 3rd Squad responds fluidly.

The pack of hellhounds coming from three o'clock is scrambled by a dark elf leaping off the walls and ceiling and once they show an opening. Chris shoots across the ground, getting close and unleashing a big swipe with his body-length sword.

The cheerful sound of monsters being split in two rings out as Iglin, who stayed on the main passage, breaks through with the support of Nina's magic blade.

"Ooooooorrrryaaaaaaaaaaaa!"

"Ghgiiii?!"

His hammer slams down, shattering three crystal mantises.

Iglin's battle-mode roar echoes in the Cave Labyrinth as we finish the combat without issue.

"All right! The fifteenth floor isn't any trouble, either!"

"Pick up drops. Quickly."

"I'll help with the magic stones, Rapi."

"Thank you, Nina."

While Iglin hoists his hammer in joy, Legi complains as she and Chris quickly gather drop items, and Nina puts her magic shortsword back at her hip before helping out with the magic stones. No gaps even in the after-battle cleanup.

The 3rd Squad has always been an outlier in terms of individual strength, and now that I've reached the fifteenth floor with them, I have to say, they really are something.

We handled the first of the middle levels' enemies without issue and made good progress. We still haven't run into any larger enemies like a minotaur, but the 3rd Squad has been working as a party well enough that I don't have to do much of anything anymore.

And apparently we've gotten deeper into the Dungeon faster than any other squad today.

"It feels like we can do anything now! Maybe we could even go all the way to the eighteenth floor?"

"Could. But don't."

"Thanks to all of us, there's only two credits left to earn! Where are the minotaurs, I wonder!"

Everyone is feeling their growth. They have confidence, but not so much as to get overconfident, and high morale, too. This is probably the optimal condition for them. The 3rd Squad right now might be fine against anything in the Cave Labyrinth.

"………"

"Rapi? What is it?"

But there is something bothering me, something other than the party's condition.

The Dungeon feels different today…I've got a bad feeling…

If anyone were to ask what it is, all I could say is "something," but my instincts are warning me.

I'm looking around enough to make Nina worry a bit—

"*KIKAAAAAAAAA!*"

"Whoa?! That surprised me!"

Chris leaps into the air as a shrill monster shriek rings out.

A cloud of bad bats born from the ceiling.

"———"

Realizing it's just a bat-type monster they fought on higher floors already, the 3rd Squad relaxes, but the warning bell in my head starts blaring.

And then—

"*KIAAAAAAAAAAAAA!!!*"

"*KIKIIIIIIIII!*"

"*YAAAAAAAAAAAAAA!*"

A terrible, dissonant chorus fills the air all through the floor.

"Wh-what?!"

"Bad bat cries, everywhere…!"

"A mass emergence?!"

Nina and Legi cover their ears at the screech of countless monsters, and Iglin looks around.

Bad bats' main means of attack is their screech that impedes movement. And the unmistakable shrieks of tens or even hundreds of them fill the air.

There weren't any bad bats. That's what felt off.

That is the answer. I didn't see a single bat hiding away in the darkness even though they were always here!

Not good!

That late realization reveals an all too slow sense of danger. The sound of rock exploding comes from all directions. It's the sound of a monster being born.

Because the labyrinth gave birth to so many bad bats, not just from the walls but also from the ceiling, the fifteenth floor's equilibrium breaks, and the walls collapse.

"Wha—?!"

"Wh-wh-whooooooooooooa?!"

The ceiling above us is filled with holes from giving birth to so many bats, and it starts to fall, too.

A ferocious hail of rubble starts tumbling down.

"!!!"

All my nerves, all my senses as a Level 5 first-tier adventurer scream out.

I push Legi and Iglin forward, grab Nina and Chris under each arm, and leap out from under the collapse with all my might.

There is a series of thunderclaps as the Dungeon roars ferociously and the Cave Labyrinth shudders terrifyingly.

"Lady Hestia?!"

The area around Central Park was lively.

Just as Hestia noticed the mood while going about her job at the Jyaga Maru Kun stand, Lilly suddenly rushed over.

"It seems there was a cave-in in the Dungeon's middle levels! It's covering a significant area and several of the School District students were also caught in it…!"

"A cave-in?!" Hestia shouted, forgetting she was still working.

"*Ganesha Familia* and *Loki Familia*, and also the School District, are quickly removing the rubble, but…the situation is dangerous."

"What about Bell?! Where is he right now?!"

Lilly grimaced, confirming the goddess's concerns.

"Ms. Lyu already went to the Guild to confirm the situation…the 3rd Squad, which Mr. Bell is part of, is currently on the fifteenth floor as part of their Dungeon Practical…"

Spinning around, Hestia looked toward the tower piercing the sky, and the Dungeon that extended below it. The number of her blessings had not decreased. The worst had not happened to Bell. But Hestia's eyes wavered, and she couldn't help but say it.

"The fifteenth floor again, Bell…?!"

She experienced a powerful case of déjà vu.

"It's no good! We're blocked here, too!"

There's impatience in Iglin's voice as he grips his hammer.

Even a dwarf, one of the people of the earth, can only throw up his hands at the mountain of rubble completely blocking the passage. The others all grow pale.

Our current location is the fifteenth floor of the Dungeon.

Having somehow escaped the murderous shower of rocks, the 3rd Squad is at least all together, but we have a different problem.

The massive collapse has blocked all routes back to the surface.

We can't even use this detour...

Checking the map of the middle floors I bought from the Guild, I mark another red X using a Blood Feather made by Ms. Asfi I bought with my own money.

The main route that we, or rather, every School District student used for coming and going is completely blocked by the rubble. The smaller paths radiating like blood vessels through the floor are all out, too. Every route back to the fourteenth floor has been sealed off.

There are areas that have completely changed shape from the collapse, too, and it's dangerous even to hang around there to see what is happening.

Most likely, there isn't a clear route back aboveground...

At least not currently.

Until adventurers with specialized gear for clearing the rubble make it down from the surface, there won't be a way back. Even now that I'm a first-tier adventurer, it's not hard to imagine the situation getting even worse if I use a full charge to bust my way through the rubble and cause a secondary collapse from the tremor.

Without specialized knowledge, all I can do is destroy things, which isn't enough to get out of this situation.

Just hoping that an instructor from the School District is conveniently on the fifteenth floor too, and that we just happen to meet up with them would be the worst plan.

I'm worried if there is anyone else trapped besides us, and if possible, I'd like to help, but...I can't drag Nina and the others around the whole floor in this situation when they're already tired...

The 3rd Squad would run out of strength first if we tried that. If I want to search for other people who might have gotten caught up in this, it has to wait at least until I get them all to a safe place first.

"Rapi, is there any other route?!"

"...There is just one more narrow passage to the southwest, but if this is blocked, then I think it probably is, too. Just moving around is going to tire us, so I would not really recommend checking there..."

"That's..."

Even though it threatens to rob them of their hope, I answer Iglin honestly. I chose to give them an accurate assessment of the situation.

We have no way out, and we're blocked on all sides, alone and without support.

It's frustrating...and I feel terrible.

If I had noticed the lack of bad bats sooner. If I had just sensed the looming irregular, they wouldn't have had to go through this.

I'm still not good enough. Ms. Aiz or Ms. Lyu, Mr. Finn or Master—they all would have noticed the signs of danger immediately and led the party to a safe place. Even though I'm a first-tier adventurer, I'm still green and lacking in experience.

I need to be more careful. I need to be more diligent. I need to sharpen my senses further. To protect myself and to protect my comrades.

Engraving that regret and reflection in my heart, I immediately shift gears and look up.

Just then, as a heavy silence fills the air...

"Nina...what do we do?" Legi asks.

"Eh...?"

"Decide our course."

What is the party's plan of action?

Legi precisely and mercilessly asks the commander charged with leading the squad.

Nina gulps, at a loss for how to answer.

"...Thinking about it calmly, there are just two choices. Set up camp on the main route and wait for help from aboveground..."

"Or pin our hopes on the other route Rapi mentioned. For me, I think I'd rather wait for help! Not because I'm trying to avoid the despair from trying to do something that doesn't work, though! Obviously!"

Iglin and Chris lay out our options. And Chris even honestly shares his thoughts.

Nina's lips and breaths quiver as she looks at me.

"Rapi…water and rations…and items…how much do we have left…?"

"…If we split it out evenly, the food won't last half a day. As for items, we have four potions, three magic potions, and two high potions…"

I take everything out of the backpack and line it all up on the ground for everyone to see.

There are also two spare shortswords Legi and Chris can use.

Iglin and the others all take out the items they have, too.

Nina's judgment to confirm our supplies immediately is correct. Top marks befitting her model-student reputation. But because of that choice, it also feels like we are strangling ourselves.

Confirming the items you have on hand is the equivalent of putting a number on your remaining life. If you lose your calm, it is easy to be driven mad by that cruel, uncaring number. I've experienced it myself before.

The only reason that this situation feels fine to me is probably because of the death march I experienced in the deep levels. Kicking aside those pointless thoughts, I put everything back into my backpack and peer at Nina.

Her sweat is terrible. Her breathing is getting shallower. The stress is getting bad.

The big decision that might well influence the lives of her party is weighing down on her, even as all eyes are on her.

Even though it isn't really right, I can't help seeing the me from six months ago in her.

I wonder if this is how Lilly felt…

When Welf was injured and I was panicking after thoughtlessly moving all around the floor, sweating terribly.

In that despair-inducing situation, the supporter who should have been weaker than all of us was calmer than everyone.

Lilly isn't here. So this time, it's my turn to help them the way Lilly helped me.

"For now, let's calm down."

It's the same thing Lilly said back then.

Everyone's shoulders jump, and they turn to look at me as I walk over to Nina.

"Breathe, Nina."

"Huh...?"

"Take a deep breath and slowly exhale. Iiiin. And ouuuut. Iiiin. And ouuuut...yes, just like that."

Smiling as I demonstrate, I think for a moment, and then hold Nina's pinky. The good luck charm Ms. Lyu did for me in the deep floors.

Her hand freezes, and then the trembling stops and she lets the tension drain out.

Meeting my gaze, Nina quietly breathes in and out several times, calming her breathing. I walk over to Iglin and hold out my hand, but he rejects me immediately, looking like he might gag. Legi passes too, hiding her hands behind her back.

Chris holds out both hands and says, "I'll take it!" so I hold his hands, too.

It feels a little awkward, but it is a lot better than before. Everyone has relaxed a bit.

"About our options. I think there is actually one more possibility."

They all look surprised.

There aren't any signs of monsters around us, so there is no need to be fully on guard for an attack for the moment. So without hurrying, remembering what Lilly said here before, I give them another proposition.

"The route back to the higher floors is out of the question, I think. But there is also the option of intentionally going lower...to go to the eighteenth floor for safety."

They're speechless in shock.

"The eighteenth floor is a safe point where monsters aren't born from the walls. There's even an adventurer town there, so if we can make it that far, we'll be safe."

Of course, everyone immediately raises their disagreement and questions.

"Wait a minute, Rapi! This is the fifteenth floor! Even the super-ultra-amazing me would be exhausted going another three whole floors!"

"There are pitfalls. If we find one of the many pitfalls in the middle floors, we can jump down into the next floor in one sweep."

"What about…the floor boss? Its home is…the seventeenth floor…"

"If the information on the Guild board today is right, then there are still two more days left until its interval is up."

"D-do you have a map, Rapi…?"

"Mhmm. I have maps covering up to the eighteenth floor."

I answer Chris's concern, Regi's question, and Nina's follow-up without hesitation.

As if remembering me checking the board back in the Guild Headquarters, Iglin looks dazed as he asks, "D-did you know this was going to happen…?"

"I didn't know. But I wanted to be ready. Just in case something happened…because that's what the most amazing supporter I know is like."

Smiling awkwardly, I spread out the maps of the sixteenth and seventeenth floors for them to see.

Lilly always carries a full backpack and does everything to prepare us adventurers.

When it was decided I would be the supporter for the 3rd Squad, I used her as my model. That was really all it was. So I proudly talk about the most amazing supporter I know.

As everyone inhales sharply, I look to Nina.

"Nina, it will be fine, whatever you choose."

"Eh…?"

"The 3rd Squad is strong. So whichever path you take, I'm sure we will make it back to the surface."

I smile at her, and her emerald eyes widen.

I just gave her a little push, but the decision is for her and for the rest of the squad to make. It feels like something I shouldn't be choosing for them. That isn't Rapi's role right now. There is a reason for me being here. Not as a familia's leader, and not as a first-tier adventurer, but as Rapi Flemish.

It isn't because I think I have the capacity to guide people. But now that I'm Level 5, I can't afford to just keep running only for myself like I have until now.

The field of view Ms. Lyu was talking about. That shared perspective and influence. The transmission of the light of hope.

Lord Hermes, Lord Balder, and Professor Leon wanted to teach me that through the School District, didn't they?

That's how it feels right now.

"Gh..."

Her long brown hair shudders. The lock of jade hair indicating her noble blood, too.

Clutching her rod in both hands as if hugging it to her chest, she forcefully looks up.

"Let's keep going."

Iglin and the others look surprised, and I smile.

"Just standing around...that wouldn't be like us at all!"

Hearing that, this time, Iglin and Chris smile, too. And I'm sure Legi is too, behind her mask.

"All right! Let's freaking do this! The eighteenth floor! This is payback for everyone who made fun of us! We'll retract the ignominy of the worst party!"

"My legend is going to be even brighter now! And Iglin, you don't retract ignominy, you expunge it!"

"That's rare...Chris being the straight man...That's a good omen."

As usual, they all have their own different reactions, but their intentions at least are united. Seeing that, Nina breaks into a smile. I nod too when she looks at me.

Our choice is adventure.

The 3rd Squad sets out for the eighteenth floor.

"Oy, this is bad…the people coming back said there's no getting through from the fifteenth floor…"

"Adventurers with some experience'll just make for the eighteenth floor…and I'm sure those School District brats will, too. H-how many people are gonna be in trouble 'cause of us faking the report on Goliath…?!"

"Th-that's not our fault! We just wanted to scare 'em a bit. Who knew this would happen?!"

Leon glanced at Babel towering before him, hearing some adventurers talking about something suspicious, but knowing that there was no point in dealing with them now. "To think that students would be trapped in the Dungeon like this."

Central Park was in chaos. While adventurers from various familias and instructors from the School District were all running around, he stood there with a platinum armor chest piece.

On his back was a great longsword.

He walked toward the white tower, lamenting the ill-timing for an incident to have happened today, on the day he was away from observation duty in the Dungeon.

"Even I can't just chalk this up as another instance of Aoharu. Please, Leon, save the children who must make the most of their youth!"

"I cannot make any promises when the situation is this dire, but I shall do everything in my power, Lady Idun."

The goddess smiled with faith in the absolute strength of the man who answered her plea with a knightly vow, and then shared everything she knew.

"Currently, *Balder Class* 7th Squad and 3rd Squad are still inside the Dungeon. The 7th are an elite group, so they should be fine, but the worst party is a concern…"

Idun was not a goddess of battle or fate, and she did not hide her unease.

But in response to her concerns, Leon simply smiled.

"Regarding that, I can say with confidence that you need not worry."

"Oh?"

And as he readied his powerful legs, before he raced off, he said, "Since *he* is with the 3rd Squad."

"OOOOOOOOOOOOOOOOOO!"

"Outta my waaaaaaaaay!"

Iglin met the larger liger fang blocking the way head-on with his hammer.

The al-miraj following it and the dungeon worm popping out of a hole in the ground were slashed repeatedly by the dark elf with her twinblades and the prum with his two-handed sword.

"Keep going, everyone!"

Nina unleashed a slashing blade of wind from her magic sword before swiftly using her healing magic.

Her support from the back lines breathed new life into the three vanguards.

Her decisions had been spot-on after she had been entrusted with actual command. In a situation where stamina and Mind could not be wasted, she was carefully toeing the line before activating her magic, supporting the three on the front lines at all times. After the painful experience on the twelfth floor, the party's healer had taken to bringing a magic blade with her, and she quickly began growing into her natural leadership potential.

The pressure from monsters has increased since we dropped down to the sixteenth floor! We had to move Legi up to the front line, so our backs are against the wall now!

Which just made it all the clearer to her that this was both the critical juncture and a terrible predicament.

They were long past the amount of time they had originally planned to spend in the Dungeon. They were breaking their personal best for consecutive battles over and over again, testing their limits and experiencing the Dungeon's true initiation, just as so many other upper-class adventurers had before them.

Their stamina was depleting. And not the sort of stamina that could be recovered with magic. Pushing their minds to the limit over the course of repeated fights, they were starting to lose focus. When a merciless wave of monsters crested on them, a struggle the likes of which they had never experienced at the School District began.

Iglin's cheek was scratched, Legi's dark arms were bare from having her sleeves shredded, Chris's neck was splashed in monster blood and covered in trickles of sweat. And Nina was even worse. Because she was using more magic than anyone, her Mind was at its limit, and a sheen of sweat poured down her body.

If Rapi, waiting right behind her, hadn't been resupplying her with magic potions with perfect timing, she would have suffered Mind Down by now.

We're making progress! It's a tightrope walk, but we're doing it! With Rapi helping, if we can just get through this, I'm sure we can make it! Just one rest would be enough, and we can make it to the eighteenth floor!

With Rapi supporting with the purple moth grenades and all the other items he had brought with him, the 3rd Squad was fighting as one. Right in that moment, the squad was demonstrating an incredible strength.

So please, just let us…!

They could handle enemies from the front somehow. With the three vanguards and her, they could deal with enemies ahead. As long as it was only one direction, they could respond.

So if nothing more would happen…

—But the labyrinth summoned death's scythe, sneering at her prayers.

"Nina, behind!"

Chris, who was fighting in the front, spun around.

His shout was filled with an almost never heard tension.

"Minotaurs!"

Hit in the back by a terrifying howl, Nina stopped breathing for an instant.

Somehow managing to turn around, her emerald eyes saw three minotaurs.

"UUUUOOOOOOOOOOOOOOOOOOOOOOOOOOO!!!"

Now of all times, they faced their first encounter with minotaurs, which unleashed a howl that threatened to paralyze them.

Nina shuddered and held out her magic sword.

And that was the end.

Having reached its limit, cracks ran through the green blade as it shattered audibly.

"______"

Nina froze. Chris and the others were speechless.

The worst possible pincer, as if it had been planned all along.

The three vanguards had their hands full with the monster in front of them. Trying to help her would mean death. And so the first prey of the minotaurs would be none other than the supporter at the back.

The powerless rabbit boy without any fighting strength.

"Ah…"

Despair cracked opened its wide jaw.

The Dungeon roared in laughter.

As Iglin, Legi, and Chris's hearts began to crumble in the moment of failure, Nina screamed out.

"—Run, Rapi!!!"

The boy had only one answer for her cry.

"It's okay."

He slipped his arms from the straps of the backpack.

"I'll manage somehow."

The big backpack fell to the ground with a thud.

He fluidly drew two spare shortswords, one in either hand. And he became like the wind.

"______"

As time slowed for Nina, she saw it.

The minotaur swinging its massive arm down at its prey, and just before it landed...the boy *blurred*. In an instant, with a teleportation that she could only imagine was her eyes deceiving her, the boy appeared right inside the minotaur's range, and his right arm became a silver flash.

BOOM! An unbelievable crash.

A thrust like a cannon going off landed in the minotaur's chest. And then it exploded.

The shadow didn't stop there.

As a cloud of ash scattered, the figure accelerated.

It closed in on the two monsters that froze with the loss of their comrade. This time, as he whizzed by, his left arm became a flash of silver.

An outthrust sword pierced its target in the chest, and another explosion rocked the room.

"OOOOOOOOOOOOOOOOOOO?!"

The final minotaur roared in fear, swinging its massive nature weapon down.

The ground exploded, creating a cloud of dust, but the vorpal bunny was no longer there.

Slipping past the edge of the ax in a bold escape, he slipped behind the minotaur and ended it.

With its magic stone pierced from behind, the minotaur disappeared into a cloud of ash, never realizing its own fate before it was too late.

"...Huh?"

It was over in an instant.

It had been so fast, so overwhelming, that they couldn't comprehend it. No one could even grasp just how strong the boy was.

The labyrinth that had been laughing moments earlier had fallen silent.

Nina, Iglin, Legi, Chris, the other monster, too. As the half-elf girl's lips trembled and let out a single sound, the first to come back to life was the dark-elf girl, who quickly slaughtered the remaining monster.

This time, the combat really was over.

"Hu…huuuuuuuuuuuuuuuuuuuh?!"

The next moment, Iglin shouted as he ran over to the hume-bunny boy.

"What the hell was that?!"

"Ummm…I just tried aiming for the magic stone…"

"Those movements…weren't Level One…!"

"Th-that is…actually, I just leveled up…"

"Why didn't you tell us?!"

"I-I'm sorry."

Legi and Chris joined too, surrounding Rapi, who—though he had held back to avoid revealing himself, all his abilities were massively boosted because of his slayer skill, which had made everything much more powerful against these particular enemies—apologized profusely.

Nina stood there slack-jawed until she regained her senses and raced over, running her hands over Rapi's body, almost hugging him.

"A-are you all right, Rapi?! You're not injured, are you?! Are you really okay?!"

"I-I'm okay, Nina. More importantly, let's take a rest!"

"Huh?"

"We need to recover and then keep moving! While the onslaught of monsters has stopped!"

The 3rd Squad all looked unconvinced, but the situation right now was an emergency. What he was saying was very much right, and their judgment was being impacted by exhaustion, so they just dropped the topic and took a short rest.

Using items, quickly recovering, they set out again.

With Chris taking the lead, using his scouting abilities to check their surroundings, they carefully advanced as fast as they could. Fortunately, they were able to find a hole in the ground before long, and the 3rd Squad quickly reached the seventeenth floor.

"There's a lot about this I don't really like…but with this, we can make it to the eighteenth floor! And if Rapi can fight, we don't have to worry about the back as much!"

"We haven't run into many monsters here, either! The goddesses of fortune are smiling on us!"

More than anything, though it hadn't been planned, Rapi's feat had lit a fire under the 3rd Squad.

Even in this predicament, they had a tailwind boosting them, and their morale had increased. They only had a couple sparse encounters that they were able to charge through without slowing down, continuing forward until they reached the big passage that was the key route through the seventeenth floor.

"Rapi, the path!" Legi called out.

"...All we have to do now is follow the path deeper into the floor."

Rapi spread out the map in both hands and answered frankly. The 3rd Squad's faces lit up with hope. Nina clutched her rod.

"We can make it...! We can do it!"

Yeah, with this, we can make it. We can make it, but...

I look around us while listening to Nina.

The path is wide, and the ceiling is high. As we walk down the passage even a giant could pass through, we stop seeing even the shadows of monsters.

It's quiet.

Too quiet.

Even with the hypothesis that the Dungeon is prioritizing regeneration over birthing new monsters due to the massive collapse affecting so much of the fifteenth floor, the silence is deafening.

And I *recognize* this silence.

"...Ngh?"

The others notice the unnatural situation, too.

Nina, Iglin, Chris, and Legi all look around nervously as they run, and then glance back at me.

Standing at the tail of the party, I just nod back at them. We have no choice but to proceed now. Turning back around, still filled with serious concern, our footsteps echo in the passage.

It isn't that monsters aren't appearing. They aren't coming out. As if they're waiting—or as if they are dreading the birth of *something.*

This is... The Guild board's information really was...

There is a terrible pain in the back of my head at a scene that feels awfully familiar.

I grimace, but even so, I push forward with the rest of the squad. Because of the silence, everyone's breathing resounds in the passage. The stones kicked by boots clatter, disappearing into the quiet darkness.

A chill strikes the squad.

Chris in the lead starts running faster, giving in to the disquieting air. Nina and the others accelerate to match speed, telling themselves that they can make it as long as the silence holds, just like a certain rookie passing through here did half a year ago.

And then—

"!!!"

"This is the Great Wall of Sorrows...!"

We reach a massive room.

The walls and ceiling are made of an enormous, twisted rock, but the wall on the left alone is different. Legi and Iglin are speechless. That beautiful, smooth, unblemished wall, the root of adventurers' sorrows.

"Don't stop, Chris! Forward—" I start to say.

But this time, truly ready to crush the party...

Crack.

"Gh—"

It happens.

That noise.

Nina and the others turn.

A giant crack appears, running vertically through the wall like a lightning bolt.

"—RUN!!!"

Urged on by my shout, they all dash.

We cut through the massive room, but the cruel cry of the shattering wall is faster.

The crumbling noise accelerates. Their faces grow pale as the noise assaults their ears. The wheezing, painful, groaning creaks become a thunderous torrent and a cry of destruction.

The next instant, it is born with a terrible crash.

"UUUUUOOOOOOOOOOOOOOOOOOOOOOOOOOOOOOOO!!!"

Goliath, the Monster Rex!

The gigantic baby that was just born notices the sickly pale students below it and lets out an earsplitting roar.

"——————————*!!!*"

The giant runs with a loud shout.

Its tree-trunk-sized legs break the ground with each step, causing tremendous quakes.

"H-Hurrrrrrryyyyyyyy!!!"

Iglin's panicky shout rings out.

Bursting into sweat as they wring out the last of their strength, everyone begins sprinting at full speed.

Goliath is in fierce pursuit!

Just like six months ago! A rerun of the deadly chase!

—But this time, my mind at least is calm.

Just run, the by-the-book approach. Counterattacking is out of the question. The party's safety is the top priority.

Even if I dropped the limitation of hiding my identity, the only real choice I have is avoiding a fight with the Monster Rex. My level is higher than it now, but fighting a floor boss is different from fighting a normal monster. I could make any number of mistakes. And even if I hang back as a rear guard, it would be moot if 3rd Squad runs into danger later because they don't have me. This isn't the time for an adventure. Risk should be avoided as much as possible.

Judging the distance between the giant staring me down at the back of the party, I continually calculate the leeway I have as the distance closes.

Run. Run. Run.

Nina and the others race like their lives depend on it, because they do, putting as much distance between themselves and the massive, murderous pressure closing in on us as they can.

Abandoning all thoughts, fear, and exhaustion, they just focus on the exit in front of us.

But then, caught in a tremor, a single prum topples over.

"Argh!"

""""Chris?!""""

Chris's face twists in fear.

Despair grips the others.

Without hesitation, I drop my backpack.

"Hyaaah?!"

"Go, everyone!"

"""!!!"""

Without slowing down, I pick up his small body. Carrying Chris in my arms, I shout at the other three, who froze for just a second.

Stunned, the 3rd Squad faces forward again and pushes themselves to the limit.

Holding Chris, who is bright red as he clings to me, I kick off the stone floor, too.

"Run, run, ruuuuuuuuuuuuuuuuuuun!!!"

Iglin's desperate shout is drowned out by the terrible noise of the giant, and as I run at the back of the party, I have to make the terrible decision.

—We won't make it.

—That pause was fatal.

—Goliath's attack is going to erupt before we can make it into the connecting passage.

My arms are full. I can't cast Firebolt. I blundered.

"Oooo."

There is a big breeze from behind. The giant has swung its arm up over its head. The blow that will shatter everything is coming.

I can hear the desperation in Nina's, Iglin's, and Legi's breathing. They can't even look back anymore.

Chris's eyes are screwed up tight, and he's clinging to my battle uniform as if he can't bear it.

So I use the brief moment when no one can sense it and let out a little chime.

One second's charge.

The pure white light enchanting my right leg.

Before the iron hammer of destruction unleashed overhead can kill me, I slam my right foot down on the ground.

"Fly!"

It explodes.

My explosive acceleration cracks the ground, filling the distance between us and the passage that is too far to reach. Slamming into Iglin's back, I push him, Nina, and Legi forward—just as the destructive blow lands right behind us.

"OOOOOOOOOOOOOOOOOOOOOOOOOOOOOOOOOOOOOOOOOOOOOOO!!!"

The wave of destruction, the violent blast of air barrels into the passage at the end of the floor.

We fly.

A repeat of that crash into the narrow cave that I didn't really want to remember.

"Kyaaaaaaaaaaah?! Rapiiiiiiiiii!"

Holding Chris tight to my chest even as he lets out a girlish scream, the world spins two, three times. We roll along with Nina, Iglin, and Legi, deeper and deeper into the cavern. The shock falls on all sides, from all angles, but this time I remain conscious, sliding down the gentle slope at a terrible speed, until finally—

""""Ugh?!""""

Shooting out of the exit, the 3rd Squad is thrown sliding across the ground before finally skidding to a stop.

Tears well up in Nina's eyes as she splays out facing up, Iglin is curled up, hugging and kissing the ground, and Legi is vacantly staring, her cute face visible after losing her mask in the chaos.

And finally, I wince from the pain in my back while setting Chris down.

The prum who is even smaller than Lilly is unconscious.

...It's...noon...I guess?

My eyes narrow at the light pouring down from above.

Standing up, as if drawn by the light, I see the broad field of green before us and the crystal mums growing from the ceiling.

"The Under Resort..."

Ten minutes later, after I divide the last potion between everyone, 3rd Squad finally starts to move again.

"What do you mean we can't stay at a lodge?!"

Back in gentleman mode, Iglin's angry voice echoes through the wood-and-crystal-lined streets. Standing across from him, unshaken by the stern-faced dwarven menace (despite being a student) is the one-eyed leader of the inn town.

"What place in the world allows boarders who can't pay? Huh?"

"Fifty thousand valis is extortionate!"

"Rivira's a classy place, a resort that puts any cheap hole-in-the-wall aboveground to shame. If you don't like it then git, you School District brats."

"Gh...?!"

Sticking his pinky in his ear, Mr. Bors tells us his demand, while Iglin's blood vessels look almost ready to burst in rage. Behind him, Legi and Chris are booing and making a fuss while I, carrying Iglin's hammer on my back, just sneak a wry chuckle.

After sitting around stunned and unable to move for a while, the 3rd Squad made its way to the western end of the floor from the entrance in the south, and with great effort, finally reached Rivira on the edge of a cliff and wetlands around night.

With the glow from the ceiling starting to fade and darkness spreading, the squad tried to get lodging, but the result is as you can see. Apparently, Mr. Bors—or really, pretty much all the residents of Rivira—dislike the students from the School District. They aren't even willing to deal with us.

Well, they will, but they're demanding an insane fee.

"If you gimme your weapons and the gear and clothes on your back, I wouldn't be against letting you stay a night."

"Gh…! Don't toy with us! We have to go back through the Dungeon to get back! Who would hand over their weapons and gear?!"

Iglin unleashes a tirade that is almost spittle-flecked, but Mr. Bors just turns away.

Nina and the others look troubled and prepare to search for another lodge, clinging to hope.

The ruffians' welcome is…a little harsh. Befitting the situation.

Waiting until I am sure the others can't see me, I go over to Mr. Bors, who started spontaneously cleaning his weapon.

"Umm, Mr. Bors."

"Ahhh? Who said you could call me that, brat? You ignorant kids can—huh?" As he starts going off, I raise the fringe of hair covering my eyes. "You're Rabbit Foot?! What are you doing dressed like that?!"

"Shh! It'll be bad if I get caught…! Don't let them hear you…!"

I beg him to keep his voice low, and his eyes spin for a moment, but he quickly breaks into a grin. He gestures for me to come behind the counter and into the back.

"You got dragged into some new pain in the ass, didn't you?"

"I wouldn't say that…But it's a bit complicated."

"If you're stuck protecting those brats, it's way more of a pain in the ass than your average quest."

I grimace even more as he pounds my back with his big hand. If you were just willing to deal with the students this amicably…

"So? You want in?"

"Yes. Could we borrow a room? I will pay you back for it later."

"The thing is, I said all that to those brats, but the truth is, there isn't any room anywhere. You came here because of the collapse earlier, right? We're all full up. Between the people who came down from there and people on their way up from exploration who can't get out, there's no vacancies."

O-oh…now that you mention it…

I had sort of sensed it from the mess on the fifteenth floor, but with all the routes back to the surface blocked, adventurers have no choice but to come here.

"In that case, could you sell us some gear for camping outdoors? We can just find someplace safe and take care of ourselves..."

"Yeah, that I can do. I owe you big time, so I'll even give you a deal!"

I can't help smiling a bit when he adds "just a little one," but there is one other thing I've been wondering about.

"About the Goliath that just came out on the seventeenth floor. Do you know what's happening with it? I imagine there are other people who will be coming here, so it would probably be best to take care of it soon, but..."

"You're too nice for your own good, or maybe too hardworking. But you don't gotta worry there. The tremors from the seventeenth floor are gone, so it's definitely down already. From what Mord said when he tumbled into town, some folks from the School District fought it..."

"Ah, Mr. Mord's here too?"

It has been a while since the 3rd Squad, exhausted as it was, actually made it all the way to Rivira, and I don't have any time to go back to the seventeenth floor, but hearing that, I can finally breathe easily. We should have reached the eighteenth floor sooner, so they must have passed on along the way, since we took the safe route into the plain in the center of the floor first instead of traveling straight west along the water's edge.

I was planning to leave them here with Mr. Bors and then go out to fight myself, but...

"More importantly, with Goliath rampaging a bit, the lines of contact are broken. I've got my guys out digging too, but the whole cavern is collapsed, so it'll take time to get things reopened."

"Meaning...we'll have to stay awhile here on the eighteenth floor."

"Yeah. If you're camping, then I'd recommend a spot around the lake just down from here. The monsters hang around in the forest where all the food is, so you don't have to worry too much about bein' attacked. If you want quick access to food, then you can set up camp in the forest like *Loki Familia*, but…"

"Ah-ha-ha…if you don't mind, I'd love to buy some food, too."

"All right, we've got a deal! Though, with you around, they'll be fine campin' out wherever!"

Mr. Bors gives me another hearty pat on the back, and I smile awkwardly one more time before buying the camping gear and food. The reason he doesn't take my familia emblem is because he trusts me not to run out on my tab, I guess.

When he disappears into the storage room to get everything together…I think back to what happened on the floor above, wondering whether I should go help.

"You really have a habit of getting mixed up in incidents, Bell Cranell."

"Whoa?!"

A voice suddenly echoes in the empty room.

Wait, that voice…

"…Is that…Fels? You're invisible…?"

"Yes. I came to check on things. Ouranos's orders. The irregular earlier was just too large. And seeing a student who looked an awful lot like a certain record holder, here I am."

Invisible thanks to the use of a magic item, Fels is apparently right in front of me. I guess Fels is just that good, but I didn't sense anyone at all.

Maybe I let my guard down just a little too much when we made it to Rivira.

"But how are you here? All the paths through the fifteenth floor should be…"

"I came through Knossos."

Ah…I forgot.

Fels has the key, so using that, Knossos could be…

"…Do you know the details of the situation?"

"Leon and the others have saved almost everyone who was trapped in the Cave Labyrinth already. I have put a few adventurers to sleep and am safeguarding them in Knossos as well. As for students, your

group is the last to be found, so you needn't worry anymore, Bell Cranell."

Fels sees right through me and my plans to return to the Dungeon, letting me know my concerns are misplaced.

"Once the connection between the seventeenth and eighteenth floors is open, the Dungeon's routes will all be restored. Until then, you may enjoy yourself in this paradise. If it was just you, I could let you through back aboveground, but I'm afraid I cannot allow students through Knossos."

"No worries. Thank you very much, Fels."

Right after that—

"Kept you waiting!"

—Mr. Bors comes back in.

"Pardon me," Fels says in a whisper and moves away as I take the food and camping gear and leave the inn.

Enjoy myself in this paradise, huh…?

For now, I should find Nina and the others.

"Is this really okay, Rapi…? All this gear…"

"It's fine. He was willing to lend it to us once I explained the situation."

I smile and fib a little as Nina looks at me in concern.

Like Mr. Bors suggested, we set up two simple tents on the bank of the lake—it goes much easier this time with my experience from camping out during the expedition.

The pseudo-sky has gotten nice and dark overhead, and the crystal stars are glittering. Taking a deep breath and looking at the illusory Dungeon night sky, Nina lowers her eyes.

"If that's true, then I'm glad…but you're really saving us at every turn."

With her long face, it feels like she's seen through my lie, and my heart skips a beat.

"Ninaaa! Rapiii! My ultra-spectacular dinner is ready!"

Then Chris suddenly calls out from the campfire where the others are taking care of dinner. I feel bad, but I quickly use the opportunity to escape this conversation and head toward the fire.

We're camping on the crescent shore at the northern edge of the lake. The tents are on the border between the shore and the plains, and the campfire is nearer to the lake's edge, which is where the other three are waiting.

"Still, though…you're really incredible, Rapi," Iglin says earnestly.

"Eh? Wh-what? Where did that come from?"

Using the food Mr. Bors shared with us, dinner is a simple risotto, a warm egg soup, and a block of portable rations to fill our stomachs.

As we sit around the fire, for some reason, everyone is looking at me.

"We're used to camping out from Fieldwork and Combat Volunteer deployments, but you're so good at dealing with stuff, and you even managed to get some things out of that nasty adventurer."

"Mhmm, incredible…"

"Is there a trick to negotiations?!"

Legi nods too, and Chris excitedly leans forward, expecting something great. I struggle with how to explain the situation and end up making a pathetic excuse.

"Umm…just keep asking, I guess?"

"What's that supposed to mean?"

Iglin looks exasperated, but Chris just laughs.

"I can definitely see Rapi doing that!"

Finally, once we finish eating, as if moving onto the main topic…

"You said you want to be an adventurer, right?" Iglin asks. "So have you decided on your path?"

"Wh-why are…?"

"I can't help it. It's annoying, but you're incredible, even though you're just a supporter…I just have to know."

I'm a little stunned, but with him looking so earnestly at me, I'm at a loss for how to respond.

To think he would ever ask me something like this…Does that mean he's acknowledged us as being a real party? But…I don't *want* to be an adventurer; I actually *am* an adventurer…

If I were really a student right now, I would probably still say *Hestia Familia*, but I can't afford to be caught, either…so after struggling with it for a few moments, I answer with the next familia I could see myself considering joining.

"Umm, *Loki Familia*, I guess…?"

I think Nina's ears prick up at that, but Iglin just keeps going without picking up on it.

"I guess that makes sense if you want to be an adventurer. I've heard their admission rates are insanely low, but I've got a feeling you can make it. If they don't take you, then they must be blind."

"Th-thanks…?"

My cheeks start to heat up a bit at that surprisingly strong compliment. I'm on the verge of collapsing into a fidgety mess, so I quickly try to shift the topic.

"Umm, what about you, Iglin? Have you decided your path?"

"I'm going to be a blacksmith."

"Eh?! Even though you're in Combat Studies?!"

My voice cracks hysterically as Iglin proudly explains his logic.

"Right now, the greatest blacksmith in the mortal realm is Tsubaki Collbrande. It's something that master smith once said. 'You have to be able to go down into the deep levels to test your weapons.' So I'm working on my smithing skills while learning how the people who will use my weapons see things, all while aiming to become a master smith!"

Ms. Tsubaki, take responsibility for what you said…!

"Mmmm, then…what about you, Legi?"

"Assassin."

"Mmmm?!"

Not really knowing how to respond to Iglin, I shift the topic to Legi, but she just offers another answer that is even harder to react to.

"I'm waiting…for a high elf. A dark one. An amazing high elf… who'll destroy the white elves."

"Eh?"

"That's why I didn't make friends. I want to be powerful…by myself. But it wasn't enough…for the Dungeon."

"!"

"I realized...strength in numbers. It's so obvious. So...thank you, Rapi, everyone."

"Legi..."

"Now...I want to train...soldiers."

If I trust in the language-deciphering capabilities I've refined while dealing with Mr. Hegni, then Legi wants to be an assassin because she wishes for the restoration of a dark high elf who will defeat the white elves, who are overwhelmingly superior in number.

I don't know how she ended up entering the School District, but even though she originally wanted the strength to fight alone, during her time in the Dungeon, she's learned how brittle fighting alone can be. So now she wants to become an instructor who trains soldiers...is what I think she's saying.

"I'm going to be an imperial knight! I'll change our land from the inside, cleansing what has rotted away under the rule of colonizers, restoring the name of Cormac and the lost pride of Ulster!"

Chris, chiming in confidently even though no one asked, is the one with the most levelheaded yet grand goal, and though it's a bit rude to think this, I'm definitely surprised to hear that coming from him.

"I'm going to restore the glory of my people's proudest band of knights! I'll be more amazing than even Braver!"

"M-more than Mr. Finn? That's a little..."

"I can do it! Because I'm a prum who's made it to Level Two already! And, well, if Braver insists, I guess I could join *Loki Familia*! Then I could be with you, and you could keep being my guardian beast!"

I smile watching Chris's chest swell with pride as he closes his eyes, just like the first time we met.

And finally, everyone's gaze turns to her.

"You know, I don't think I've ever heard you mention it. What are you aiming for, Nina?"

"........."

Nina's response as she looks down at the cup of soup still in her hands is silence.

After a few moments, she looks up and flashes a lonely smile.

"Nothing, really..."

"........."

Silence fills the air.

Out of all of us, she alone seems lost.

Exactly ten minutes.

Ten minutes since Iglin and I were on guard when the next shift came and I took a nap.

Compared to the five-minute rest in the deep floors, ten minutes here on the tranquil eighteenth floor is luxurious. My thoughts are clear again, as if the muddy slog from before has been washed away. Physically, I'm really that exhausted to begin with. That's just part of being Level 5 now.

I slip out of the tent, careful not to wake up Iglin, who is sleeping soundly...and see a single girl sitting in front of the fire.

"Nina."

"Rapi...? We just changed lookouts a few minutes ago..."

"I just couldn't really sleep...Where is Chris?"

"In our tent. He kept blinking and looked sleepy, so I told him to rest."

The two tents should theoretically be split between boys and girls, but...well, I guess it's okay if it's Chris?

Nina's long, brown hair sways as she turns back around and stares out at the lake in front of her. After asking for permission, I sit down next to her, leaving a little bit of space between us.

"Nina...did something happen?"

"........."

"Earlier...you seemed not exactly in high spirits."

She doesn't answer. The girl who was so bright and cheerful and kind to everyone at the School District is just quietly, coldly staring out at the lake.

"If you have something bothering you…I can listen. You've helped me so much all this time."

Working up my courage, I push in. And also, I tell her that I want to repay her.

After not moving since I sat down, Nina slumps her head.

It looks almost like she is burying her face in her lap, but then, her one jade lock of hair trembles, and she slowly looks up.

"I just…can't find a dream."

I turn in surprise and see Nina still looking forward, smiling.

A weak, delicate smile that might crumble and fade any moment.

"I think everyone who enrolls at the School District has some sort of worry or anxiety. Not knowing what they want to be, not knowing their future…but the School District lets those students see all sorts of dreams."

"…Dreams?"

"Mhmm. So many countries, cultures, jobs, research…the shape of the world. And as students discover the goals they want to achieve, they begin to leave."

The word *dream* echoes in my ear as Nina murmurs softly.

"So…maybe it is just hard for people who enrolled without any real reason."

The smile on her lips looks terribly self-deprecating.

"I have an older sister."

"…That woman at the Guild Headquarters?"

"Mhmm. Her name is Eina. My wonderful sister."

I know, though for now I pretend not to.

"I'm not the only one who thinks so, either. Everyone is proud of her."

And now, there is clearly a shadow in her smile.

"I can't remember a time before she was enrolled at the School District. I never got a chance to see her face or hear her voice. So that day in the Guild…was my first time meeting her."

"………"

"But I already knew she was amazing. Everyone in our hometown always said so. She's so smart; she's so bright. Whenever I heard those stories, I was always so proud of her, as if her achievements were my own. Father and Mother, too…they were always so proud of her."

Does she know what her face looks like right now? Does she have the courage to peer into the water and see for herself?

"Our mother…is frail. My sister went to the School District for Mother, and for Father, who is always working so hard to take care of Mother. To get a good job. My sister might not have had a dream, but she did at least have a proper goal. And I…didn't. The reason I enrolled in the School District is because she did. Because I just thought I should follow the path that she took…that's all I was thinking when I took the exam for the School District."

My eyes widen.

Nina confesses that she's simply been following in Miss Eina's footsteps.

"Coming here so casually, enrolling, and trudging along all this time…I regret it."

Hearing her say she regrets it stuns me. As passionate about studying and as hardworking as she is, has Nina been suffering all this time?

"Do you know the first course I took, Rapi?"

"…I don't, sorry…"

"Theological Synthesis."

"!!!"

That's the subject she advised me against when I was picking my courses.

"Because my sister passed it, and everyone praised her for it. So I tried it, too. I thought, surely I can do it."

"………"

"But I was wrong. That wasn't true at all. I couldn't understand anything. I couldn't learn to read hieroglyphs like her."

She continues sharing her past, painfully, as if cutting into herself with each word.

—It's a little hard to recommend it…

—The word is only around one in ten people who take it pass…and even fewer people learn how to properly interpret hieroglyphs.

The advice she gave me…that wasn't something she had heard from others. It was something she had experienced firsthand.

"I took the practice exam for a job at the Guild, too. Chasing after my sister again. But no matter how much I studied, I couldn't get good marks. I couldn't compare to her. So I ran away again, just like with Theological Synthesis."

"………"

"My sister was so amazing that even after she graduated from the School District, lots of people still remember her. Just like back home. So I keep copying her, just following the path that she took…but I can't be like her. She's far more incredible than someone like me."

Her eyes are starting to become like fountains. Tears fill her emerald eyes, accompanying the flow of emotions she can no longer hold back.

"I did everything my sister did when she was younger, so I just blindly followed in her footsteps. Thinking that would be easier. But…it wasn't."

"………"

"I just copied her and didn't decide anything for myself…I'm so pathetic."

…You're wrong.

She's probably misunderstanding.

Lord Balder and the other deities at the entrance interview, when they heard her desire to enter the School District, would have been able to know if she was lying.

So the real reason she entered the School District is…

"I was in the Education Department originally…but I switched to Combat Studies."

"Eh?"

"It was just a coincidence…Completely by chance, Professor Leon saw me studying for Magic Theory and spoke to me. He gave me a staff to hold and told me to try channeling magic. I managed to cast a spell. And I was better at athletics than I expected, too…And lots of people told me how good I was."

"…So you switched to Combat Studies?"

"Mhmm…When I heard my sister struggled with athletics… I became obsessed. I trained my combat abilities, not because I'd found a dream, or because I liked it, but just to protect the little place where I could be me."

That is probably the thing that feels the worst to Nina.

She's ashamed of herself for staying in Combat Studies, not because she has some higher goal, like Miss Eina, or a dream, like Iglin or Legi or Chris, but because it's just an escape.

It's all to protect her sense of self, so when we talked about our paths, she began to feel like she was being left behind.

"My sister's letters came to me, at the School District. At first, I wrote back…but a lot happened, and I stopped being able to write."

"………"

"I thought I was lame for only copying her…and I hated myself for clinging to things she couldn't do just to protect myself…!"

"…"

"Reading my nice sister's letters, I couldn't write anything back…!"

A sob creeps into her voice.

Clear droplets flow from her eyes and down her cheeks, landing on her slender legs. Burying her face in her lap, her shoulders tremble and her fingers clutch her arms.

Venting everything that she has been holding in all this time, she cries.

I don't say anything. I can't sidle close to her, and I can't hold her shoulders or wipe away her tears.

I don't have an older brother. I don't have any siblings. Gramps was my only family. I can't sympathize. I can't even begin to understand the anxiety and pain she is feeling.

But…

"Agh…"

Taking my overshirt off, I put the battered battle uniform over her shoulders. Just so she doesn't get any colder. The surface of the lake is rippling, as if a breeze is blowing. It feels like the temperature has dropped a little bit.

And moving a little—really just the tiniest bit—closer, I sit down again.

"Nina...even if you hate yourself..."

Thinking back to all the time I've spent at the School District, I just put my honest feelings into words.

"It's thanks to you that I've been able to enjoy all of this."

"!!!"

"Thanks to you, I've learned the joy of studying. And thanks to you...I found a new goal for myself."

I sit cross-legged on the ground, not looking at her, my eyes fixed on the surface of the lake.

"And you've helped the three of them so many times too during the Dungeon Practical."

"Gh...!"

"I think the way you try to be kind to everyone like your sister... has helped a lot of people."

The gleam in the sky fades, as if the stars are falling.

The crystals that are actually falling from the ceiling create ripples in the lake. Dozens, hundreds of little ripples.

Like beautiful tears.

Nina looks down again, her voice trembling...and then, she slowly looks up and turns to me.

It is small, but there is a little smile blooming on her face.

"Rapi...you sure know how to make a girl cry."

"...Sorry..."

"It's fine...I'm just a little surprised."

"...Sorry..."

"Ha-ha, why are you apologizing?"

"...I don't know, but I'm sorry..."

"Don't be. I'm...happy. Thank you, Rapi."

I don't know what to say, seeing her smile, the damp tearstains still visible on her cheeks.

I'm still looking forward, but my face is completely flushed.

Noticing that, she giggles softly. She slides over just a little bit. I start to move away just a little bit, but her outstretched fingers grab me, and I give up.

My face is still red from embarrassment. It's really hot considering I'm only wearing a sleeveless undershirt.

As the idle question of whether Lady Idun might come do something about this crosses my mind, the two of us continue looking out at the gleaming blue lake.

"I think," Nina starts, speaking in a tone different from earlier, "people who have found what they want to do must be happy."

"Hmm...?"

"Lots of bad things might happen, and it might be hard to keep going at the things you like. But even so, I think that's true for everyone."

Looking over, I see her face in profile. She is looking up above the lake, at the sea of crystals that make up the night sky here.

"I think people who walk straight ahead, instead of aimlessly wandering, deciding for no real reason, are dazzling. All of you are so much more amazing than someone like me."

"........."

"Maybe it's no place for a half-elf without a dream to comment, but..." The girl without a dream to chase smiles a little as she peers up at the fake night sky. "But even so, I think people with dreams are happy...and cool."

To me, she looks almost sad...or maybe...hollow.

"........."

Following her gaze, my eyes narrow as I stare at the sky, fake, but beautiful nonetheless.

The next morning.

The blue crystals in the ceiling start to shine and brighten, emitting light that resembles early morning aboveground. After Nina drifted off to sleep, lying down with her head on my lap, I stood watch by myself.

I kept the fire going all night so she wouldn't get cold.

"...Aoharu."

"...Aoharu."

Legi comes out of her tent, walking over to us, speaking Idun-ese with a flat expression.

My eyes glaze over as I decide to match the greeting.

"...Hey, Legi. If we get the chance for a little bit of adventure later, would you be interested?"

Not understanding the point of the question, Legi cocks her head a bit, but adjusting her mask, she nods.

"It's the Under Resort...after all...might as well see...the new... together."

I smile and thank her.

Careful not to wake Nina up, I leave her with Legi and head to Rivira.

"You've got some really weird tastes."

When Mr. Bors hears my request, he looks fairly exasperated.

"Is it too much...?"

When I smile awkwardly and look up a little pleadingly, he grins.

"Not like we're going to get the path between floors cleared today anyway. I've got nothing to do, so I'll go along with it! I'll say it as many times as I have to, but I owe you more than I can ever repay!"

He wraps his thick arm around my neck and makes a little circle with his fingers.

"No point looking a gift horse in the mouth! We can make it a proper protection quest!"

I thank him as the thick arm around my neck threatens to strangle me.

When I get back to the surface, I'll have to work hard to pay all this back from my own wallet.

"""""Field trip?!"""""

When I say that after coming back from Rivira, everyone looks stunned.

"Mhmm. Since we came all the way to the eighteenth floor, would you like to go a little deeper?"

"I can understand the temptation, but…the Dungeon's a completely different beast past this floor, right?!"

"There have been squads who made it to the eighteenth floor in incidents, but no other students have ever explored deeper! Mrgh?! Meaning, this is my chance to leave my mark in new territory?!"

"I said I wanted adventure…but danger?"

"R-right, Rapi. It was so difficult just getting here…"

The party is largely against the idea. But there's also a bit of interest if it can be done safely, judging from Chris and Legi. So…

"When I went to Rivira, there were some upper-class adventurers who were heading down. They offered to let us come with them if we're willing to help out…"

"""…!"""

"And if we can bring back some drops, we might get higher marks…"

"""…!"""

Nina and Chris, followed by Iglin and Legi, all react to my explanation.

Even though it's my idea, it still feels a little crazy. Miss Eina would never let me hear the end of it if she found out. But at the same time, it feels safe, too.

Ordinarily, no matter what level you are, entering a floor you've never seen is dangerous. But with Mr. Bors and all those second-tier adventurers who have so much experience protecting the party, I'm sure we can safely go at least several floors below this one.

As long as I work hard to support them too, I might be able to show them something they've never seen.

"Heeey! We're here!"

"The adventurers look like they're ready to go…so what do you want to do?"

There are at least twenty upper-class adventurers waving as they approach the camp.

Seeing that, the members of the 3rd Squad look at each other, and after thinking over it long and hard, they decide to go.

"Th-these weapons are amazing! Even though they've been used so roughly this whole time…there aren't any nicks or cracks!"

Seeing one of the adventurers from Rivira handle a large mammoth fool without issue, Iglin, hammer in hand, shouts in wonder. What particularly draws his attention are the adventurers' weapons.

"Don't underestimate Orario's weapons. They're way tougher than any of those fancy things you guys make at the School District!"

"Focusing on durability more than the cutting edge? No, there isn't any compromise on the strength, either…!"

Getting permission to check the animal-man's weapon, Iglin immediately starts taking advantage of the study opportunity.

I guess that's not something a future blacksmith can pass up. He isn't the only one getting worked up. Chris and Legi have commented in surprise several times already about what the adventurers are using and the way they fight.

"This potion is way more effective than the ones provided by the Compounding Department ! It tastes awful, though!"

"Wait…what was that?"

"Just using the monster's fire to ignite it. Weapon and item strength all comes down to how you use them."

The three of them are stunned by the knowledge and wisdom of the adventurers they previously looked down on as ruffians.

And since it is technically a quest, Mr. Bors and the others aren't doing anything rough and are carefully protecting the 3rd Squad from all sides, even though they don't really like students. I won't say it's like a tour bus, but it is going smoothly.

"Hey, Rapi! What is that?! That mushroom's bigger than a house!"

"It's a poison mushroom, apparently. I think I've heard it's edible if you have a good enough Resistance ability…"

"It's edible?!"

And Nina is getting excited at all the new things she is seeing, too.

At the School District, information about the Dungeon beyond the Cave Labyrinth isn't available to students, so everything is exciting, wondrous, and teeming with the unknown to them.

There are all sorts of mysteries and fantasies lurking in a single moment in the Dungeon. That is what I wanted them to know.

It's a little haughty, and maybe just my selfishness, but I wanted Iglin and them, and Nina especially, to be interested in some part of it.

I'm sure that is what the concept of a field trip—what Professor Leon mentioned—is really about.

Opportunities like this could bring about a new sort of goal or dream.

The location is the twenty-fourth floor. The deepest part of the middle floors. Legi and the others can't hide their tension.

"Hey, Nina. Yesterday, you said you only just copied your sister and that you don't have a goal…but I don't think that's true."

"Huh?"

As we descend into a faintly blue cavern, Nina is right behind me.

"I think…you want to be something other than what Miss Eina is."

"!"

I can sense her breath catching as I keep walking forward.

I'm sure she's been compared to Miss Eina ever since she was young. Compared in some way or another to the bright older sister whose face and voice she didn't know.

I think children are more sensitive and sharper than adults imagine.

And Nina, who was probably smarter than most kids, became very conscious of the comparisons those adults made, even if they didn't mean it that way, and built up a lot of stress without realizing it.

I doubt the adults had any bad intentions. But after being compared in everything, feeling uneasy in a way she couldn't comprehend, becoming so nervous she could no longer grasp what her parents were really saying to her, Nina enrolled at the School District.

But I think she also misunderstood something while doing that.

She's decided that she's just following Miss Eina's path because she doesn't have her own dream, that this is just a bad habit she's aimlessly fallen into…but I'm sure it's because she's desperate to show everyone that she's even more amazing than Miss Eina, to get them to acknowledge her.

Rivalry, jealousy, and aspiration.

Even experiencing so many failures and setbacks, Nina still hasn't let go of her true goal.

"So you don't need to hate yourself."

She believed that if she got better scores and had greater achievements than Miss Eina, people would say how great she was instead of her sister.

She wants to scream for all the world to hear that she is Nina Tulle.

"You have the things you are good at. You should be proud of them. Because you're an amazing girl who doesn't lose even to Miss Eina."

"Ahhh…"

Reaching the edge of the cave, I turn around, and Nina stops, dumbstruck.

Mr. Bors and the others in front look back dubiously as she freezes and the rest of the 3rd Squad stops moving.

I hold out my hand as she stays frozen in place.

"You're here because even though you thought you were only running away, you never stopped trying your best. So, shall we?"

Finally, after several seconds, she slowly, hesitantly holds out her hand. Taking it, I lead her out of the cave.

"——"

What appears before us is the Great Falls, the largest waterfall in the Dungeon.

"This is amaziiiiiiiing!!!"

"Whoooooooooooooooa!!!"

"…Wow."

Iglin, Chris, and Legi were all full of excitement.

And Nina's eyes shot wide open too; she was awed by the sublime sight.

The gemlike falls extended through so many floors, it looked like it might pass through the entire world. The endless spray of water splattered against crystals, like a scene in ancient myth telling of the grand ocean.

Blue, inlaid, gleaming.

Beautiful, cruel, majestic.

And expanding out far below was the New World and the Water Metropolis.

"Incredible…"

After losing themselves in the great falls for a minute, their excitement continued even as they started moving again.

Masses of blue crystals seemingly carved out of the ocean, but different from those on the eighteenth floor. An eternal current where white eels and mermaids that all looked like sisters swam, while vibrant coral and blue petals formed fantastical images. It was so enchanting. The students' chests were getting hammered by the new and the unknown that surrounded them.

The adventurers protecting them didn't leave anything to chance, either. Relying on their plentiful experience, they were always on guard, taking out monsters before any could become a problem. And more than anything, this was a field trip to experience something new rather than a search for magic stones and drop items. Taking the shortest route possible, they continued forward, forward, peering into a different world. They were lucky as well that they hadn't run into as many monsters, and they reached the waterfall basin on the twenty-fifth floor unbelievably quickly.

"It's so beautiful…"

Looking down from right near the entrance to the floor, the Great Falls were undoubtedly sublime, but looking up from the basin, it was utterly breathtaking.

They'd never seen anything like it before, even while sailing around the world with the School District.

Nina felt like she could begin to understand why adventurers might be enthralled by the Dungeon where they were always risking their lives.

"How is it, Nina?"

"Rapi…what is this…?"

"A reward, I guess?"

"Huh…?"

"A reward for you and everyone else. For how hard you've worked."

The boy who usually felt like a little kid smiled like a reliable, kind older brother who had his eyes hidden behind his hair.

"This is a present for you, who worked so impossibly hard and managed to find something you were good at, even if you still haven't found your dream."

"…!"

"Because you are in the 3rd Squad, and because you've become strong, we were able to give this to you. This is the proof of your growth. Even if you continued to fail, even if you didn't manage to achieve what you set out to do, because you've grown stronger, we were able to experience this new world," the rabbit boy who was their guide explained. "Nina, I can't say anything grand about what your dream might be or what you should do to find a goal. But…I think if a person can be inspired by something, anything, then that person is blessed."

"I-inspired…?"

"Yes. Excited, passionate, making your heart race, wanting to cry…if you can feel something like that, if something inspires you, then you can keep your head up and try just a little more."

He spoke carefully, as if recalling his own experiences, digesting each and every memory.

"If this present gives you a little bit of courage…then that's enough."

"Rapi…"

Finally, he smiled awkwardly. So awkwardly, and even a little lamely, that it was clear even with the hair covering his eyes.

Nina's heart ached. Even though she had been so sad last night, it was so warm now. She couldn't move her lips right at all, and she clutched her right hand to her chest.

"—Oh! You're in luck, brats! It's a blue dragon!"

Just then, Bors called out as he peered deeper down the falls.

Nina and the others turned around for a moment, and far below, down past the twenty-sixth floor, a slender figure was swimming through the air, rising into view.

"Hide!" Bors ordered.

The students were caught by surprise, but they obeyed the adventurers who were already running and hid behind clusters of crystals jutting out of the ground like boulders.

Moments later, the dragon rose to the twenty-fifth-floor basin and continued its ascent.

Nina and Rapi watched it in awed silence.

"Is that…an aurora?!"

The long dragon was maybe ten meders in length. It had blue-and-white scales and long, winglike fins that were moving slowly as it swam through the air. But the most eye-catching aspect of all were the red, green, blue, and purple folds of light that trailed behind it.

"Blue dragon…! A rare monster from the lower floors!"

"Right, also known as an aurora dragon. It's up there with carbuncles in rarity."

Rapi had known of them, but it was his first time actually seeing one, and he couldn't hide his shock. Hiding behind the same cluster, Bors grinned.

It went without saying that Nina, Iglin, and the students' eyes were locked on it, but even some of the upper-class adventurers were staring.

Seeing the aurora and the sublime great falls together was more beautiful than any scene in the world. Spray from the falls splashed through the aurora, looking almost like a spirit's mischief.

"An aurora in the Dungeon…I can't believe it…" Iglin murmured in awe.

"Supposedly," the animal person next to him explained, "that dragon shits magic power out its tail there, which refracts the light from the crystals in this floor, and that's what creates that pretty thing."

"Terrible explanation…"

"But even so, it *is* captivatingly beautiful."

The description sapped Legi's excitement, but Chris's eyes were still gleaming as he described the thrill he felt in a whisper.

The way it floated through the air, seemingly free from the bounds of gravity, resembled voltemeria, a rare monster from the twenty-seventh floor, but its elegance was incomparable. Its round, cute eyes were perfectly clear as it continued to release the aurora that illuminated the adventurers and students.

A moment of inspiration…

Nina gripped her chest as she continued looking up.

Her heart raced as she recalled what Rapi had said moments ago, and she started to feel a hard-to-describe heat.

Nina didn't know what answer her heart was leading her toward as she just seared the most beautiful, otherworldly scene into her eyes.

"*—Gsha!*"

"Tch?! Whoa?! Monster! Watch out!"

Just then, behind everyone who was busy staring at the dragon and its aurora, a single blue crab had sneaked up on them and leaped forcefully into their midst.

Iglin spun around wildly, sensing it right after it appeared, and swung his hammer down.

When the hard shell refused to give way entirely, he slammed it down again, and one more time.

A loud, clanging sound echoed in the basin.

The blue crab finally stopped moving.

Then the dragon's eyes turned downward.

""""""""Ugh.""""""""

The adventurers and students hiding behind the crystals froze like deer, and the clear, cute, round eyes of the dragon turned an aggressive red. It opened its big mouth wide, revealing rows of sharp fangs.

""""Not good!!!""""

Bors and the adventurers immediately leaped out from behind their cover.

The next to move was Rapi, who was stunned for an instant before pushing the rest of the 3rd Squad out from behind the cluster where they were standing dumbstruck.

The next moment, a gleaming, multicolor storm erupted from the dragon's mouth.

"*GHHHHHHHHH!!!*"

A blinding aurora beam burst forth in a spray of light, swallowing up the cluster where they had been standing moments earlier, corroding it.

"Wh—?!"

"The crystals are melting?! A-a heat beam?!"

"No! It's a magic breath! The light that dragon spews is a mess of poison, paralysis, and all sorts of other afflictions!"

Bors answered Iglin and Chris's shock with a spittle-flecked shout while continuing to run.

The true nature of the enchanting aurora was a corrosive light that cruelly ate away at the dragon's prey by causing several different negative debuffs.

Like with the mist the floor boss Amphisbaena used, an unusual breath ability was a common trait for monsters in the Water Metropolis.

Nina and the students gasped at the beautiful and mysterious poison the Dungeon had created.

"AAAAAAAAAAAAAAA!!!"

Far overhead, the blue dragon was going wild.

Unleashing breath attacks from more than twenty meders overhead, it took its time targeting its prey that was running around the floor. The crystals corroded all around them. The water's surface took on a hideous color and started giving off a putrid smoke.

Rapi dodged a swirl of light and—

"L-let's run! It can easily target us here! Let's go into the labyrinth!"

"No! We have to stop it here!"

But Bors immediately shot him down.

"What?!"

"That dragon's long and thin! It's not Amphisbaena! It can follow us into any path we take!"

"...!"

"Dealing with that breath inside a narrow passage is way scarier! It's better to fight it here!"

Even with all his knowledge, Rapi's lack of fighting experience was visible in his educated guess, and Bors and the other Rivira adventurers immediately gave his suggestion a thumbs-down.

""""So it's up to you now!""""

"What?! Y-you're not going to fight with me?!"

""""We didn't bring any bows or magic swords.""""

"This is outside the terms of the quest, so take care of it yourself, client!"

"That's…?!"

Rapi groaned as Bors and the others took cover in the relative safety of the entrance to the labyrinth area after drawing a clear line. And while that was going on, the aurora blasts continued to pour down, forcing Rapi to keep dodging.

There's no sign of it coming down from up there…! It would be reckless to run up the wall, so I guess there's no real choice but to use magic, but…!

The adventurers' judgment was correct. With the blue dragon maintaining its altitude, it was impossible to attack it directly. It would take magic or bows and arrows or some other long-distance attack to take it down.

And knowing Rapi's true identity, they had made a natural and obvious demand—hurry up and use your Firebolt already.

But if they find out my identity…!

Remembering his promise with Balder, Rapi was caught in the middle, but he quickly made up his mind.

Holding out his right arm, he aimed his cannon at the long dragon.

"*B-Blasphemous Burn*!"

Stubbornly sticking to the script to the end, he used his fake incantation while unleashing a lance of fire.

But the crimson flame and lightning missed its slithering body, hitting nothing.

Gh…! It's faster than sirens and harpies, even!

He unleashed a barrage of shots, but they were all dodged.

The enemy was a dragon, the strongest of all species of monsters. Its potential and its flying ability were incomparable to other winged species' from the same floor.

And more than anything, the distance. It was a long range, a distance that Bell was not comfortable fighting at.

He had used Firebolt mostly to control a chaotic fight at close range, or occasionally at midrange. But long range was Bell's worst distance, and against a quickly moving target high overhead, the difficulty was jacked up even higher. It was difficult for Bell to substitute precision sniping like Hedin's with a quick attack magic wielded by someone who wasn't a pure mage or even a magic swordsman.

Why'd I have to find a new challenge now of all times...?!

Just then...

"Whoaaaaa?!"

"—gh?! Iglin!"

The deadly aurora closed in on the fleeing dwarf.

Rapi kicked off the crystal shore, shattering the ground as he pushed his comrade's body out of the way—and that was all. He could not escape the enormous range of the attack himself and was swallowed up by the corrosive light.

"Ghhhh?!"

Crossing his arms, he shielded himself.

The shortsword in his hand crumbled in moments. Eyes wide, he tried to escape immediately, but the corrosion reached all the way to the ground.

...?! My feet! It's like a swamp!

Having caught its prey, the dragon increased the force of the aurora, corroding Rapi's surroundings at a terrifying speed.

Unable to kick off the ground, and discovering that he was actually starting to sink into it, Rapi's face tensed.

My body...can take it...! But my gear...!

The first-tier adventurer's body with its naturally high resistances was able to endure the corrosive light so well that it was infuriating the dragon. His skin was tingling and stinging a bit, but that was all. On the other hand, the shortsword and the battle uniform on his back were both starting to rot away.

An unexpected struggle in just the lower floors.

In the Dungeon, the unknown was a threat to adventurers regardless of level.

"Rapi?!"

Nina cried out, barely able to see the shadow of a person in the swirl of light. Sitting on the ground where he had been pushed, Iglin turned pale, and Legi and Chris blanched, too. They started to rush out immediately, but their arms were grabbed by heavy hands.

"Wait! Don't go out there! If it's Rabbi—that Rapi kid, he'll be fine!"

"How could he be fine?! Let me go! Let me go!"

Bors and the others stopped Nina and blocked Iglin and the others.

The ruffians were still keeping to the letter of the quest—protect the students—and managed to hold the struggling girl back.

They had grasped it. They saw the first-tier adventurer's aim was a test of wills.

But Nina had not. Of course not. She didn't know the first-tier adventurer that even these adventurers acknowledged. The person she knew was the kind, gentle boy who had guided her here.

"*—Lullaby of wind, cradle of flowers.*"

And so, she sang.

"...!!! What do you think you're doing?!"

The noble song that she had been permitted.

"*Splendor of old, majesty of yore. White city protecting Mother, atop the floral hill.*"

Closing her eyes to focus on her magic, images of her roots flashed through the half-elf girl's mind.

Her homeland, filled with pure air, unprotected by a city wall, high on a promontory, where countless white petals danced in the blue sky.

Nina's origin and her blemish, manifested in the nostalgic tears cried into a pillow, the terrible yearning for a home she had once left, that she longed for again after so many failures and setbacks, but that she could never bring herself to return to after failing to become anything.

"*Blossom ye flowers. Blossom for this seed that cannot bloom. Sing, O light, to illuminate the noble traveler.*"

The girl who could not write her own future, jealous of the travelers, yearning to be like them, came to at least pray that their journeys be fortunate.

So as not to turn her back on the nobility in her veins, she never hesitated to devote herself to others. Unfulfilled and unable to discover a dream, she entrusted her maddening emotions in others, subconsciously using others. The shallow girl's wish was a foolishly gentle elf's song.

"Noble blue. Purest white. Purify miasma, and here bequeath a laurel."

And in all that shallow, foolish devotion, she had met him. The boy who had told her that her path was not shallow, was not foolish, but was incredible, too.

Rapi has given me so much!

The boy who had said that he had been saved by her. That was wrong. It was the opposite. She was always being saved by him.

I haven't given him anything back at all!

So Nina had to keep helping him. She wanted to be by his side. She wanted to teach him so much more, to be taught so much more.

That was Nina's wish.

"Whoooa?!"

"Nina?!"

Feeling the growing magic power—and fearful of an Ignis Fatuus—Bors immediately let Nina's arm go.

Chris was astounded seeing her sublime figure, more gallant than ever before as she held out her staff.

The next instant, she started running.

"*Bloom, second sacred mount—*"

Attempting the spell she had only just learned, she raced to the light even now eating away at the boy.

She braved danger out of a simple wish to save him.

As she was about to plunge into the light, at the last moment, she finished casting.

"*—My name is Alf!*"

Her single lock of jade hair gleamed with magic power, and she unleashed her spell.

"*Lagriell Krisheim*!!!"

A field of white flowers forced the sinister aurora back.

Standing in the stunned gaze of the long dragon and blocking the similarly shocked boy, a domain of dancing white feathers, or perhaps pure white petals, burst into being.

"Wh-what the hell's that?!"

"Purifying magic! Nina's barrier that can cure everything!"

Bors was taken aback while Chris and the other students leaned forward excitedly.

Lagriell Krisheim. A rare magic that Nina had manifested. As Chris had said, it could cleanse any and every debuff. A midsize healing barrier that not only cleansed negative effects like poison or paralysis, but even prevented curses and psychological attacks—demarcating the boundaries of a sacred elven field.

A bright field of flowers in place of a royal wood. The indelible scene of her frail, beloved mother had left a tremendous impact on the heart of the girl who had always wished to someday be able to save her.

"Nina…!"

Awestruck, Rapi's body was already fully healed.

Not only did the barrier cure poisoning, it also enchanted all those inside the barrier with a cleansing light that provided continuous healing, banishing all traces of impurity from its bounds. Even the aurora of the blue dragon, which had such a higher potential than the half-elf girl's.

"Ughhhhh…!"

Her knees trembled. The aurora roared, trying to crush the barrier of light and Nina's protection.

But it did not fail. There was no hint of it giving out. Because in that moment, Nina was burning with a sense of duty like none she had ever experienced. She had a goal. The desire to protect the people precious to her until the very end.

The dragon finally grew fed up with the unyielding field of white flowers. Stopping its aurora breath, it quickly descended, intent on crushing it directly with its fangs.

Nina's eyes widened. Her Lagriell Krisheim had no way to prevent direct physical and magic attacks.

Just as she was about to clench her emerald eyes shut, a slender arm supported her back as she started tilting.

"Thank you, Nina."

Grateful to the half-elf girl who had lent her support in the test of wills he had set up, the boy stepped forward himself this time. What he drew from his hip was the black knife he always kept close at hand.

"OOOOOOOOOOOOOOOOOOOOOOOOOO!!!"

"Hah!"

The moment the fangs were right in front of his eyes, he deflected them with a tremendous slash, protecting Nina, whose eyes widened in shock. Then the boy grabbed on to the dragon's long body.

Not letting go as the aurora dragon quickly ascended, he held on to a fin, climbing toward the dragon's head.

"——"

Nina seared the sight into her eyes: the boy rising through the air while the dragon created a terrifying, beautiful aurora in its wake, and the stunning waterfall and towering crystals in the background.

It was a mysterious, fantastical scene, almost like a page taken out of a heroic epic; it made her heart flutter.

"Nina, we cannot answer to your troubles."

Professor Leon had once told her this. When she had been at her limit and struggling hopelessly with the environment of the School District, that was the moment he had recommended Combat Studies to her. What Leon had told her then was to never stop questioning.

Leon and Balder and the others would never give her the simple answer she desperately wanted. They refused to tell her what to do, what she should set her sights on. Even though she would have been able to stop feeling the way she did and just blindly pursue whatever they suggested if they had only said the word.

The instructors at the School District would not turn Nina into a puppet.

"If I were to give you any advice…Nina, when the time comes, be honest."

That was all he had told her, as if praying that the right moment would come someday.

"When your heart is trembling uncontrollably…that is the moment when you've found your dream."

* * *

Her dream lit a heroic flame.

"*Firebolt*!"

While the dragon was trying to shake him off, Rapi leaped out above its head, firing a scarlet blaze into the black knife.

Suddenly, the sound of a loud bell rang out.

Particles of white light gathered, and an enormous wreath of flames clung to the divine blade.

The dragon recoiled from the blazing light, unleashing a final aurora blast from its mouth.

A four-second charge.

Letting his body fall naturally, the adventurer faced the dragon's breath head-on as he unleashed his attack.

"Argo Vesta!!!"

A crimson slash.

"———————*Aaaaaaah?!*"

The sacred flame slash swallowed up the aurora before blasting the dragon into oblivion.

Looking up, Nina and the others averted their eyes at the blinding flash and the explosion's blast.

The floor trembled, and even the great falls seemed to groan in terror.

There was a rustle as a rain of gray particles filled the air.

The dragon's corpse had been turned to ash as the boy splashed down into the basin at the bottom of the falls.

Seeing that, Nina sprinted over.

Bors and Iglin and everyone else gathered too, cheering.

"Rapi!"

"Nina…are you all right?"

Wiping his face, his clothes a mess, the first thing out of the boy's mouth was still concern for others, and Nina really should have been upset at him.

But just right now, in this one moment, she listened to the ringing in her heart.

That smile.
That kindness.
That dream.
Nina's heart was trembling, and so she said it without hesitation.

"I want to become an adventurer!"

She shouted it while standing right in front of the stunned boy.

"I want to see all sorts of new things by your side!"

Her tongue had slipped a surprising amount.

"Huh?"

""""""""Huh?""""""""

It wasn't just Rapi. All of the 3rd Squad, and even Bors and the adventurers froze, staring at the half-elf girl.

But before she realized what she was saying, her face turned bright red…

Because of the aurora, the boy's clothes, gear, and *magic items* were completely worn out. And so, the top of the boy's head—the wig he was wearing, slipped to the ground with a thud.

"Ah."

""""""""Ah.""""""""

This time, trading places with the boy, the girl's eyes widened in surprise.

The red eyes that had been hidden behind that hair this whole time were revealed.

The long rabbit ears disappeared too, revealing hair like virgin snow, shining in the waterfall's spray.

Rapi—or rather, Bell, froze.

The 3rd Squad stopped mid-motion.

Bors and the adventurers from Rivira just shrugged, and then the next second, there was a thunderous shout.

"""""Whaaaaaaaaaaaat?!"""""

EPILOGUE
AND SO I START TO RUN
© Suzuhito Yasu

The early morning, before the sun begins to rise.

Still a little out of sync after spending so much time in the Dungeon, I am summoned to the headmaster's office.

"Good job in the Dungeon Practical."

On the top floor of Breithablik. Lord Balder is sitting behind a large, ash desk as he thanks me for my work, but I can't help feeling apologetic.

"In the end, my identity ended up coming out..."

"Yes, I've heard. However, strangely enough, the 3rd Squad isn't saying anything at all about the first-tier adventurer who appeared on the twenty-fifth floor. Given that, it will not even rise to the level of rumor."

I don't know if it would be right to call it a barefaced lie, but I have to smile a little as the god of light tells me that.

After my identity came out on the twenty-fifth floor, the rubble blocking the eighteenth floor and the Cave Labyrinth was completely cleared, and the 3rd Squad was able to return to the surface. No one said much on the way back, and I was way past feeling awkward...but none of them blamed me for concealing my identity.

It's just, none of us really knew how to interact with each other after that. That's how it felt to me, at least.

"A field trip after an accident in the Dungeon...an incredible idea. I wonder whether it is because you are an adventurer, or if it is simply because you are you."

The other person in the room, Professor Leon, glances over the report while chuckling wryly.

I've heard how he did more than anyone to save the many people caught up in the accident. He, along with some other helpers, was the one who came to meet us on the eighteenth floor.

"And you expanded Nina's vision and her outlook. As expected."

"Sir?"

"Yes. As expected, you surpassed my expectations."

My eyes widen a bit as he winks almost impishly, smiling in a way I've never seen him smile before.

Did he…really have such high expectations of me?

Is it because I'm a first-tier adventurer? Or because I earned the title Record Holder?

I don't know.

But in the end, he says this to me.

"I would like to adventure with you myself next time, *Bell*."

That sounds like a promise.

"Incidentally, were you able to speak with Nina after that?" Lord Balder asks.

"Ah, umm…it was a little awkward, so we didn't really speak much…" I stumble a little bit, but then smile. "But she did tell me she was going to talk to her sister."

I look out the window toward Babel, where the sky lightens over a city where the sisters will finally be able to reunite.

Fall had passed and it was unmistakably winter.

Most people were still struggling to get out of bed as Eina walked alone through the park on her way to work at the Guild Headquarters, white breath forming near her lips.

It was a time when scarves and mittens became required clothing.

She was wondering to herself if she would be able face her precious family as a proper sister when the cold passed and spring finally came back around—

"Sister."

"!"

—When the time came much sooner than she had been hoping.

This park was a shortcut on the way to the Guild Headquarters. With a little investigation, it was simple enough to learn that most Guild employees passed through it on their way to work. Nina was wearing her School District uniform, and she had been waiting for Eina to show up.

Standing beside each other, the almost totally leafless trees lining the street watched over the two half-elves.

The sisters stood in the middle of the street, staring at each other.

"...Eina..."

"...Mhmm."

"...I'm sorry, I really don't remember you at all." The younger sister averted her eyes a moment, answering honestly, but then she looked up again and smiled awkwardly. "So...it's nice to meet you. I'm your younger sister, Nina."

Just that was enough to make Eina's emerald eyes tear up, even as she donned an easy smile.

"I remember you from when you were a baby, so I guess I'll say, 'It's been a long time.' I'm Eina, your older sister."

Even though they were sisters by blood, they had started with a greeting like strangers. But the two who looked so similar despite their age difference both smiled. It was like looking in a mirror.

"I'm sorry I couldn't answer your letters. The truth is, I was always glad to get them. But I was scared to reply."

"Really?"

"Mhmm. I was always just copying you. Always just chasing after you. And I just lost my nerve and made myself suffer."

Breaking into a broad smile at her older sister, who listened with a gentle smile throughout, Nina told her about everything.

About how she had copied Eina.

About how she loved studying but wasn't as good at dealing with things as her.

About how she had experienced so many failures.

About how she was actually good at athletics.

About how she could never become Eina Tulle.

And about how she now had a dream of her own, as Nina Tulle.

Instead of the letters she had not been able to write, the ones she had never answered, Nina shared everything.

So many words that would never have fit on any number of letters spilled out of her.

For some reason, tears welled in her eyes as she spoke, and Eina grew teary watching her, too.

"I learned so much during the Dungeon Practical! Someone really important to me taught me so many precious things!"

"I see…It sounds like you had a wonderful encounter. Is that important person a classmate from the School District?"

"No, it's Mr. Bell Cranell!"

And she dropped that bomb.

"—What?!"

Exploding the tranquil moment that should have lasted from start to finish, Eina shouted hysterically.

Nina cocked her head. She really wanted her sister to know, so with her cheeks flushed for reasons other than the cold, she started talking excitedly.

"Mr. Bell Cranell, no, Bell, is an incredible adventurer! He's the model of a first-tier adventurer! He saved us so many times…!"

"U-um, Nina? Are you…?!"

"I've decided! I'm going to set my sights on joining *Hestia Familia*!"

"Ehhhhhhhhh?!"

She was so caught up in her own world, she didn't even notice her older sister's shock, creating a scene of Aoharu. She beamed as she took Eina's hands.

"So, Sister! I want you to be the one to register me as an adventurer when the day comes! It's a promise!"

"W-wait, Nina! Please, wait! Bell has feelings for Ms. Wallenstein, and I, well, there's this and that, and you should probably not go for him…!"

"I'm going to see all sorts of things at his side!"

"Ninaaaaaaa?!"

Beyond the reach of her sister's shout, the little sister who still didn't know turned and started running.

Exhaling white breath, her cheeks red, there was nothing that could get in her way as she ran down the road that stretched straight ahead, chasing her dream.

It was not just brilliant—there would be difficulties and setbacks in store for her, but even so, precious, irreplaceable treasures were waiting too on the other side of her adventures.

"I'm going to do it! I'm going to be an incredible adventurer!"

Now a full-fledged dream chaser, the girl set off at a run.

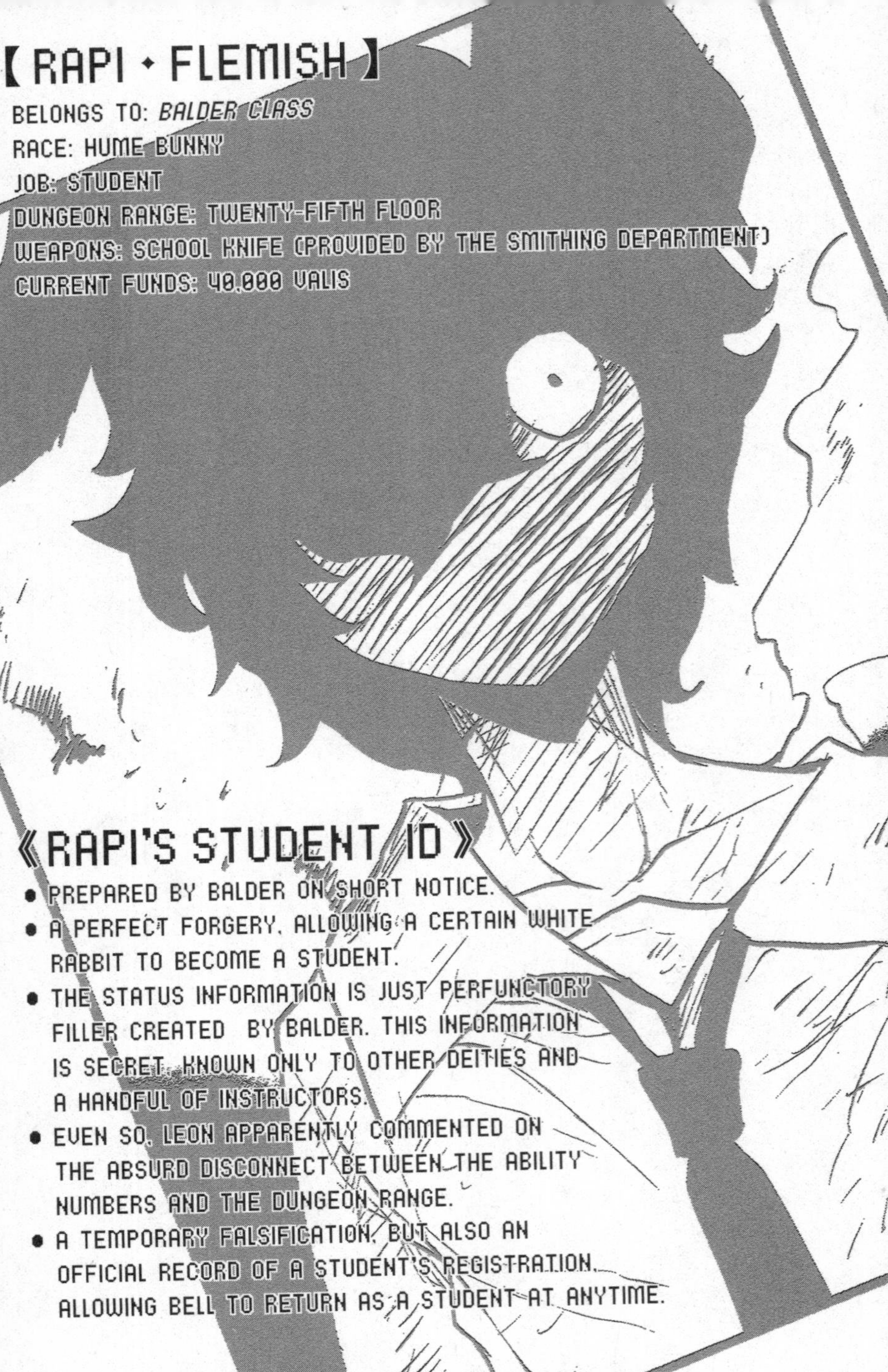
【RAPI • FLEMISH】
BELONGS TO: BALDER CLASS
RACE: HUME BUNNY
JOB: STUDENT
DUNGEON RANGE: TWENTY-FIFTH FLOOR
WEAPONS: SCHOOL KNIFE (PROVIDED BY THE SMITHING DEPARTMENT)
CURRENT FUNDS: 40,000 VALIS
《RAPI'S STUDENT ID》
• PREPARED BY BALDER ON SHORT NOTICE.
• A PERFECT FORGERY, ALLOWING A CERTAIN WHITE RABBIT TO BECOME A STUDENT.
• THE STATUS INFORMATION IS JUST PERFUNCTORY FILLER CREATED BY BALDER. THIS INFORMATION IS SECRET, KNOWN ONLY TO OTHER DEITIES AND A HANDFUL OF INSTRUCTORS.
• EVEN SO, LEON APPARENTLY COMMENTED ON THE ABSURD DISCONNECT BETWEEN THE ABILITY NUMBERS AND THE DUNGEON RANGE.
• A TEMPORARY FALSIFICATION, BUT ALSO AN OFFICIAL RECORD OF A STUDENT'S REGISTRATION, ALLOWING BELL TO RETURN AS A STUDENT AT ANYTIME.

STATUS

Lv. 1

STRENGTH: 130 DEFENSE: 110 DEXTERITY: 140 AGILITY: 170
MAGIC: 110

《MAGIC》

【BOLTFIRE】

- FLAME MAGIC
- CHANT: "BLASPHEMOUS BURN"

《SKILL》

Afterword

The new arc in Volume 19 is the school story I've wanted to do ever since becoming an author.

I wondered while writing whether the contents of this story were something I should have done during Volume 1.

The protagonist harbors a secret power, enrolls in school, makes friends with his classmates, and supports them from the shadows before finally letting loose and showing them his strength at the very end. It's a classic formula, and also an overdone, cliché sort of development. But maybe by doing the classic first-volume contents in Volume 19, it hits a little differently, or at least feels not quite so cliché.

The protagonist who has been running forward all this time beneath your watchful gaze has become so strong. Thanks to all his adventures and the advice of so many dear comrades, the boy who used to be so pathetic has grown so much. If you get that sort of feeling thinking back over all the stories, then I'm glad.

Changing the subject a little bit, when I'm writing, I take care not to project myself into the feelings and thoughts of the characters.

And because of that, I struggled mightily over whether I should write about a certain topic in this book, and in the end, I didn't include it. It may be selfish, and unnecessary from your perspective, but I would like to write a little bit about it here.

The idea of dreams and goals showed up a lot in the back half of this volume, but I don't really think those are particularly needed. It's great to have them, no doubt, but they aren't really crucial.

If you are feeling uneasy about having an aimless life, please don't worry. I think that feeling of unease is the first step in moving forward. Much like an author who has a deadline looming and starts feeling the pressure to start writing. I think not feeling unease or anything might be the most dangerous place to be in.

If there is someone reading this who is uneasy and struggling with whether to take a new path, "just because" is a good enough reason to start. Whether that something is studying, or clubs, or a job, or sports, or even part-time work.

There may be some who think it's irresponsible of me to say that, and while it is embarrassing, allow me to share a small anecdote.

While writing this book, I searched for a bunch of material from my time in school. One of the things I found is an essay I wrote in elementary school. Apparently, my dream was to become a schoolteacher. I couldn't believe my eyes when I saw that.

During my time as a student, I was really bad at studying. Honestly, I hated it.

True story, there was one test where I was one place away from being dead last in my entire school year. I buried the grades in the back of my desk and never showed it to my parents. And the assignment I hated most was writing book reports.

As terrible a student as I was, I somehow managed to end up with a job working with light novels. Me, the student who was so awful at classical literature and modern literature alike.

It's all because I just started for no particular reason. Of course, I had some interest in what I was doing, but actually starting was really just because I felt like it.

So even without something grand like a dream or a goal, just loosen up a little and give something a try. If you're interested, be bold and make the leap. I don't know if it will work out, but the amount of effort you put in is the amount of growth you'll see in yourself. Embarrassing moments or bitter experiences can be terribly stressful, but even those can become an asset. If you ever feel frustrated or disappointed, rest assured that is proof of growth.

Maybe you resent or are jealous of someone, or maybe you want to blame it on circumstances, but whatever you do, if you can turn those feelings into motivation, into effort, then that's wonderful.

If you dive in, try to hang on, and if you find it really isn't right for you, then try looking for something else. If the search itself becomes exhausting, then try talking to someone. It could be your family, your friends, or even a complete stranger. And once in a while, I suggest looking out at a clear sky. I think that can make your heart feel a little lighter. I don't know everything will always go smoothly, but please don't forget that just by doing something, you are leveling up.

Now that I've gone on at length, please take everything I've said with a grain of salt. This is just my personal experience. People are far more complex and far more varied than I could ever describe on my own.

But if you are ever feeling terribly nervous, if you ever need to find courage and the words of one dumb author manage to cross your mind, then that's enough.

With that, allow me to say my thanks.

I am deeply grateful to my editor Usami, the illustrator Suzuhito Yasuda, and all the people who helped bring the drama CD to fruition. It is thanks to all of you that we've managed to get through twelve consecutive months of releases. I am truly grateful. And I am humbly grateful to all the readers who picked up this book and so many of the other stories as well.

I laid out foreshadowing in this book (that I'm worried whether I'll be able to fully take advantage of). Most likely, the School District arc will end in the next volume. I hope you will pick up the next story as well.

Thank you very much for reading this far. Now, if you'll excuse me...

Fujino Omori